The Belfry Haunting
By Chris Sherrit

All rights reserved. No part of this book may be reproduced in any form or by any electronic or mechanical means, including information storage and retrieval systems, without written permission from the author, except in the case of a reviewer, who may quote brief passages embodied in critical articles or in a review. Trademarked names appear throughout this book. Rather than use a trademark symbol with every occurrence of a trademarked name, names are used in an editorial fashion, with no intention of infringement of the respective owner's trademark. The information in this book is distributed on an 'as is' basis, without warranty. Although every precaution has been taken in the preparation of this work, neither the author nor the publisher shall have any liability to any person or entity with respect to any loss or damage caused or alleged to be caused directly or indirectly by the information contained in this book

This is a work of fiction. Names, characters, places, and incidents either are the product of the author's imagination or are used fictitiously, and any resemblance to actual persons, living or dead, events, or locales is entirely coincidental.

The Belfry Haunting

Trigger Warnings

This book contains content that may be distressing to some readers, including but not limited to references and depictions of **violence, alcohol consumption & abuse, drug abuse, racism, rape, and blood & gore depictions**. If you or someone you know might find these themes triggering or overwhelming, please consider your emotional well-being before continuing.

1

Why did nobody turn on the lights? Perhaps a fear of the dark? It certainly wasn't due to a need to save costs on electricity.

"Deborah?"

"Yes, Dr Dietrich?"

"Who switched the lights off on ward B?"

"Oh, I'm not sure, sir" Deborah investigated the cold sterile white corridor for some reason the doctor couldn't understand. As if an educated man like himself wouldn't be able to distinguish between light and dark.

It's only been six months since the last safety meeting. Am I going to have to demand another?

"Could you remind your colleagues that the lights should be left on at all times throughout the wards? Only the treatment rooms and the basement floor should have the lights switched off when not in use."

"Of course, Doctor."

As Deborah turned to leave, Doctor Dietrich chased a finger after her. "And Deborah? I really don't mind the lights being left on in the entire building at all times. We are doing important work here, and I'd rather not be hindered by a lack of vision or the need to repetitively flick switches."

"Very good, sir. Anything else?" The woman waited for the doctor's response; her body language made it obvious she didn't care for this perilously overly anal inquiry.

"No, that will be all." Dietrich sighed. *Silly woman*, she probably wouldn't tell the rest of the staff what he had said. Probably go moaning to her fellow nurses that her boss was being an asshole…again! Well, let the silly woman do so, as long as the damned lights are on.

It wasn't like he was running some everyday practice or even operating a public hospital. This was Lockwood, for heaven's sake. The things they were doing here were going to change the world. Leaps and bounds would be made in medicine and psychology that nobody could fathom. The world would look back in time and remember Lockwood, of that Dietrich was certain. His name would be synonymous with excellency and his work would be considered elite in the field for centuries; he knew it. They were already renowned for the treatments that had been carried out here, revolutionary treatments that had changed the course of medicine. Lockwood would help him change the course of humanity. Admittedly, the treatments were initially met with disgust, scoffs and outright refusal. His peers didn't understand; they didn't have the bravery he did. The results would speak for themselves.

Once Dietrich made one of these discoveries, then he knew, then his father, *damned wretched old cad*, would respect him. Maybe, just maybe, his father would tell him he was proud of him, that he loved him. Dietrich wouldn't tell a soul how he hated how much he yearned for this approval. Worst of all, he hated himself that he was intellectual enough to realise it in himself.

"Meh, you've spent how many years on this, Viktor?" The old pile of wrinkles would more likely say. "I completed my work in half the time and at half the cost."

No, Doctor Viktor Dietrich would have his day; it was close, he could feel it. He was sure of it.

Returning from ward B, Viktor headed to his office. It was late, he'd drawn the blinds already, and he didn't care for looking out across the grounds in the darkness. He had no need to look at the moon tonight and ponder his latest qualms. No doubt there would be little for him to attend to; the patients would be asleep, the staff quietly letting the hours burn away. He could relax and sift through his research, maybe even get a little bit more done. All that would happen tonight would most likely be one or two patients having nightmares and wetting the bed, nothing for him to worry about. The orderlies and nurses could tend to those gormless dribblers.

A warm feeling of power rose in him as he entered his office. Books of his father's loomed over his desk. An ever-present reminder: *I'm better than you ever will be, son!* A light cushion of light from his desk lamp let Viktor rest his hands in as he slumped down into his armchair, the dark red leather groaning under his weight.

Knock, knock, knock!

Can't a man get a minute to himself?

"Enter!"

Elizabeth poked her head in the door.

"Hello, Doctor."

"Ah, Elizabeth, please come in," he smiled, forgiving his frustrations. He always had time for young Elizabeth, time he hoped his wife never found out about.

Her shoes slid across the floor as if Elizabeth was fighting against being pulled into some unseen quicksand; something about the woman suggested an unease. In herself? In her position? In the affair they were having? *How many times have I told her to lift her feet?*

Viktor stood from the desk, circling to perch on the other side.

"All patients are in their beds?"

"Yes, sir."

"All orderlies have reported to their stations?"

"Yes, sir."

"All nursing staff on duty have reported in?"

"Yes, sir."

Viktor frowned. Normally, when Elizabeth approached him so cautiously, it was to deliver bad news. He paused, retraining his thought, the corner of his mouth raising. A sense of arousal teasing inside.

"Well then, Lizzie, it appears we have time to discuss *work* again." he raised an eyebrow as he reached for her hand. Lightly pulling her as he rested his full weight on his desk. Elizabeth avoided tripping on the carpet under the doctor's desk, a light breath escaping her as her shoes slipped on the carpet.

"Oh, Viktor, I would love to, but I don't think we can."

This woman, honestly, so dramatic. Maybe I need to prescribe her something for her...hysteria.

"Heavens, woman, what's the matter?"

"Well..." she looked down to her side for confidence, security, courage. Viktor knew it well, a textbook defensive technique. He observed her as she crossed her arms, cupping her elbows, another sign. She continued after a breath. "My fellow nurses are all here and running things smoothly. All the orderlies are in their stations for the evening, but it's Jonathan, sir. He mentioned he heard something strange going on in the basement. He was collecting chairs for his colleagues and said, well, he's quite shaken, sir."

Jonathan, which one, ah! Yes, the most recent orderly we took on from Africa. Where was it? Ghana? Yes, that must be right. Silly sod's probably gone and got himself scared by a rat or something.

"And a scared orderly is something I need to deal with?" Viktor stood from the desk, placing his hands on his hips. His doctor's coat splitting, his waistcoat watch swinging like a pendulum. Elizabeth's eyes fixated on it, hypnotised.

"No, sir. It's just the rest of the orderlies...and...and some of the nurses. They said they've heard the same thing. Some of them from the basement, some of them on the wards. Some of them from the patients."

"Noises? Why hasn't this been reported to me already?"

"They thought nothing of it; it wasn't until Jonathan brought it up that we all realised we'd all heard similar."

"And you?"

"Beg your pardon, sir?"

"Have you heard the noise?"

Biting her lip, Elizabeth confirmed with a nod.

Ah! The poor woman has been spooked as well. No doubt a creaking water pipe. Always an explanation, the unfortunate downside to Lockwood is, of course, the imposition it leaves on people. It's ability to induce unease within its patients. Has it really extended to the staff as well?

"And this noise, what is it?"

"Well, there are three noises that have been experienced."

Great, now there's multiple noises, the human mind has an amazing ability to draw comparisons and create unrealistic links only to manifest images of terror. Why is it always those of poor upbringing that are susceptible to these blights. Perhaps I should construct a new experiment to test these supernatural experiences. Bully Dietrich, Bully!

"Three? Ellaborate." Viktor sighed, his frustrated breath forcing Elizabeth further into herself.

"A wet click, according to orderly Thompson, it sounds close to the sound of wringing a rabbit's neck."

Vitkor sighed again, grunting a confirmation to continue.

"The second is a scrape, not quite nails on a chalkboard but close."

"And the last?"

"The last is a breath, sir."

Viktor chortled. "My, my, Elizabeth. A breath? Might that not obviously be one of the patients exhaling in their sleep? One of your colleagues hiding in the dark? You know, I've already told Deborah to let the rest of the staff know that the lights should be left on at all times. Certainly, lights should never be switched off on the wards. Not even while our patients sleep. Too many complain of monsters in the dark; the rest seem to get infected with their panic. No, the lights must always be on."

"That's the thing, sir. I heard the breath, it was when I went to the basement to restock the gause. The lights were indeed on. I switched them on myself when I went down." Elizabeth lifted her head. Scared of the truth, scared of her own need to explain.

"Not a soul was down there with me, and I heard a breath, light and close to my ear. When I turned around, there was nobody there to see. I thought nothing of it initially, and then the lights went off by themselves. It was then I heard the breath again, right behind my ear. I swear it said something to me."

"Elizabeth, you've been working too many hours; you must be exhausted and on the brink of hysterics."

"It said the name Cargill!" She stamped a foot.

Viktor halted his next attempt to calm the woman.

"Cargill?" Viktor asked, the now quivering woman nodded.

"What's the date?"

"October 2nd, Doctor, why?"

Viktor shoved the nurse out of the way and bolted for the door. How could he have been so stupid, so arrogant? *No, poor Viktor, stop beating yourself up. You've been focused on your work. No, this is not your fault.*

As Viktor tore through the corridors and raced for the basement, his little devil voice whispered in his ear.

It'll be your fault that she gets out tonight!

2

For most of us, death is an ending.

For some, it is a lingering, a never-ending transitional state. Perhaps death leaves unfinished business, perhaps it leaves a message not passed on to a loved one or an answer to a long-standing question.

The human race can but hope that their transition will be as quick and trouble-free as possible. Those instantaneously passing onto the great beyond should count themselves lucky. Those passing from the mortal plane into the vast chasm of nothingness that is non-existence, doubly so.

The winds whistled through Belfry with their typical spine-chilling friendliness. Abigail pulled her coat tighter, knowing full well that it wasn't going to do much to prevent the cold. Still, it's not always about practicality; sometimes it's about the mental act. A lesson that had taken her longer than she'd like to admit to learn.

A keen observer, Abigail Rennie had regularly wondered why people did things the way they did. Why did her father always tap the top of his can of beer three times before opening it? She'd looked into his excuse. "Keeps it from frothing over, honey". It wasn't true; it did nothing. No matter what level of shaking you give a can, if you tap it three times and then open it, it'll still cover you in its contents.

Why did people look at their nails, breath on them and then wipe them on their collars? It wasn't polishing your nails, it wasn't cleaning them. If it was, then it was only getting your collar dirty, surely. If your nails needed polishing, or you felt polishing would improve their look, then do you really think your breath was a worthy solution? No, people were arrogant and liked to show off; that was the truth.

Why did people insist on forming queues and common pathways through things like shopping centre doors? Multiple sets of doors welcoming customers in out of the cold, and what do people do? They all formed up in a line to walk through the one set of automated doors. Why suffer bumbling up behind others when you could easily open one of the manual doors and be inside quicker? Subconscious behaviour to follow others was something that benefited humans centuries ago. There is no need for us to continue these actions now.

Human, a strange species indeed. Anyway, having observed people for so long, she'd finally discovered that people just did things sometimes for no good reason. Quite often, doing them subconsciously. It had only taken her eighteen years to figure out. *Only.*

Why did she have to walk home? Johnny had his licence now; he could have driven her home, right? She wouldn't have to walk through this blasted weather. *Bloody Scotland, never gets a good day. Always bloody rain or bloody wind...or bloody both!*

Abigail sighed. Why was she so grumpy tonight? Yes, Johnny did have his licence now. He didn't have his own car yet, though, did he? Only occasionally got to use his parents' car when they let him. No doubt had to complete all his chores and give a very valid excuse to drive. Poor boy, his parents knew as well as Abigail just how clumsy he could be. Taking the Mercedes out to drive his girlfriend home wouldn't have cut it for Johnny's father. The best chance the boy had was to help his mother pick up the shopping. Then his dad could stay at home and have another beer while he watched the football. Typical man!

It wasn't just the weather; it wasn't even the fact that she had to walk home from Johnny's. *It's only a fifteen-minute walk after all.* Abigail let the cold cool her temper. What was it then? She groaned in gradual realisation as her stomach gripped, the small of her back crunching inwards.

Great! The latest addition to being female that made the world an ever-present bastard. *My period!*

"Oh, hello, dear." Abigail's mother whistled as she opened the door. Unwilling to remove her protective covering, Abigail closed the door with one hand, the other making sure her coat was tucked around her waist. She marched into the living room and plonked down on the brown and orange striped sofa. Kicking her boots off onto the blue, brown, and orange swirled carpet, Abigail crossed her legs as best she could, tucking her feet under her knees to preserve some warmth. If the cramps didn't make her feel nauseous, then the old carpet and furniture very well might.

"Cold out?" her father asked from his armchair, eyes still fixed on the television. Abigail mused at how her father seemed unable to refrain from holding the TV remote at all times while he watched, his thumb primed on a button to change the channel at a moment's notice.

"Just a tad!" Abigail confirmed, frustrated with herself at the standard Scottish reply. Never would a Scot suffer the weather; we are proud Scots and will not be stopped by the mere movings of the Earth and atmosphere. The only time the weather will receive exaggeration will be in a Scots jest. Pah! Damn the weather.

"That time of year, eh?" her father added. It was unclear if even he was aware he'd said it. Abigail ignored him, shivering off the last of the cold. She considered broaching a conversation with her father but decided against it. He wasn't the chatty type. If he couldn't give a one-syllable reply, then one word would have to do. Besides, he was too engrossed in the advert on the television for a new three-piece suite. Abigail wouldn't deny that it looked comfier than what she was currently sitting on. *Looks a hell of a lot nicer than this ugly striped thing.*

Thankfully for Abigail, it was only the sofa and carpet that gave her the ick. She didn't blame her parents for the furniture's appearance; they had been the same carpet and three-piece suite that the house came with. The Rennie's had put away pennies as best they could to make the pounds available to alter as much of the house as they could.

The living room wallpaper was the first to go. Orange and brown flowers that caused a dizzying unease in Abigail as a child. Her mother had made the decision not to wallpaper it with some other "groovy" design but paint the walls a flat orange instead.

"Cantaloupe, dear," her mother corrected her when she'd put the first tester brushes onto the wall next to the other possible candidates. Abigail and her father both smirked and nodded.

"Aye, orange!"

Summer had come and left, autumn taking its odd hypnosis over Belfry. Though tonight was a cold night, wind chilling your bones, tomorrow would bring only a calm breeze. The sky would be overcast, no doubt, but what light broke past the clouds would bounce off the orange leaves littering the streets and give the town a welcoming brightness.

Abigail loved autumn; it fit her well. The cold during the day was sharp and chipper, the brightness lifted her spirit. She bid her parents goodnight and made her way to bed. Looking forward to what she could get up to the next day, and more excited to be tucked up cosy under her duvet.

Maybe she could get Johnny to take the car out, they could go for a cruise, blast some music and feel like free adults.

Maybe Nadia would give her a shout and they could take the dog out for a walk down near the river.

Whatever the day held, that would be fine. She was no longer in school, and that meant she had more freedom, not enough, though. Tomorrow evening, though, there would be freedom. Freedom for her to forget how restricted this town made everyone feel. Tom had picked up two crates of beer, which, combined with the bottle of Smirnoff she had stashed underneath her bed and the bottle of Gin Nadia had stashed under hers, meant one thing.

They were going to have a fucking party!

3

It was Friday, October 1st, 1974. Fridays had been a favourite day of the week for Abigail and her friends for years. Last day of the week, last day of the week to go to school. That was how it started. Back then, they'd be looking forward to sneaking out of their houses and going to the river to drink. They'd all been drunk before, but now, now they weren't underage teenagers. They were all eighteen; they could legally drink. It didn't stop them from wanting to get together somewhere around Belfry, somewhere that wasn't a legal drinking establishment.

It wasn't like any of them had a proper job to earn enough to drink in the single pub of Belfry, anyway. Well, Tom did, but Abigail considered him on the edge of the group's friendship. He'd attached himself to their group, and they weren't going to kick him away. He was able to supply booze and weed. They just had to put up with his crappy

The Belfry Haunting

banter, and they'd be able to get drunk or high whenever they wanted. Unfortunately, Abigail would have to put up with the odd bit of uncomfortable flirting from Tom. Thankfully, Johnny would be there tonight, though. Tom wouldn't stand up to Johnny; how could he? Tom was the idiot dropout who sold drugs to make money. Johnny was the coolest guy in school, or had been, they were only eighteen, though. Still fresh out of school, Johnny's supposed coolness kept his lackies loyal.

"Bacon? Eggs?" Abigail's mother said as she came down to breakfast. The table was set as if they were about to have a fancy meal. Frowning, Abigail sat, blinking her vision clear and noticing a jug of orange juice sitting in the middle of the table. Her father hid behind the paper as usual. The cover slapped with a big headline about a bomb going off in England.

"Help yourself, Abby, mum's got the kettle brewing as well if you fancy a tea," her father's voice hopped over the page. Her mother set down a dish full of scrambled eggs, another of bacon and sausages.

"What's all this for?" Abigail asked.

"Oh, can't a mother cook a nice breakfast for her family?" her mother grinned.

The paper dropped, her father scoffed, raising an eyebrow at Abigail.

"She's got a new job, she's celebrating."

"You got the job?" Abigail leapt to her feet.

"I start on Monday," her mother hugged her. It had been years since she'd worked. Sure, she'd helped out at the school every now and then, but that wasn't work; it didn't pay anyway. She was just helping out the kids during break time, which gave her a chance to keep an eye on Abigail.

She'd applied for a job as a receptionist for a hardware company. Brushed it off when she came back from her interview, expecting no call back. Would be reporting into one of the executives for the company, she didn't think the guy liked her, thought he was just looking for a pretty girl to be his assistant.

"I'm so happy for you," Abigail said, glad to realise that she was telling the truth. *Thank god I'm getting control of that teen angst…I am right?*

Her mother let her go and filled Abigail's plate with food before sitting down and filling her own plate.

"There's something that I need to let you know, Abby."

Abigail mumbled an acknowledgement as she shovelled her breakfast into her mouth. Delicious, smoky bacon merging with the buttery taste of the eggs. *Perfect start to the day, now if I could only get mum to make a cup of coffee instead of tea, that'd be peachy. Still doesn't know I prefer it, though; she'd string me up. What's so bad about coffee?.*

"In order to do the job, I'm going to need to spend a lot of time away from home."

"That's alright, Dad does with his job. Why shouldn't you?"

"You're mother won't be working around Belfry like I do," her Father peered over the paper.

"That's the thing, Abby, the job I applied for was in Dundee, I'd have been an hour there and back each day, I might have been able to manage that. They gave me a job in Glasgow, though, sweety."

"Oh! That's cool, wait, that means you'll be driving much further."

"No, no, honey, I won't. I'll be staying in Glasgow through the week."

Breath sucked out of the room. "What?" Abigail didn't understand why she needed to work so far away. Why couldn't she get a normal job right here in Belfry? *As if there was anything that paid well or had any ounce of interest about it, duh!* Questions filled her brain, swelling, warming, uncomfortable. The biggest of all. W*hy am I so worried?*

"We could move," the words spilt from Abigail's lips before she could control them. Her father scoffed, and she frowned in frustration at him.

"We can't move, honey. We don't have the money to up and move like that. Your dad has his job here as well."

"So? Why can't he get a job in Glasgow as well?"

Her mother sighed, those eyes peeling layers of pain from Abigail's heart. Soothing her, "Your father has worked here all his life, sweetheart."

The paper finally dropped, the goatee on her father's face peeled to one side. "Look, it's alright, Abby. It would be a real struggle for the family if we up and moved to Glasgow. There's no guarantee I could get a decent job there either. Nothing that pays as well as I'll get running maintenance here."

"You're a glorified janitor, Dad." Again, Abigail wished she could reach out and catch the words as they left her mouth. She was frustrated, confused, it all felt too sudden and not in her control, like her entire life was being uprooted. *What is wrong with me?* The strong demeanour she worked so hard to present was beginning to fade.

"Good one," her father chuckled. If there was one thing more frustrating than feeling lost at a sudden change in her life, amused agreement was it.

"Now, Abby, your father works very hard helping out everyone in the town."

"Isn't like there is anyone within a hundred miles that'll come fix anything here as well", the paper flapped back up as her father pulled back out of the conversation.

"What do I do?"

"Oh, bless your soul, sweetheart", her mother lay on the doting parent voice thickly. Okay, maybe there was something else more frustrating than her dad's self-mockery. "You don't need to do anything, you'll stay here. Dad will come home and make dinner, and you can go and hang out with your friends all you like. How does that sound?"

Abigail's eyes drew circuits around her breakfast. Did the eggs hold any solace, the bacon an answer? Why did she feel so on edge? She needed to do something, to distract herself. Her stomach knotted. *Wait, am I jealous?*

"Of course, you could make dinner as well if you like, Abby. You're a better cook than I am," said her father.

"I put a shepherd's pie in the oven every other month." Abigail winced. Her father lowered the paper enough to show his raised eyebrow.

"See, like I said, better cook than me," he chuckled, raising the paper again. At this stage, both Abby and her mother doubted he was actually reading anything.

"Do I have to get a job here?"

"Only if you want to. We won't force you to do anything you don't want to," her mother replied. *Ugh, just be difficult for once in your lives. Be interesting, challenge me, give me something to give my life some level of excitement.*

"Of course, a third income into this family wouldn't hurt," her father's voice again, she could almost see his smirking face being pulled. *Fuck you.* She grinned, never having sworn aloud in front of her parents.

Abigail picked up the rashers of bacon from her plate and nudged the remaining eggs and sausages forward. The chair pierced a screech as she stepped away from the table.

"Where are you going?" her father asked, the paper crumpled into his lap.

"Out."

"Out?" her mother asked. "Out where?"

"I don't know. Nadia's? Johnny's? Just out, alright?" Abigail didn't look over her shoulder as she marched to the coat rack, grabbed her jacket and slipped out. As the door closed, she could make out her mother's voice calling after her.

"Alright, dinner will be at seven."

Her father's exhale of happiness followed, happy that he'd be able to polish off the breakfast remains from Abigail's plate. Abby bit her lip, knowing that her parents would do the same thing that all parents did. *Oh, she's just overreacting like all teenagers her age do. She'll come round.*

Bullshit!

4

Take a stroll down Belfry High Street, if you could call it that, and you'll find a collection of odd and interesting-looking shop fronts. *Knicks and knacks* has a wide array of strange-looking artefacts in the shop window. A pink flamingo wearing a sombrero and sunglasses, a diorama of crickets playing cricket, another of crickets reenacting the last supper, various tools hanging from the ceiling with questionable stains on them, a child-sized doll riding a tricycle glaring out with snake eyes, a porcelain nightmare. The grandfather clock behind it would look normal if it didn't have a monochrome gradient painted at an angle down it. Rumours say it was Andy Warhol's old family grandfather clock.

Plaice of mind, the oddly named fish and chip shop that also sells knitting supplies. Why the strange additional side hustle? "Pfft, people like to knit, eh?" owner Bill Petrie tells anyone who asks.

The antique store next to *Knicks and Knacks* holds arguably fewer antiques, more rejected possessions than anything else. Nothing in the window is more than ten years old. Various kitchen appliances, three vacuum cleaners and a naked mannequin fill the window. The oldest thing in the shop is undoubtedly Mr Belvie, ever vigilantly watching the passersby while swigging from a hip flask. Nobody honestly knows how old he is. He couldn't tell you himself.

Wilson's fine goods and exquisite car dealership says everything you need to know about it. There are no fine goods in the building. Unless you would consider a plastic cheesegrater with the Queen's initials on it and a heavily inflated markup. As for "exquisite cars", well, Terry Wilson would tell you the sport stripes he tried to paint on one of the Volvos showed its "European pedigree".

Safe to say, Belfry is a strange place. Live here long enough and, like the locals, all the strangeness would become a comfortable commonality. Why have so many different businesses been mashed together in a containing only one pub? Why not? It gave the place something to call its own. Tourists, which was a phrase Abigail had snorted at countless times due to their rarity in town, would say that it gave the place character. What sort of character that was varied depending on who you spoke to and what you wanted to believe.

Amusingly and strangely enough, the one thing that had the most normality to it was the old abandoned hospital up on Boswell Hill. Abigail's mother always referred to it as "the old hospital", but Abby and everyone else in town knew it was the old asylum, Lockwood. There hadn't been a person in there in years, save for the odd homeless passerby looking for shelter. Word had it that those wandering carefree people of the world, calling themselves "nomads", would frequently stop there for shelter, though nobody ever saw them leave. For Abby and her friends, it had been a spooky place to play games. Daring each other to run across the grounds at night, bang on the windows, whoop like banshees and smash anything they found that could be smashed. When they grew of an age and started taking an interest in the opposite sex, it progressed to sneaking into the security guard's hut to make out, smashing rocks and bottles against the walls and generally getting up to no good. Y'know, wayward teenage stuff.

Abigail stood on her tiptoes at the pub window once she'd walked onto the town high street. Why a pub window needed to be so high, she didn't know. It was either a bad design choice or a purposeful one. Windows high enough to let light in but keep the prying eyes of angry wives away. Of course, every wife knew that if their husband wasn't around, then he was at the pub.

The Crying Witch, a name satirically adored by the locals, was the only pub in Belfry, but it wasn't the only place to get alcohol. With Belfry's strangeness and the businesses' "adaptability", you could pick up a crate of beer in three or four of the high street shops on most days. Any of the little shops on smaller streets and corners would probably sell you a bottle of vodka as well. It was less about finding the right shop and more about knowing the right people. Of course, with Belfry being so small, everyone knew everyone, so the subtleties of keeping on the right side of shop owners were key.

Still, it was nice to have a proper pub to sit and relax in from time to time. The televisions only ever showed football, obviously. No news, no films, no culture, just football. Not even a different sport, no rugby, no field hockey, not even darts. For that reason, Abigail and Nadia usually wanted to drink at different locations.

Nobody in the pub, Abigail noted, not anyone she wanted to see at least. Big Ronnie, the pub landlord, sat behind the bar on a stool, engrossed in whatever game was on. The usual patrons held up the bar, Vic O'Henry, Neil Connors and Ben Budny. Ben wasn't his first name, but nobody could pronounce or understand the correct Polish pronunciation. "Bennie boy" was the usual call sign for the pale skeleton of a man. He was the easiest one to keep on the right side of and ran a corner shop just off the main street. Always wanted to be welcoming to any customer who stepped into his shop. An over-the-top smile and a warm weaselly "Hyello, velcome to my shtore, ples let me know if you need hyelp". The poor man acted as if running the most welcoming shop in Belfry set him above the rest. How he hadn't realised that in a town of this size, that just made him easy pickings was an enigma. As mentioned earlier, he was the easiest one to keep on the right side of. He loved having the kids come into his shop and would always try and push some sweets into any sales, sometimes even popping them in for free. It felt like it was he who was trying to keep on the right side of the locals. Keeping on the right side of Bennie also came with another benefit; he was the easiest to get booze from.

Vic O'Henry would rarely sell you vodka, nor a pack of smokes, nor even a bloody lighter. *Grumpy old Irish prick*, he did have the best selection of meat and veg in Belfry though. You had to put the work in with that man to get alcohol from him. Nadia had managed once after being dared to, and it had taken her two weeks of offering to help carry in stock, casually flirting with Vic as she did so. Batting her long eyelashes and giggling as she bit her knuckle at whatever shit joke he made.

Nadia swore never to do anything like that again when all her work rewarded her with was three cans of Stella Artois. She managed to joke about it now, though the beer wouldn't wash away the dirty feeling she had inside, pretending to like poor old Bennie.

No, Bennie was you're best bet. Johnny swore he'd overheard a couple of the other locals have a go at him for selling to underagers when he was watching Aberdeen play Hearts on the telly one night.

"They were all giving him a hard time, like," said Johnny, his eyes wide, some of the hottest gossip the town had in a long time. "Vic nearly lost his voice shouting at him to stop selling booze to kids. Lucky for Bennie, Ronnie jumped in, corrected him. We're not kids after all, eh? Anyway. Bennie took it all like a champ; it seemed like none of it fazed him. Like he'd been through far worse in his life. He let them all have their moans that he was enabling them, downed his beer and told them all it was better than us going out and doing drugs. It was Ronnie who took over at that point. Banned him for a week. I thought one of them was gonna smash him in the head when he waddled out. Poor old guy."

"How old is Bennie, anyway?" Nadia asked.
"Fuck if I know."

"That's probably why he's so unfazed, he's been through it, eh? Probably got caught by the Nazi's and stuck in that camp, eh? Asswash or whatever it was." Tom Winters butted his thoughts in.

"Auschwitz. I doubt he's a concentration camp survivor." Abigail said, barely able to lock eyes with Tom, his idiotic humour grated against her.

"You never know." Tom stood his ground.

"Oh, stop it, you two." Nadia ended things. Abigail tried to ignore it, exhaling a long sigh as she sat back and looked at Johnny. He leaned in and whispered.

"He could be right, you know. I heard they had tattoos of their ID numbers on their arms. Have you ever seen Bennie without long sleeves? Just saying." Johnny leaned back, eyebrows raised. Abigail smiled and blew him a kiss. *Sure, doll. You let your pretty face believe that bullshit.*

So, nobody at the pub? Abigail guessed the next best place any of them might have been. She could have called ahead, checked in with Nadia and seen if she was home, likewise for Johnny or even Tom. The brisk air was welcome, though. She just needed to get out of the house.

As she expected, turning off the main street and heading down Auchniyell Lane, rounding the large bushes, there they were, sitting on the roundabout in the kids' park. Before you ask, no, they weren't loitering like teenagers up to no good and bullying children. There were no more young kids in Belfry to enjoy the park. It was theirs as far as they were concerned.

"What's the news?" Tom said as he clocked Abigail from the roundabout.

"Same old," she replied. The gang gave a collective "Aye" in bored confirmation. Abigail walked past the roundabout and to the bench facing it, a cold steel viewing place for parents to watch their children shout and giggle. Fresh blood enjoying their youth under the watchful eyes of their loved ones. Now just a rusted ruin that inhaled your hopes and dreams to leave you with nothing but the cold encompassing arms of ennui.

Johnny slumped off the roundabout, ever the clumsy kid, and leaned over the back of the bench, giving Abigail a kiss.

"Geez, get a room, you two." Tom blurted. The resounding lack of acknowledgement rendered him quiet, for now at least.

"Where's Gary?" Abby asked.

Nadia unfurled her legs, sitting on the bench next to her and sighed.

"Has to help his grandmother move some stuff, get rid of his grandfather's old stuff."

"Can't his folks do that?" Tom again.

"Dumbass." Johnny jumped on him before Nadia or Abigail could. "his dad's in a wheelchair and his mom is well...y'know." Johnny's confident voice faded. If one thing could bring the young boy down, it was depressing situations like Gary's.

"She's a fucking whale?" Tom chuckled.

"Hey!" Nadia stood, hurling an empty bottle of Pepsi at him.

"What? She is."

"Tom, shut the fuck up, alright. Dude's doing the best he can with a family that's struggling." Johnny jumped to the rescue again. *What's with him today? He normally stays out of these things or hides a laugh with Tom,* Abigail thought.

"Not my fault." Folding his arms, Tom sulked. His foot skidded the roundabout to a stop.

"Yeah, and it's not like your family is the polar opposite, is it, Tom?" said Abigail, finally happy to contribute, clocking eyes with Nadia and smiling.

"Where is your dad again?" Nadia asked, fully aware of the badger she was poking.

"Don't!" Tom's lips curled inwards.

"Haven't seen old Mr Winters around Belfry in a good while. Why did he leave again?" Nadia clocked Abby's eyes again, a sadistic smirk of mutual amusement.

"Fuck you." Tom rose, starting to storm off.

"Hey, hey. Everyone just leave it fucking be, alright? We're going to all get together tonight and have a good fucking laugh, alright?" Johnny commanded. Abigail turned to him with a confused grin. *What's got into him?*

"Hey, everyone! Sorry, I'm late." Gary rounded the same bush Abigail had earlier. He jogged to Nadia and gave her a kiss. Tom stared, finally clocking eyes with Gary.

"What's up, Tom? You look like someone pissed in your bed last night or something." Gary said innocently.

"He's just been telling us how hi-" Nadia started to stir again.

"Guys, come on. Are we all set?" Johnny controlled the situation again. "Gary, you picked up everything on your list?"

Gary grinned, pulling a little piece of paper from his back pocket.

"Of course, picked it all up this week. No problem, folks. Did you guys all get your stuff?" he held out the list as if it were proof.

> ~~Cider~~
> ~~Crisps~~
> ~~Cola~~

"Good job, bud," Johnny said, trying to keep things positive. Silence played a too-long note.

Johnny interrupted, "Well, guys? Like Gary said, did you guys get everything?"

"I've got my stuff, Johnny." Tom boasted. "What are we going to do with Chambord anyway?"

"Cocktails, my friend. I found a recipe for Sex on the Beach." Johnny grinned, and Tom smiled and nodded as if he'd just been told the dirtiest joke on the planet. Abigail looked at her boyfriend again, with another quizzical look. Johnny returned a wink, and Abby snorted.

"Yeah, I've got my gin," Nadia added.

"Vodka's good to go," Abby added.

"And I've got the rest. Alright, we're all set for a kickass Friday night."

"What's happening?" Said a voice nobody in Belfry had ever heard before.

5

Raised eyebrows stared in the direction of the voice. It was so strange, so foreign. A twang that took more than a few seconds for anyone to recognise. Wasn't Irish, there was only Vic in Belfry who was from Ireland. It wasn't anyone from England, didn't have either the posh silver spoon-fed roll or the harsh tones of anyone down south.

"Excuse me," Nadia said, unclear if it was a question or a statement.

"I was asking what's happening?" The voice returned.

American!

A tall boy, broad, blonde hair, etched from every teenage girl's dreams, his age unclear, stood with his hands in his jacket pockets on the edge of the park. *How long has he been there?*

The Belfry Haunting

"Oh, nothing." Nadia turned her back to the boy, flashing Abby a wide-eyed look that meant they'd have to talk about this later.

"I don't mean to be rude. Just sounded like you guys had something fun going on tonight?" The boy kicked off the climbing frame he'd been hiding under, ducking to keep his head from banging off a beam, his wide shoulders turning to face the gang.

"Here, are you American?" Tom stepped forward, his tone a mix of curiosity and a ridiculous need to establish male dominance. The boy smiled.

"Guilty as charged," he spread his arms, an eagle's wingspan.

"Cool, where abouts you from?" Tom relaxed his shoulders, unaware he'd instantly submitted his apparent masculinity to this new stud. Johnny circled the bench, putting himself between the girls and the new boy. A new contender.

"Florida. Orlando, more precisely."

Nadia turned her head to Abby again, seizing a chance to interact. She quickly whispered, "He's cute"

"Nice to meet you, man. I'm Gary, must be new here in Belfry" Gary walked over, not a care in the world for all the dick swinging. It was one of Gary's qualities Nadia found the most endearing, his constant and total ability to coast through life being nice to people. Abigail was only slightly jealous of the quality. *Still, maybe Johnny's taken a page out of his book tonight. He's been less of a bell end so far.*

"Gary? Hi," the American shook his hand, a strange exchange for two teenagers. At least everyone presumed the boy was a teenager. It would be even more strange if he were an adult trying to socialise with a bunch of kids, after all. "I'm Troy"

Of course, he's named Troy. Abigail stifled a laugh. Still, she couldn't deny that Nadia was right. He was cute. The cutest guy she'd ever seen in Belfry, though that wasn't difficult if she was being honest. Of all the boys around here, plenty had taken their swing at a chance with Abby or Nadia. Unsurprisingly, it was one of the things they laughed about the most. The feeble attempts the boys at school made to court them were laughable. Abby's favourite failed attempt was still Norman McGabe giving her his Optimus Prime action figure when they were twelve. "A gift", she received during lunch break. She'd never spoken to Norman nor expressed any interest in transformers, still, she awkwardly accepted the gift and then left it on the teacher's desk later in the day. *I'm assuming Norman picked it up at the end of school, but I don't know, though. No idea where Norman is these days either.* All attempts at flirtation after that followed in an avalanche of embarrassment and failure.

All until Johnny, of course. The rest of the school accepted it as the most likely outcome; he was the best-looking boy in Belfry after all, until *now*. His looks weren't what drew Abby to him. Nor was it the fact that he was the most popular boy in their year. In fact, Abigail disliked herself more for being with him due to those facts. No, it was Johnny's confidence, even though he was such a clumsy boy. He'd have very easily fit in the Three Stooges as Curly if it weren't for him being physically built like a brick shithouse. He was popular with the boys at school because he was so big, because he was a good footballer, and again due to his build. Troy, however, made Johnny look like a perfectly average human being. Johnny's frame was wide and lean, not the tall mass of muscle now before them. Still, at school, with the addition of Abigail at his side, he'd been lorded over by some boys, most of all Tom Winters. He was the prince of Belfry.

Abigail didn't agree with the expectancy that Johnny should be with her. She didn't consider herself the best-looking girl in school. Nadia was more beautiful than her by a long shot. She could honestly admit that now without any tinge of bitterness. Why Abigail, being a few inches taller with long brunette hair, was more appealing, she didn't know. She'd guessed that the boys were more accustomed to the pale white skin of the north. She knew she wasn't ugly as well. She wasn't overweight; she considered her face to be fairly symmetrical. Her choice of clothes wasn't overly revealing. To Abby, though, Nadia's exotic looks were far more beautiful.

It nearly caused the two of them not to be friends, though Abigail hadn't told Nadia that. Meeting at the nursery, the two of them had formed an early bond over playing with different coloured bricks. The boys wanted the blocks to build monsters and robots, and the other girls wanted to build cars to take their characters to the hairdressers. Abby and Nadia simply wanted to build their homes and put their happy families inside. Nadia's mother had suggested a play date for the two of them outside of nursery, and the two became fast friends.

It wasn't until mid-way through primary school that Abigail started to notice that people looked at Nadia differently. Nadia stood out in the crowd. Abby knew it; the way she carried herself, even as a young girl, was like there was a barrier around her. Nothing could hold Nadia back. More and more, Abby would notice boys looking at Nadia during those last years at primary school, though. Comments tossed her way. The first hint that all the boys were creeps with thoughts stemming from their crotches.

The Belfry Haunting

"You're eyes are so beautiful" was a common one from older boys; it made Abby's skin crawl.

"Oh my god, I love your hair!" Some of the other girls started to comment. Even the young boys in Abby's class were spending longer than a normal pause fixating on her. Abigail couldn't understand it. Sure, she was a beautiful girl, but did that warrant all this extra time staring at her? Why didn't Abby get an equal share of these looks? It was her first taste of pure jealousy, and she didn't like it. She didn't hate Nadia for the way she felt, but she made the decision to avoid those feelings in the simplest way. To stop hanging out with Nadia.

"She's becoming a gorgeous young lady, that's all, sweetheart." Abby's mother had tried to reason with her on a particularly grumpy and difficult day. When Nadia would phone, Abby would no longer talk to her directly. Any attempt to arrange sleepovers would be met with a different excuse for Abby's absence. Feeling poorly, had to do her chores, was seeing her grandmother, whatever one hadn't been used in a while. Abby would sulk in her bedroom after each phone call, unaware that she was the one who was bringing this on herself. The phone calls reduced in frequency and eventually stopped altogether. Abby felt lost.

The well left in her chest was difficult to fill. She struggled to make friends with others, none of them sharing the same sense of humour that she and Nadia had. What hurt even more was that Nadia didn't seem fazed by the lack of Abby in her life. She'd skip across the playground giggling with the other girls, pointing at other boys in class, and whispering messages.

It wasn't until secondary school that the two of them reconnected. Abigail could still remember it vividly. They'd both walked to school, Abigail holding back a little behind Nadia, though they walked the same route. They were assigned to different registration classes. Another peg hammered into the coffin of their friendship, Abigail had thought. There were occasional classes they would share, though in none of them did they sit together.

After the fourth day, the pupils in her year started to mingle together a bit more. Groups forming, new friendships being made, Abigail hadn't managed to make any real, tangible strides towards that. The most she'd gotten was a few "classmates" in different subjects, meaning the pupils who were forced to sit next to her in each class. She didn't want to get chummy with them; she had no idea how they'd grown up, what their interests were, what their dislikes were. Bubbling at the top of too many conversations with kids her age was too much discussion about the opposite sex. She wasn't sure if she was a late bloomer or if the

The Belfry Haunting

concept was just entirely foreign to her, but she had no interest in boys. They were stupid. They did stupid things, they liked stupid things, and whenever they tried to talk to you, they said stupid things.

During lunch on that fourth day, a young boy from their year strided up to Nadia in the lunch hall. Fully in sight of everyone, the other kids in her year, the sixth years, the prefects and even the teachers. Craig Pointer, supposedly the hardest boy in Abby's year. How this could have been established after only four days, she had no idea. Nor did she understand how he was apparently the best-looking boy in the year. He wasn't much to look at, he was obnoxious, he had a stupid laugh, and Abby swore he had a weird smell to him. *No biggie*, she assumed her distaste was due to her lack of interest in boys in general. *Must be still to come*, she reassured herself.

Tugging on Nadia's hair, Craig scoffed, "Wow, it isn't a wig!"

Nadia turned, placing a hand on her head to soothe the pain in her scalp. "Why would it be?"

"Because look at you/" he said, a smirk on his face.

"What do you mean?"

"Well, you know, look at you, you're a smelly paki. It's not a wig, I guess, but it still feels weird." Craig said as if it were the most normal thing in the world. Nadia gasped as Craig turned to his gang of reprobate friends "Hey, guys! It's not a wig, but it feels fucking nasty, like some frozen strands of piss." The little group of young boys giggled and cheered.

Abby had seen it all happen as she leaned against the wall of the school hall, amidst the other outcast children, unaware of where they sat in the social ranking, before anyone else could step in, before the teachers overheard and made their way over, an instinctual urge made Abby walk over. An urge that forgot about all of the feelings of jealousy Abby had. An urge to help her friend.

"Hey!" She shouted within three feet of Craig, the young boy startled. Spinning around with hunched shoulders, no doubt expecting some disciplinary action about to take place. "Oh, hey, what's up?" he tried to click on his charm.

"What's up with her?" Abby asked.

"Oh, her?" Craig looked back at Nadia, small sparkles of tears beginning to blossom in her jade green eyes. "Yeah, she's a smelly paki, huh? You aren't, though. You're fit as fuck, like." His eyes trickled down Abby, she felt an acid burn in the back of her throat, pure disgust.

"No, I didn't mean what is wrong with her, I meant why are you bothering her?"

"Huh?" The boy was confused. A girl was challenging him? No chance. "Whatever, fuck off. I wouldn't even kiss you anyway, never mind shag you," he shrugged, looking over his shoulder to his backup. The gang of boys smirking at Craig's action. Digging her nails into her palms, Abby balled up all the words she wanted to see to the petulant little shit. Forming them into a burning energy, it grew and grew in her chest before descending to her legs. She tensed her legs to hold herself to the ground and avoid exploding.

As the boy turned back to the situation, Abby seized the moment. A swift, vicious kick to the boy's groin, a sharp high high-pitched yelp squeaked out of Craig's mouth as he fell to his knees. The gang of boys and all the remaining onlookers bellowed a collective "ooft!" Abby didn't stop there. Grabbing Craig's head by the ears she thrust her knee as hard as she could into his face, all those play fights that went too far with her brother finally paying off. She never told anyone that she felt a sickening crunch though she doubt she'd have to tell anyone. The audible *crack* made quite a few faces wince.

"You bitch!" Craig spluttered through blood gushing from his nose. In his panicked state he pooled the blood in his hands, as if his brain might spill out.

"Fuck off, I felt more from your damn nose than I did between your legs. Neither of us want anything to do with you, you filthy fucking maggot" Abby said.

She was, of course, grabbed by the teachers, along with Nadia and Craig. The whole situation had to be worked out, and parents had to be informed. Craig's father threatened to get the police involved, finally backing down once he'd displayed his knowledge of expletives when several teachers mentioned that they would wholeheartedly provide the police with a full report of Craig's actions towards Nadia, and how Abby had been attacked and defended herself. Abigail's chest felt so tight hearing all of the adults talk about it. She was fine when it was Craig, an immature boy, but adults? She didn't have the confidence to stand up to them. Not after she'd expelled her energy and anger like that.

"Fine then, fuck off. I don't want my boy going to some paki loving fucking freak school anyway," was the reply. Craig was not seen at school again. Not seen in Belfry again. Many joked that he *had* been the hardest boy in that year, if for only four days.

"Thanks, by the way", Nadia had said to Abby when they left school after everything was settled that day. Abby understood then, Nadia wasn't different, but she was treated different. Some people treated her as special because of her looks, and some people treated her as less than a person because of how she looked. To Abby, she was just Nadia, the girl she'd grown up with.

"No need, Nads," Abby replied.

"So was it really smaller than his nose?" Nadia asked. Abby grinned and snorted out a laugh. The two of them chuckled, doing their best to hide it from their parents as they walked home. Things began to balance back out after that. They hung out again, and Abby noticed fewer boys were taking an interest in Nadia. Was it because they were in secondary school now? Was it because they feared what Abby might do to them if they got on the wrong side of her? Was it because Abby was developing earlier than Nadia, and they were taking an interest in her? None of it mattered to her.

"So what's cool in Belfry?" Troy pulled his hands out of his jacket and cracked his knuckles, stuffed his hands in his jeans pockets, easing his jeans down low enough to flash his torso. Abby grit her teeth, frustrated that she'd lingered on the sight. It almost looked like he had those weird lines at the pelvis, *the Adonis belt* Abby had discovered. *Damnit, girl. Stop looking!* Thankfully, her attention was suddenly grabbed by Nadia elbowing her in the ribs. Nadia was blushing; she'd obviously noticed as well. Thankfully, the boys had been too engrossed in each other to pick up on either of them. Abigail snorted a laugh at Nadia. She always found it so funny when Nadia blushed; she'd lower her head, and her eyes would shift from side to side.

"Fuck all, mate." Tom chuckled as if brushing off his shoulder.

"Well, not that much if you're a normal, sane teenager. Which…you…are?" Gary asked.

"What, normal and sane?"

Gary laughed in apology. "Teenager, I mean"

"Oh, yeah. I'm seventeen."

"Fuck off." Tom blurted.

"What?" Troy grinned in a low defensive posture. One that Abigail instantly recognised, yes, he was indeed a teenager. Only a kid with that level of insecurity would lower themselves to the challenge from someone like Tom.

"You're built like a brick shithouse, that's what. Christ, you're bigger than *me.*" Johnny said.

"Oh." Troy's head seemed to lower further into his shoulders. Not only was he an insecure teenager, but he also apparently embarrassed easily. *Damn, he's cute but has no balls. Ah well.* Abby thought, standing and pulling Nadia to join her. Nadia muffled a refusal until Abby yanked her to her feet.

"No, no mate. You look fucking big, like it's a good thing." Johnny reassured him, slapping his shoulder. "We're all eighteen, and as you can see,

The Belfry Haunting

aren't as much of a unit as you are is all. How'd you get so big?"

"You work on a farm, right?" Gary guessed, Johnny nodded an expectant agreement.

"No, I, um, I'm part of the football team back home."

"You play footie, mate? Sweet. Hey, lads, boy's a fucking unit, bet he's a mad defender or something." Tom tried to grasp some masculinity again.

"Sorry, unit?" Troy asked.

"Another word for you being so big. You're a big dude. Again, a compliment." Gary said.

Troy let out a little snigger, dipping his toes into the friendship group a little further. "Oh, back home, we say corn fed. Don't have a lot of farms in Florida either, by the way."

"Too hot for it." Abigail raised her voice from the bench. The boys split, all turning to face the girls. "Yeah, hi, we're here too." Troy was stuck in the middle of their quizzical gazes.

"Yeah, that's right," Troy confirmed. Abigail walked over, pulling Nadia with her, their arms interlinked.

"I'm Abby," she put out her hand. Let down again by the boy as he shook hers with an oddly soft hand. Skin far too supple for what she'd expect of a tough-looking football player like Troy.

"Nice to meet you." Troy blushed.

"And this is Nadia." Abby nudged her forward. Nadia snorted a hello and shook his hand as well.

"Nadia, nice to meet you." Again, he blushed. Best guess, this boy had had few interactions with girls so far. Though Abigail didn't feel attraction for the boy, she was curious. His traits didn't align with the stereotypical American football teenager. She'd expect him to be flaunting his muscles and have cheerleaders swooning after him. *Wait, is he actually a normal kind of guy?*

"Fancy a game, Troy? I can nip home and grab my ball." Tom shoulder barged the American.

"Oh, um, I don't really know how to play."

"What? You said you played football."

"I'm guessing you mean soccer?" Troy began to whimper again. Tom nodded.

"He means American football, dumbass", Abigail said.

"American football?" Tom spoke the words, unknown disgust in the taste.

"She's right," Troy murmured.

"Not seen it?" Johnny asked. Tom's face didn't budge; confirmation, he knew very little after all.

Johnny wrapped an arm around Tom's neck in a headlock and began to explain the rules to American football, occasionally turning to Troy for confirmation or getting interrupted when he was incorrect. The group shifted across the park to the swings, Troy stood awkwardly on the edge of the group but talking and answering questions none the less.

"Oh right, like rugby for pussies then?" Tom laughed. Johnny looked at Troy to see if he wanted to challenge him. Troy shrugged.

"Do you guys have guns back home?" Tom rolled into the next blip of thought in his mind.

"My family don't, no. I have friends who do, though"

"Have you ever shot one?"

"Yes."

"Fucking cool, bro."

"Do you drive a car?" Gary asked.

"I was away to start driver's ed."

"He could drive us to Lockwood." Tom's excitement stunned everyone.

"We barely even know him," Johnny said.

"Aye, but he could drive us up We could get a jump on things now if he does. Troy, would you drive us up to Lockwood? We're going up tonight to get pissed and have a laugh. You drive us up and I'll give you some of my booze. What do you say?"

"Sorry, I said I was just about to start, but before I could, we had to move, and so I never actually started" Tom frowned, confused frustration thrown at Troy.

"Tom, settle down, it's fine. We'll get up there tonight. Don't worry." Gary calmed his friend.

"Do you want to join us tonight?" Abigail asked.

"Where?"

"At Lockwood?"

Troy bit his lip, struggling to keep up with the conversation. "What's Lockwood?"

6

Evening had arrived, finally! Friday evening at last, the gang had succeeded in getting their plan to go ahead as they'd hoped. Johnny had left the park early to go home and do his best to convince his parents he should be allowed the car that evening. They'd given him a hard time and made him promise to do double the chores next week, but they'd agreed.

"I'm sorry, you all speak quite fast. It's hard for me to understand." Troy said, squished in the back between Gary and Tom.
"Yeah, we know. Could be worse, though?" Gary said.
"Really?"
"Aye, could be some cunt from Aberdeen." Tom blurted, still looking out the window. He eventually turned to look at Troy. Seeing his

confusion, he added, "Aberdeen, northeast of here, folks there speak even faster."

"And speak that weird farmer talk." Gary chimed in.

"Doric," Abigail spoke over her shoulder from the front. She was also sitting in the middle, but thankfully, there was enough room in the front of the bench seat for her, Nadia and Johnny. Troy had smiled when they'd picked him up from the main street in Johnny's dad's Ford Zephyr.

"She's a beaut," he'd said, scanning his eyes over her contours and classic look.

"Aye, a beautiful piece of rusting shite," said Tom.

"Are you wanting a fucking lift?" Johnny put Tom back in his place.

"I'm sure you'll pick it up as you talk with us more." Nadia smiled over her shoulder. Troy smiled back, blushing again. Nadia had thankfully perked up a bit and was more talkative. However, Abby did wonder if Gary might be starting to pick up on the effect the American was having on his girlfriend.

"Thanks, did you have any trouble picking it up?" Troy asked. A chill of silence crawled through the car.

"What do you mean?" Nadia asked, a polite hint for the boy nestled in her tone. *Don't poke any further on this topic; you've been warned.*

The Belfry Haunting

"Well, you've picked up the accent pretty well."

"You mean *my* accent. I was born here."

The chill crept back through the car, this time only targeting Troy. He smiled again, warmth melting the chill from his blushing cheeks.

"I'm sorry, I, uh, back home, I, uh, it's normally people from, uh…I'm sorry."

Eyes bounced off each other and the car finally erupted in laughter. The awkwardness subsiding. Abby always gave Nadia an extra look after exchanges like these. Knowing that deep down, behind the acceptance to just avoid tensions growing, Nadia wished people would just let her be.

"My mother is Indian and my father is Iranian. Don't worry, I'm used to it now."

"Aye, us Scots are fifty fifty, half of us love diverse cultures, the other half are still asshole racists for some reason." said Tom, Abby looked around the car stunned. Of all the people to say such a thing, he was the last she'd pick from the group, probably one of the last she'd pick from Belfry. *Five points to Tom Winters.*

"Oh, so you're half Persian, that's so cool." Troy perked up. Nadia frowned at the boy with a slight smirk.

"Yeah, so?"

"I had a Persian friend back home. I got invited round for, what was it, now…nori…"

"Nowruz?" Nadia smiled.

"Yes, it was awesome, there was so much food. Oh god, you guys gotta try it." Troy fell back into the group.

"Food?" Tom perked up, "You never told me there was food, Nads."

"That's because I didn't want an asshole, horny stoner ruining my family celebration, Tom."

Tom inhaled, ready to retort, before his face pained in worry.

"What is it?" Johnny said. He'd been focusing on the road. Tom ignored him, or perhaps didn't hear him in his worry. Patting his chest, his stomach, his legs. His hands worked into the left thigh pocket of his cargo shorts. *I'm going to have to tell him those shorts are part of the reason he never gets any from girls*, Abby thought.

"Phew!" Tom exhaled.

"Seriously, dude, what is it?" pressed Johnny. Tom pulled something from the pocket and leaned into the centre of the car to get everyone's attention, though he already had all eyes fixed on him.

"Thought I'd forgotten this," he said before unfurling his hand. A clear plastic bag tumbled out, holding a fistful of weed. The boy's grin suggested he'd just saved the party. *And here I was thinking we'd all agreed to pull back on the weed.* Abby told herself she'd just not partake, though she knew that she'd probably crumble under the peer pressure.

"Sweet!" Troy reached out, Tom whipped the pack back and slapped the boy's hands.

"Hey, hey, hands off till we get camp set up."

"Oh, sorry." Troy slumped down again.

"He's fucking with you," Gary said while giving Tom a stare down. Tom snorted.

"He's right," he reached into his right thigh pocket and pulled out another clear plastic bag containing ten joints rolled and ready.

"No, no. No smoking in the car," Johnny piped up. "I don't want to get shit from my dad for leaving the car stinking."

"I thought he smoked, too?" Tom asked.

"Occasionally. Mum gets pissed off at the smell, though, and has a go at him; he then has a go at me. Look, just leave it till we get there, alright?"

"Party pooper," Tom mumbled as he returned the bags to his pockets.

"We're nearly there anyway," Abby said. It seemed like Johnny and she were the only ones paying attention to the road. Tom too busy showing off, Troy too busy getting distracted by the weed and Nadia, Nadia too distracted by Troy, and Gary too distracted by Nadia. He'd definitely started picking up on Nadia's eyes lingering on the boy's shoulders and triceps.

"There she is." Johnny tried to raise excitement in the car as they took the last turn. The road clearing of what little civilisation Belfry had to a long, winding route. Walls guarded the land they approached. On a raised mound of earth stood their destination, looking over Belfry with its slowly rotting windows. The sign on the pillar they approached was barely readable after years of neglect. The metal plaque faded and rusted. Dead vines curling their grasp and drooping over the letters.

"What is this place?"

"Lockwood, our own private party palace," Tom chuckled.

"Ignore him, it's an old abandoned insane asylum," Nadia said, unable to stop biting her bottom lip as Troy leaned forward to get a better look, his shirt revealing more of his firm chest.

Johnny slowed next to the pillar and pointed out the window while nodding to Troy.

Lockwood Asylum.
Hospital for the mentally disturbed
Est. 1423

"Disturbed?" Troy wasn't conscious of saying the word out loud.

The Belfry Haunting

"Yeah, just an old way of saying insane people," said Gary as the pillar disappeared behind them.

The Lockwood grounds, that being the land which entailed basically large open grass areas, were surprisingly well kept in comparison to the building and surrounding walls. Trees lined the edges, a defensive forest leaning in, drawn to the energy hidden within the asylum. Withered and sharp, they did not look welcoming, though it was late in the year. *Trees just look creepy this time of year.* Old buildings, though? They looked creepy all year round. Lockwood defiantly stood, a creation that almost scoffed at the town it had been built in. Arrogantly surveying the peasants living below it within its brick bones, vine-wrapped buttresses, and turrets hid cobweb-encased hospital supplies. Abby had only seen a small part of the asylum. Both too afraid and not interested enough to go exploring an old abandoned building. It was a wonder how, after so long, the building still stood so confidently. *Why don't they tear this down or repurpose it into some flats or something, I don't know,* Abby thought. Accepting, as a second thought, that flats would serve no point. *Who wants to stay in Belfry?*

What little Abby had seen of the interior was every bit the exact picture everyone had when they thought of the insane asylums of every horror movie. Long corridors with a horrible mix of white and that vile, faded turquoise colour. Stretchers haphazardly left at angles drew an unease in your gut. There may well have been some circuit breaker that could be switched to bring the lights on, but none of the gang had been brave enough to find it.

Darkness was every bit a part of the experience of the gang hanging out in the building. Of course, they took a few torches, mainly so whoever needed to nip outside for a piss would have some visibility. Tom brought along a portable standing light he'd knicked from a garage to sit in the middle of them while they "partied".

Party was a push, Abby thought. They lingered around in the lobby, drank, smoked. Occasionally, Johnny and Abby or Nadia and Gary would slink off into a dark corner to make out. Tom would occasionally scuttle over to perv, resulting in a bit of badgering of the horny single boy. The badgering would continue until he got bitter and threatened to cut them off from his supply of weed.

"Nobody comes here?" Troy asked, helping unload the supplies from the car.

"Nah, no reason to," Tom boasted.

"Apart from old man Dougie," Gary corrected. Tom lingered in the silence, waiting for an answer. Nadia walked past and noticed his gormless expression.

The Belfry Haunting

"The caretaker looks after the grounds. Glorified gardener, really, and that's a push. He just mows the grass. Don't worry, he'll be at the pub by now."

"Really, he doesn't know you guys come up here?" Troy asked, falling in line with Nadia.

"He does, hard to keep it hidden in a town like this. One of those 'everyone knows everyone' situations, y'know?" Troy nodded "Besides, he doesn't care. Better things to do than try and move on a bunch of teenagers up to no good. He isn't the police after all."

"Better he just has a drink and we all leave each other be," Johnny chimed in, dropping his drink down in the doorway, holding the door open for the others to enter the building.

"And the police?" Troy enquired.

"Pub as well," Tom answered. The gang didn't elaborate further. No need, Troy was picking up on the trend. Friday night, adults were in The Crying Witch.

Tom marched into the lobby, plonked down the portable light and dragged the plug to a socket on the wall behind the reception desk, the only one the gang had ventured far enough to try; luckily, the mains supply to the building still worked.

"Ladies and gentlemen. Let the party begin!" The young boy shouted to sighs and moans.

"Give it a rest, Tom," Johnny said.

"Wow, you guys are really boring," replied Tom.

"You guys don't seem very hyped up about tonight," Troy chortled as he scanned over the waiting room seats, trying to find one with the least amount of dust.

"This guy gets it," Tom said, grabbing a bottle of beer, pulling his lighter out of his pocket and popping the lid off. He did the same to another and walked the beer over to the American. Clinking his bottle against it and swiftly throwing it down his neck.

"Hard to get enthusiastic when this is the peak of our week," Abby said.

An echo of something clattering boomed out from one of the corridors.

"What the fuck was that?" Nadia said, nearly dropping her drink. The gang fell silent, eyes scanning across the reception desk. The 'Welcome to Lockwood' sign resting on it, the old telephone, and the metal trays holding folders of presumably old patient notes.

"There." Nadia pointed, near the corner of one of the corridors, a tall figure stood. Half hidden by the wall, half silhouetted in darkness.

"H-h-hello?" Tom stuttered.

No reply. All eyes were fixed on the figure. Johnny slowly reached into his back pocket, pulling

The Belfry Haunting

his torch and trying to avoid any sharp movements, raised it to the figure.

"Oh, for fucks sake," Tom blurted as Johnny switched on the torch. "A fucking coat rack?"

The gang released the collective tension in a harmonised breath.

"That was fucking scary," Troy said, Nadia looked up to his eyes, Abby thought she noted a little disappointment. *Probably expecting him to be the tough courageous type.*

"I wasn't scared." Tom puffed his chest.

"Aye, right. *H-h-hello?*" Johnny laughed. The gang joins him. Any chance to berate the daft boy.

"No, I wasn't. Hey, at least I tried to do something."

"Yeah, welcomed the fucker to our party." Gary slapped Tom on the back, clinking his beer against Tom's.

"So what was that noise?" Troy asked as the gang settled into seats around the reception area.

"Just an old building," Abby reasoned ", Old buildings make old noises."

Troy scoffed, forcing his fear down "Yeah, right, of course!" His eyes darting back to the coat rack.

Abby sat down next to Nadia, kicking her feet up on the table, still covered with old magazines of solutions for women to deal with the difficulties of being the 'modern housewife'. She clinked drinks with Nadia and the two threw back large gulps. Abby didn't want to ask the gang, but she thought she had heard a whisper, some voice amongst the old buildings' noises.

7

Johnny was getting on Abby's nerves. She couldn't tell if he was just being an overly horny boy or if the drink was making her irritable, or both. She'd fought back enough thoughts through the night that perhaps it had been a little bit of jealousy that Troy and Nadia seemed to be hitting it off.

Gary now sat beside her, the two of them watching Nadia and the American talk about bands they listened to. Troy had seen plenty of live bands in the States. Nadia, by comparison, had seen two, both on trips to Glasgow. Troy had never heard of Jethro Tull or Joy Division, not until Nadia softly sang a few of their songs. Nadia's eyes lit up when Troy said that his favourite gig he'd ever been to was Led Zeppelin.

"Is she?" Gary asked.

"Yup, sorry, bud," Abby confirmed, the two of them keeping their eyes on their friends.

"Should I do something?"

"Do you think you should?" Abby asked.

"I don't know."

"Do you trust her?"

"Of course," Gary shifted in his seat, rolled his shoulders.

"Nothing to worry about then, huh?"

"Is he good-looking?" Gary sat up a bit.

Abby thought about how to respond. She'd always liked Gary, he had nothing about him that should make her dislike him, a big tick in her books. Plus, he was really good for Nadia. Supportive, caring, a genuinely nice guy.

As for Troy, well, he seemed perfectly pleasant, she wouldn't admit that his accent gave her a feeling like she should dislike him. Like it gave him a smugness, though Abby put that on herself rather than him. She took a long drink and sighed. Gary shifted his gaze to her.

"Yeah…he's gorgeous," She stood up and walked to Johnny. He was chatting away to Tom in the doorway as they shared a joint.

Abby approached, Tom noticed and instantly offered the joint, but she waved it away.

"Good for now, thanks."

"Pfft, lightweight," Tom boasted. Abby flipped her middle finger at him without looking.

"What do you think of this Troy guy?" She asked Johnny. He took more time than he'd be proud of for the words to process through his inebriated mind.

"Troy? He's...he's cool. Right?"

"Are you asking me what I just asked you?" She snorted.

"Yeah, Troy's cool," Tom backed up Johnny.

"What's wrong with him, like?" Johnny frowned. Trying to see between all the colours to make out Abby's expression and adjust himself accordingly.

"Well, he's kind of flirting and hitting it off with Nadia," Abby said as the two in question let out a loud laugh. It echoed off down the corridors, bouncing back with what Abby swore was a third laugh joining in.

"So? That's not our problem," Johnny squinted.

"Oh come on, you don't think Gary is having a bit of a shit time?" The three of them looked across the room. Gary's eyes were still fixed on his girlfriend and her growing interest. She hadn't wanted to get involved, but Abby couldn't put up with how much of a sad puppy dog Gary was becoming.

"So? Guy can't stand up for himself, then maybe he shouldn't be with a woman," Tom stated.

"Shut up, you twat! If you had a girlfriend, you'd be having to fight guys off of her because she'd be trying to run from you," Abby's tongue whipped. She hadn't meant to lash out as strongly as she had.

"Okay, okay. Calm down, you two. So what do we do?"

"I don't know, you guys force him into a beer chugging competition or something. I'll take Nadia away and chat to her. Just keep an eye on Gary, alright?" Abby said, seeing a glint in his eye across the room. A twitch in his eyelid suggested his patience was wearing thin.

"I got this," Tom blurted, stepping out of the huddle.

"What? Tom, no!" Abby rasped too late.

"Hey, Troy! Initiation!" Tom held the last syllable as he marched into the centre of the room, pulling the American to his feet. Nadia's attention broke, a damsel broken from her trance.

"What?" Troy said, stumbling as he got to his feet. It was clear that though the young boy spoke a good game, his drinking habits were no match for those of the gang.

"Initiation. We've all done it. Prove to the gang that you're cool and can hang with us!"

"Initiation?" Troy's brain seemed even slower than Johnny's at processing anyone's words other than Nadia's.

"Yeah, initiation." Gary slinked out of his seat, smirk on his face. Troy looked around the

The Belfry Haunting

room, and Abby noticed that when he looked at Johnny, Gary winked at Tom. *Oh god, what have I started?*

"Oh, right, yeah. Like hazing back home. We had that for the rookies in the school team."

"Rrright, right. Just like back home. Except you guys did what? Dunked their heads in a toilet? Made them carry your school books for the week? Something like that?" Gary said, slapping his hand on Troy's shoulder.

"Something like that." Troy looked puzzled as Gary and Tom circled him.

"Guys, come on, stop. Troy's cool," Nadia piped up.

"Just our bit of fun. You know what the gang is like, Nads." Gary's tone is uncomfortable to listen to. Nadia retorted, disgusted by her boyfriend. Abby felt an acid burn in her stomach. Gary was never like this. What was he doing?

"No, no. It's ok. We've all just been hanging out anyway, right? This is a party, so let's do something cool." Troy rolled his head, Dutch courage flowing through his veins in lulls.

"That's it, a party!" Tom chuckled, "So, all you've got to do is go down that corridor," Tom said, grabbing the boy in as near a headlock as he could manage, dangling from Troy more than wrangling him in, pointing down the corridor they'd all stared down a couple of hours ago in fear.

"Just go down the corridor?"

"That's it."

Troy rolled his shoulder, Tom flopping off him.

"Ok, sure." Troy turned a slow circle, locking eyes with everyone. Lingering a little too long on Nadia's before Gary stepped in front of her.

"Go on then," Gary pushed.

Troy started a slow stumble towards the corridor, looking back over his shoulder, curling an awkward smile back at his supposed new friends. He disappeared into the darkness of the corridor. Nadia quickly turned to Gary and slapped his arm.

"What was that all about?"

8

Five minutes since Troy disappeared into the darkness of the corridor. Abby couldn't help but cast her gaze in that direction regularly, hoping the American would appear again. *Oh, please be okay. The last thing we need is bullying a foreigner into getting hurt.* She hoped he'd swing back into view, a silly drunk smile on his face or jumping into the light with a daft 'boo!'. The gang would all jump, laugh, and things would go back to normal.

Except it wouldn't, Abby knew that the rest of the night that lay ahead was going to be filled with frustration, difficulty and probably a fight between Gary and Troy when he eventually returned. Gary wasn't a tiny guy, but he certainly wasn't as big as Troy; nobody she'd met was. Gary wasn't even as big as Johnny. The boy had been in his fair share of fights, but Troy had the look of a guy who'd take his fair share of hits during games.

Something about the way he held his shoulders suggested he'd been in rough situations.

Regardless, she'd capitalised on the opportunity and had taken Nadia to a corner of the room while Tom and Johnny drank and talked about whatever silly, drunk teenage boys talk about. *Boobs, probably.*

"I wasn't flirting with him, Abby," Nadia reasoned, trying her best not to raise her voice at the accusation.

"You both clearly were!"

"So what if we were? Are you jealous?"

"What? No. I mean, he's cute. Wait, no! What about Gary?"

"What about him?" Nadia hiccuped.

"Oh, I don't know. Maybe the fact that he's your boyfriend and you're flirting with another guy right in front of him?"

"First off, like I said, I wasn't. I wouldn't do anything with Troy. Secondly, maybe Gary needs a little push. Honestly, Abby, he's been so annoying lately. Pathetic, like. Boy doesn't have any balls to him anymore."

"What? You've never mentioned this before." Abby stepped closer.

Nadia sighed, "Ok, promise you won't tell anyone else? Like…no big deal about this, alright?"

"Of course."

"Okay, so Gary and I were making out the other night and things got heavy and then we were going to have sex and he pulled out his…thing, you know?" Abby realised she was holding her booze better than Nadia tonight. She smiled and nodded, "Okay, so he pulled it out and it was like…not…you know…hard!" Nadia looked over Abby's shoulder to ensure the boys were still exchanging testosterone.

"Was he drunk?"

"No, we were both sober, hadn't touched a drink, we've both been saving our booze for tonight."

"So what did you do?"

"I kind of, I don't know. Just lay there, like waiting, you know?"

"Waiting?"

"Yeah, waiting for him to get hard."

"I'm guessing he didn't manage?"

"He tried. I felt a little bad for him to start with. He was trying to fix it, but it was just him pulling on his thing. After a while, I stopped feeling sorry for him, though. It was just depressing, and he looked so pathetic."

"Nadia, oh god. That's terrible."

"I know, I kind of realised at that point that I don't think I'm in love with him anymore."

"What? Really?" Abby asked, her face stunned in surprise. Johnny glanced over, noticing something going on, grabbed Gary's shoulder and pulled him away from catching a glimpse.

"Yeah, he's great and everything. We get along really well, but I don't know. I just don't have the feelings anymore."

A scream cut through them. Abby straightened her spine in a natural reaction. The girls looked to the boys, their startled eyes looking back and directing them to the corridor Troy had gone down. *What had it been, ten minutes? Fifteen now?*

"What was that?" Gary stepped back.

"Must be Troy, right?" Johnny reasoned.

"I'm getting sick of this place," said Nadia.

A cold rushed through the gang in a wave. Breathlessness catches them all.

"You go," Nadia said, to whom was unclear. Her hands quivered just hoping that someone would help out, fix the situation, tell her that Troy was fine.

"What? No, I'm not going," Tom answered, eyes still fixed on the corridor. Johnny took a step back, distancing himself from Tom.

"Yeah, Tom, you go," Gary added, also slipping back in line with Johnny.

"Fuck off." Tom glanced back, frustrated, fearful eyes shooting to the other boys. His legs pinned in place.

The Belfry Haunting

"Tom, just go, if Troy's in trouble, then the sooner someone gets to him, the better," Abby said. She'd noticed Nadia's trembling. She felt like she was doing the same, though her body was frozen still. "Gary, go with him. The two of you will find him quicker," she said. *And safer,* she thought.

"Fuck it, fine, come on," Gary said, stepping forward and grabbing Tom's arm. Tom flapped and fussed as he was pulled into the corridor, the blanket of darkness swallowing them up. Footsteps scuffing and sliding into silence.

Johnny, Abby and Nadia stood in silence, waiting, yearning for the boys to return quickly and laughing off an explanation that would make for a hilarious story in years to come.

"Should I go?" Johnny asked, feeling the need to establish some masculinity. His tone made it clear that he had no intention of following the boys.

"No, stay here," Nadia said as she wrapped her fingers around Abby's hand. *She feels so cold.*

Seconds passed, minutes followed, too many minutes for comfort. Abby, Johnny and Nadia shifted to one of the waiting benches facing the corridor. None of them spoke a word. As the time passed further and further, Nadia's breathing became more sporadic. Her grip clenching around

Abby stronger and stronger. Johnny rolled his lips and bit them, taking long breaths.

Finally…sound came echoing up the corridor.

Footsteps!

Abby and Nadia gasped in relief at the noise, quickly cutting themselves short.

Running footsteps!

Running footsteps coming closer, how many? Three sets of feet at least, *maybe more? Is that the sound of something slapping on the floor as well? Bare feet? Hands?*

Heaving breaths followed the echoed footsteps closer and closer. *How long is that corridor?*

"Go, go, run!" A voice. *Gary's voice?* Instructions thrusting urgency. Johnny jumped up from his seat, stepping forward towards the corridor. His fists clenched. Abby jumped up after him, Nadia yelping as she jolted forwards, still holding onto Abby's arm. *Is Johnny going to fight someone? What the hell is he doing?*

Before she could question him, Troy, Gary and Tom burst from the darkness. Their chests inflating at an alarming rate. Gary ran to Nadia, wrapping his arms around her before grabbing her hand. Troy slowed his pace, scanning over the group, making sure everyone was present. Tom bolted straight past everyone and out the door.

"We've got to go!" Gary blurted over his shoulder, yanking Nadia.

"What happened?" Johnny asked.

"Just run!" Troy said as he pushed Johnny. The gang asked no further questions, turning to run out the door.

Abby blinked, trying to grab a breath so that she could run and follow. Looking up to see Tom standing just outside the main entrance, his body illuminated. Standing as a silhouette, his shoulders pumped furiously. The gang bolted to him, unsure if they run to safety or more danger. *Troy and Johnny are still running in that direction, must be right,* Abby tried to think logically, stumbling over breaths as she followed. *What did they see anyway?*

"Stop!" A voice bellowed.

9

Falling in line next to each other, the gang grabbed at one another in solidarity. Light blinding them. Squinting their eyes, Johnny and Troy each held up a hand to try and see what was going on. Nadia peeked back over her shoulder. There seemed to be some hint of shadows moving in the reception area. *A person? More likely, some animal that had been living inside? A badger, a fox? Dust kicked up from them running away? Maybe. Maybe something following them?*

"Well, well, well." The voice bellowed from behind the light.

"Fuck you!" Tom shouted. His jaw shaking from the adrenaline, though Abby could see his confidence was flooding back. That faint whiff of owning the world without knowing the true reality. He straightened his back, his posture stronger somehow.

"What do you kids think you're doing here?" The voice, no longer a bellow, pulled to the side of the light. A figure stepping in front of part of it. Abby sighed, realising it was someone stepping in front of a car with its full beams on.

"It's fucking Dougi,e" Tom stated.

"Hey, man, look. There's something in there." Troy remained anxious, pointing back into the reception area.

"A Yankee?" The figure now identified as Dougie stated. It returned to the darkness behind the full beams, a low clunk flicked the car lights to normal. The gang, blinking away the pain of brightness, could now see the caretaker's car parked fifteen feet or so away. Dougie leaning his arms on the open car door. A smug smile on his face, the detective who has just stumbled across the serial killer red-handed.

"Hey, man, I'm not kidding-" Troy tried.

"Don't get many yanks around these parts," Dougie said, slamming the door closed and leaning against the car.

"Why are you talking like some old western sheriff?" Tom challenged.

"Shut your mouth, boy," Dougie commanded.

He was tall, thin, not a hugely intimidating man, not by a teenager's standards. A beard that could look like it had a place on the man's face if it weren't for how unkept it was. Johnny had once drunkenly joked that it looked like some runover badger had been glued to his chin; lucky for Dougie, it hadn't stuck. For how chaotic his face was, his brown work trousers looked pristine. His "Lockwood security" jacket reflected a little light. A navy blue polo shirt underneath and large, round spectacles completed his look. That gang had often joked that he looked like he was trying desperately to dress up as some American FBI agent, like they'd seen on TV. *How ironic,* Abby thought.

Douglas Bell stroked his moustache, pleased that he had the kids silent and obeying his orders.

"What are you kids doing here?" He asked.

"Dougie, come on, don't be stupid," Johnny said.

"I'll have none of that lip from you, Mr McCintosh!"

"You know why we're here. You've seen us here before." Nadia tried to help.

"I'm sure your mother would be very proud of you, Miss Hussain. Aren't your type supposed to be well behaved and avoid troublesome youths like these?" The man said. The gang's backs straightened, ready to back Nadia.

"Hey, fuck you!" Tom shouted.

"Ah, yes. Belfry's pride and joy and top dog fuck up. How are you tonight, Mr Winters? I'm assuming you wouldn't have anything illegal on your person, would you?" Dougie's eyebrow raised as his eyes trickled down to the boy's leg. One of the bags holding Tom's supply of weed poked out of his pocket. Tom fumbled, shoving it deep into his pocket.

"Ah, fuck this. You're not the cops. I'm out of here," Tom said.

"Yeah, come on, guys," Johnny said. Troy lingered, too used to American police holding such authority over kids across the pond. Johnny patted him on the back to reassure him.

"Why are you here anyway?" Abby asked.

"This is my job, Miss Rennie." Dougie folded his arms. The gang walked past him, leaving their stuff in the reception. Nobody was going to clean it up, Dougie never went inside. Nobody did except them. *No chance I'm going back in for a while either,* Abby told herself.

"Yeah, but you never come up here. Only ever see you during the day, mowing the grass."

"Fucking gardener," Tom whispered.

"I have been employed by the owner of these grounds to maintain and look out for any vagrants such as loiterers, teenagers or drug dealers." Dougie's eyes pierced through Tom.

"Well, I'm sure your employer would be happy to know that you are drunk on the job ninety per cent of the time," Abigail said, her brow furrowed.

"How dare you. You kids are the ones who are drunk!" Dougie's tone changed. Defensive, slurred, weak.

"Aye, so that's why you reek of booze, eh?" Gary snorted.

"Who even is the owner of these grounds?" Nadia asked.

A car horn blurted, almost comically timed if it hadn't cut so aggressively into the situation. Dougie whipped his head in its direction, his face dropping its attempt at an authoritative 'don't fuck with me' and moulding into a whimpering '*yes, master*'.

A black Rolls Royce sitting down the road, just passed the entrance, flashed it's lights twice. Abby and the gang felt a sobering breeze, cold seeming to seep into the darkness. An even darker night casting down upon them.

Dougie waved, stepping in the direction of the car.

"It's fine, everything is alright," He called down.

"Who's that?" Johnny's voice trembled.

"You kids better get out of here before things get worse," Dougie said, and Nadia tugged on Abby's arm. Snapping out of focus, Abby nudged her friends, shimmying to the side as Dougie walked down towards the car. The gang stumbled onto the grass, Tom nearly going arse

The Belfry Haunting

over tit. They'd never fled from the asylum, let alone over the grass. As far as they knew, the walls around the grounds had no breaks save for the entrance.

They made it to the treeline and hunkered down in shadows. Watching the caretaker make his way down the path, careful not to slip on the wet grass, he arrived at the car.

Dougie leaned over at one of the back windows, the moonlight blinking away from it as it slowly edged open.

Abby could make out Dougie gesticulating, yammering lots of words. He looked panicked, as if death stared back at him from inside the car. A desperate man pleading for his life. A sudden flick of a hand emerged from the window for a split second, pale, near white flesh shooed the man away. Dougie didn't move; the window edged itself close again.

The car grunted to life, its engine a low growl. Even at this distance, it still rattled through Abby's chest, shaking her heart. *How did we not hear it coming?* Its wheels carrying it up the hill, a cat stalking its prey, up to the front door. It parked next to Johnny's car. The driver's door opened, and a man in a black suit stepped out, his eyes scanning the treeline. The gang gasped as they dropped out of sight.

"What the fuck is going on?" Troy whispered.

"Shut the fuck up," Tom replied.

"We don't know. Just be quiet." Nadia tried to calm Troy, his fidgeting causing uncomfortable rustles.

They waited for what felt like an age. Abby had heard of this feeling before, her best estimation of it was being the opposite of when she'd sat in class, either finished with her work and having to wait for others or just in utter boredom and waiting for the class to end. This had a much different feeling to it. An urgency, a risk. There wasn't the threat of screaming internally at ennui, a very present, very real threat to life loomed. *This is fear.*

Gary, as quietly as he could, lifted his shoulder to push against the ground. Raising himself up to peak over the grass mound, he hid behind.

"They've gone." He whispered.

"Really?" asked Abby.

"I can't see them at all." He raised his head further, "Dougie's car's gone," he shifted his head, eyes bouncing white dots in the night. "So has that black car."

"Thank fuck. I'm getting the fuck out of here," Tom spoke, his voice sounding so loud, breaking from such silence.

The Belfry Haunting

"Wait, my car. I've got to get my car," Johnny said.

"Fuck that. I'm outta here," Tom refused, "Who's with me?" He stood, moving off through the treeline towards the entrance of the grounds. Gary rolled to his feet, Nadia following quickly behind him and gripping to the back of his jumper.

"Guys?" Johnny pleaded.

"No, fuck that. I'm sorry, Johnny. I'm not scared of that gardener creep Dougie, but that black Rolls gave me the fear. I'm off," Tom swatted.

"Sorry, Johnny, we'll get ourselves home", Gary shrugged. Nadia looked back to give another excuse. Unable to gasp a breath to speak, she gave up. Glancing at Abby apologetically.

Johnny stood, watching the three of them disappear and reappear occasionally in the moonlight. Three figures dancing between the trees. Abby and Troy sat up in the grass.

"You guys are going to help me, right?"

"I don't know the way back, so, ugh, yeah." Troy regretfully admitted.

"It's ok. We'll get your car and get home," Abby said. *I fucking hope we do.*

"So what's the plan?" Troy asked.

After much silence and exchanged glances, Abby suggested that they circle around the other direction in the treeline until they were far enough around to run out of the trees to the back of the asylum. From there, they could hug the wall back around to the front, hop in the car and race off before anyone noticed them.

"Sure," Troy agreed, happy that there was at least a semblance of a plan.

Johnny sighed and nodded. They circled back around the building. *Again, another first* Abby thought though she wished she didn't have to see anymore of this damned asylum.

Abby called out when she figured they'd travelled far enough, and after a count of three, they rushed the back of the asylum. Breaking from the shadows of the trees felt like they'd become suddenly exposed. Abby appreciated the courage soldiers must have had to emerge from the trenches onto the battlefield.

The back of the building felt like a hunched beast. The three of them approached from behind, not understanding the danger they were putting themselves in by testing fate.

Though they were bathed in the moonlight, not a soul saw them. They hit the back of the building hard, Johnny winding himself. Troy bounced off with such force that Abby checked to see if he'd left a dent in the wall. The rock-solid building showing not a care or any sign of damage.

Pressing themselves against the walls, they worked around to the side, ducking down to scoot under any windows. As Abby followed at the back of the group, her eye caught a flicker. Above, somewhere inside the asylum. She slowed her pace to get a better look.

There.

There it was again.

A light on one of the higher floors, *the third floor, the fourth?* The layout of the building was too confusing to tell. The light flickered off the window, dirt and dust giving it an opaqueness.

A cone of light marched down from the end closest to reception. Presumably, whoever had been in the Rolls?

At the other end, Abby thought she could see the figure of someone, someone tall. *Are they looking at me?* The figure raised an arm, not towards the cone of light, towards the window. *Oh, fuck w*as all Abby's mind could muster as she felt the hand reaching for her.

She picked up her pace, glancing back over her shoulder as she got to the corner, the beam of light marched down the corridor, the figure that she'd seen now gone.

"Come on!" Johnny rasped, grabbing Abby's coat by the shoulder.

The three teenagers sighed in relief as they reached the front of the building. There was Johnny's car, just where they'd left it. Along with it was a feeling that the coast was clear. Not that any of them trusted it. They edged towards the car,

Johnny carefully removed his keys from his pocket, slid them in the lock and unlocked the car.

After the three of them had cautiously shimmied into the car and eased the doors closed, each of them gently plugged their seatbelts in. Something neither Abby or Johnny normally did *yes we know it's unsafe.* They didn't know about Troy but he certainly hadn't buckled up on the way out.

Johnny's breath slowed, trying to control himself. He gripped the key. Taking several more long breaths, he nodded.

"Let's go!" He said before turning the key, the engine giving a chortle before coughing to life. Johnny gave no wait in slamming the car into gear, whipping it back in a wide reversing arc before thrusting the gear into first and gunning it down the path. None of them looked back. Their eyes locked on the entrance, the same thought repeating in their minds.

Please, please, please, please.
Get us out of here.

10

Troy managed to direct Johnny to his house once they'd gotten close enough to town. The only words spoken, his directions.

"Thanks," Troy said, not moving from the back seat of the car. Johnny's hands still gripped the wheel, knuckles just beginning to fade from white. Abby's eyes rested on the dashboard, seeking peaceful reassurance that they were in the clear.

"Hey, don't tell your folks about this," Johnny said to Troy.

"No, don't worry. We didn't do anything wrong anyway. Are you guys alright?" The American asked.

"Fine," Abby said, wanting the situation to be over. Troy held his silence as he looked at Abby, then back to Johnny, unconvinced by her answer.

"It's fine, we've just never had things get fucked up like that before. I've never seen that car before either. Must be the old guy who owns the place, I guess."

"So?"

Johnny looked at Abby, her eyes still on the dash. Sighing, he answered, "I'll tell you tomorrow. Meet me at the park."

Troy lingered a little before opening the door and stepping out. He leaned in before closing the door, ready to say something. The tension stopping him, giving a soft wave, he closed the door and started walking up the path to his place.

"We're going to be so fucked," Abby said as Johnny pulled away.

"Don't worry, we'll be fine. It was just Dougie."

"Dougie's never acted like that before."

"He's been pissed at us plenty of times," Johnny scoffed.

"I mean, when he saw that car."

"So, we don't know anything about that. If it's the owner, then maybe the guy's an asshole, and Dougie is scared of him. Most people hate their bosses, right?"

Abby watched houses pass by as they headed through town to her house. Johnny was right, they'd been flustered, that was all. They probably overreacted because they were drunk and high. Something in Dougie's reaction still didn't sit right with Abby, though. Nobody cared when a passerby came to Belfry. Didn't matter if you were a lowlife or a hotshot. You were just some prick passing through. *Yeah, sure, go see the hills and the landscape. Go see the caves nearby and the forest. Oh, you've never seen such beautiful places? That's nice. They are fucking boring and there's nothing to them.* Goodbye and peace be fucking with you.

"What are you going to tell Troy?" Abby tried to shift the conversation a little.

"What do you mean? I'll tell him about the asylum."

"Everything?"

"Why not?"

"You don't think he'll react funny to us?"

"We haven't done anything. Why should we be worried?"

"That place, I don't know. It's better left an untold story, don't you think?"

Johnny rolled his lips as they pulled up to Abby's house.

"Yeah, maybe you're right."

11

Saturday, normally a day of peace in Belfry. The majority of the population nursing sore heads and funny tummies, though that wasn't particularly different to any other day. The number of hangovers and their severity certainly increased substantially on a Saturday.

It was the first Saturday in a long time that Abby and the gang woke up feeling worse than a hangover. Their heads not pounding, their stomachs not turning and threatening to explode. Instead, their bellies yearned for hearty meals, their shoulders and backs ached from pinching tension. Their minds drifted in haunting emptiness.

Still, Saturday meant the same thing it always did: meet up at the park as usual.

Abby was surprised to find she was the first one to arrive; normally, there would be others already there. More often than not, she'd be last to arrive; she always slept later after a night of inebriation. They'd each bring a bag of remedies from the shop, lugging their plastic bags to the bench or swings to try and work off their hangovers. Piecing together the hilarity and chaos from the night before. If things were really bad, they'd either go to the pub for a cooked breakfast or simply not turn up at all. Coiling themselves up in bed to try and sleep through as much of the self-induced torture as possible.

It wasn't long after Abby arrived that Gary and Nadia showed up. Both of them carrying plastic bags with sandwiches, crisps and sports drinks. Gary swore by plying himself with high amounts of electrolytes to get through a rough morning, ever the aspiring athlete. To his credit, he was always the one who recovered the quickest and best. None of the rest of the gang followed suit; it was all about having something cold and fizzy for them. Something to chill and calm the throbbing pain, a pleasant sweetness to ease the drinking. Swallowed in gentle, controlled sips. Gary didn't have a sports drink today, though, pulling a milkshake from the bag, he waved a feeble greeting and opened the drink to begin chugging.

"God, I'm starving today," he said, wiping his upper lip.

"Yeah, me too," Abby agreed. She'd taken her own supply: a scotch pie, a mince and mealie pie, a bag of crisps and a bottle of mango juice. She would never normally go for the pie, usually opting for a healthier alternative. Of course, healthier food never nourished her recovery. Today, though, she could feel her body yearning for carbs. Energy she needed to restore what was depleted from their escape last night.

The three nodded to each other as they ate and drank, each aware of the other's unease. None of them wanting to poke at it for fear that they might poke at their own.

"What up, fuck knuckles," Tom shouted as he appeared. A big, stupid grin slapped across his face.

He looked frustratingly fresh by comparison to everyone else. He even looked fresher than he did when he was sober. He marched to the swings, plonking himself down and gliding back and forth, his bag of goodies swinging like Santa's sack.

"Why are you in such a good mood today?" Gary asked.

"Oh, I don't know. Just feeling tip top," Tom said, his smile playful but innocent. His shoes screeched on the rubber mats as he slowed himself to a stop, pulling out a large sub roll filled with roast beef.

"Had myself a shower this morning, and when I looked in the mirror, I don't know. I just thought I looked good," he said. Abby wasn't going to tell him he was right. His skin looked brighter, clearer of spots. His hair sat nicely on his head, not the normal mad explosion of scruffiness. A slight quiff at the front. *Has he been scared straight? Or normal? Or handsome?* Tom unwrapped the roll and thrust it into his mouth, taking a gigantic bite. His whole face moved as he chewed. It looked a little odd, like an imitation of a human doing normal things, but different. Something off-putting at the edges of the picture, just slight blurriness that suggested it wasn't quite real.

Johnny arrived, Troy walking at his side. *Had they walked here together? No, Johnny told him to meet them at the park. Oh god, I hope those two don't become best friends. Tom will freak.*

"Aye, aye, where you two bum boys been?" Tom said.

"Tom, shut the fuck up," Johnny barked. Tom stopped sharp, a dumb, stunned expression. *There's the normal Tommy,* thought Abby.

"Why do you always go with racist or homophobic insults?" Nadia asked.

"Huh? I don't know. Cuz I'm stupid," Tom said, stopping himself. Looking as if he wasn't sure why he said it. The rest of the gang looked at him. *Why had he said that?*

"We're all shaken up by last night, then?" Johnny asked the gang. A feeble attempt to lift spirits.

"I hate Dougie." Tom broke the silence. "He's always stirring up shit with us."

"Well, we are the ones trespassing," explained Nadia.

"Still," Tom reasoned, and Nadia nodded in acceptance.

"I don't understand. We just got busted, right?" Troy chimed in.

"You don't know the full story," Gary explained. Troy held his gaze as if it was an answer, waiting expectantly for an explanation. Sensing the nervous energy, the gang clearly uncomfortable on the topic. Abby sighed.

"Fuck it."

"No, you don't have to explain." Nadia rested her hand on Abby's arm.

"If I don't, Johnny was going to. Better it come from me." Abby rose from the bench, taking a few steps and breaths to prepare herself. Troy's anticipation growing, he leaned back on the frame of the swings. Expecting the anticipation to turn sour, no doubt some bullshit boring story about to get told.

"That asylum used to have a bunch of people in it, right?" She glanced at Troy, he gave a single nod. "And they did weird, crazy things to people in there. Nobody really knows for certain, but there are all these stories of experiments. People being drowned in freezing water, then in boiling water. People being subjected to blinding light and deafening sound. People being segregated away into rooms with no light and isolated from all noise. People being opened up, forced to eat disgusting creations, having body parts removed, having other people's body parts grafted onto them. All kinds of disgusting shit. Some of it is rumour and some it must be somewhat true. When the place closed, Belfry never spoke of it again. No need to. No want to."

"We've been going up there every few weeks or so to drink, mostly when we can't be bothered getting haggled in the pub. We drink, we smoke, we try and have a laugh. It's a change of scenery. We're just teenagers letting loose, you know?" Troy sighed and nodded again. He was more intrigued by the horror stories of the asylum than of what the gang got up to. Hoping for something he could take back home that might entertain his friends. Maybe scare some folks and get a laugh.

"Thing is, we *actually* go up there because I asked. I asked them to go up there with me every now and then so that I can feel closer to him." Abby lowered her head, Troy nudged off the frame, interest looming.

"Who?" he asked.

"My brother." Wind blew through the park, the rusted swings creaking. Immobile objects objecting to the conversation, already aware of the feeling it left. Lingering negative energy. The gang was used to the cold breezes in Belfry; Troy was still getting used to it, shivering slightly. It was a strange, cold wind, he thought; he'd never felt like he could smell cold before.

"What happened?"

"He was older than me, though we're older now than he was when he…left. We were nine and ten years old, Mickey was fourteen. He looked after me, kept an eye out for the rest of us. When his friends would try and bully us or pick on us, he'd stand up for us. I don't know why; he could have been my asshole brother that I hated. He could have only looked out for me, but he chose to look after all of us. He did, however, like winding us up, playful older brother and all. He dared us to go up to the asylum with him. Dared us to go searching through the building with him. I can still remember the feeling of his hand as he held mine when he walked me through the corridor."

"I don't think we would have gotten much further than you did last night before something spooked me and sent me running. The gang were waiting for me in reception, just like last night. Mickey was going to show them it was all fine, and then we would all go snoop around. When I turned around, expecting to see Mickey following after me, he wasn't there."

"He must have got lost? I damn near got lost in there," Troy said.

"We don't know," Johnny interjected, silencing Troy and letting Abby continue.

"That was the last day I saw my brother. He disappeared and was never seen again." She sniffed back tears and let out a little chuckle. "It sounds ridiculous, right? Something out of a bad horror movie? The police went in and searched the place after I told my mother. Nobody found, no signs of distress, no signs that he might have broken a window, hopped out and run away. His picture was plastered around town, even though we all know each other. Nearby towns were contacted and asked if he'd been seen. Nothing. Just gone!"

"I, ugh, I'm sorry." Troy picked up on the melancholy the rest of the gang was giving off.

"So, yeah. Sorry to make it a real bummer, but that's why we were there last night. Everything that happened was a little too heavy. A little too reminiscent."

"Did you see that same black Rolls Royce that night?"

"No, that never happened. We ran home from the asylum when Mickey disappeared."

"So none of you know who it is?"

"Must be the owner, right?" said Gary.

"Wait, what did you see?" Tom asked.

"What do you mean? I saw the black car, same as all of you," Troy squinted.

"No, when you were in the corridor. You screamed. That's why we came to get you."

Troy frowned "I never screamed."

12

The gang faced Troy, their telepathic link making them all look at the boy the same way. An outsider, someone they no longer knew if they could trust.

"What scream?" the American asked.

"You screamed when you were down the corridor. When we made you do the initiation," Johnny said.

"Yeah, thanks for that, by the way. Freaked me the fuck out."

"You scream like a girl, man," Tom laughed.

"I swear, I didn't laugh" Nadia held up her hands.

"So who did then?" asked Gary. An aggressive accusation sitting on his shoulders.

"I don't know, but it wasn't me," Troy backed up. For such a large boy, it looked odd for him to be so defensive. "There must have been someone else there."

"Who? Like the damn witch?" Tom chuckled.

"Wait, what? Witch?" Troy took another step backwards.

"Alright, alright, everyone, calm down." Johnny raised his hands.

"You guys aren't telling me something." Troy's fists balled, his shoulders and pecs flexing.

"Troy, it's alright, calm down. Tom is just winding you up." Abby jumped in.

"No, what about the witch?" Though his tone suggested a serious concern, his grin suggested otherwise.

"Look, ignore him. There is some stupid story about a witch that lived here hundreds of years ago. When weird stuff happens, the locals like to joke it's her stirring up stuff. It's why the pub is called The Crying Witch, locals like to latch onto and joke about that sort of thing," Abby explained. It looked like it did little to calm Troy. Perhaps he had just decided to take a disliking to Tom. *Easily done.*

Nadia gasped.

"Oh, Abby. Shit. I just realised. I'm so sorry." Nadia blurted with her hand over her mouth. Abby wished nobody would have realised. She wished she didn't have to explain about her brother.

The Belfry Haunting

She'd considered asking if anyone else had seen the figure in the window last night, though decided against that. *Why can't I just be left alone? Lead a quiet and boring life.*

"What?" Johnny asked.

"It's today!" Nadia's eyes flared at Johnny, not wanting to state exactly what she was meaning.

"Alright, someone please fucking explain. I'm getting sick of these secrets. Someone explain before I open a can of whoo-"

"It's the anniversary of my brother's disappearance!" Abby raised her voice. Troy frowned, realising he'd actually felt a little shock and fear at how loud the girl had become.

"Oh, Abby, I'm so sorry. I totally forgot," said Johnny as he walked over to her, wrapping his arms around her.

"It's fine," she replied. The gang all lowered their heads, Troy loosened up, sympathy poured from his eyes. "Honestly, guys, can we not make a big deal out of it. I was hoping you guys wouldn't remember. I just wanted to go and get wasted at his spot. It felt like it was all starting to drift off into the fog. Not now, though. Now it's brought it all back." Abby tried her hardest but couldn't stop the quiver in her lower lip, the reddening of her cheeks. Blinking several times to try and mask the tears, shut them off before anyone saw them. Scratching her head to distract herself, both hands grabbing clumps of her hair and scrunching it tight. *No, no, no. Why is it still so hard?*

Johnny embraced her, pulling her head into his shoulder to help her hide her tears.

"So what do we do now?" Gary asked, hoping enough time had passed that moving on from Abby's outburst was acceptable.

"We find out who the guy in the black car was," Johnny said. Abby lifted her head from his shoulder, a Rorschach blot of her face left in Johnny's hoodie. She nodded and stepped away from him.

"Yeah, I agree. I need to know," she said.

"That's an option." Nadia showed her support for her friend, lingering a look at Abby before turning back to the group. "Or we could just leave the whole thing and forget about it?"

"What's the matter, Nads, scared?" Tom hunched over, wiggling his arms and legs like some marionette gone rogue.

"Fuck you, Tom."

"Just give me a chance," Tom joked, winking at her. Gary stepped in front of her.

"Maybe she's right. Maybe letting this all go is the best option," Gary said, squaring up to the yammering clown.

"No! We go and find out who this old fucker is," Abby stated.

"I'm in," Troy said, collective eyebrows raised at him. "What? Not like I've got much else to do here. Plus, I want to find out what screamed in the corridor last night that you all think was me."

"Yeah, yeah. Keep trying to cover it up, Loverboy." Tom laughed.

"Loverboy?" Troy asked, Tom didn't answer. Abby shot Nadia a glare, a scowl shot back in confusion.

"Look, you guys can come with us or not. I don't care. I'm going, that's all. If the Yankee Doodle wants to come along, fine!" Abby said, marching off. Troy exhaled sharply, raising his arms at Abby's comment. She wasn't entirely sure where she was heading. Johnny wobbled in an embarrassing display of confusion and cowardice before accepting his fate and running after Abby. Tom followed after Johnny. Troy looked between Gary and Nadia, shrugging before scuffing his shoe on the ground, shoving his hands in his pockets and strolling in the same direction.

13

Who cared if Nadia didn't want to join Abby. Sure, she'd assumed she'd stick by her and be her best friend about it all. Be with her as they tried to figure out who the owner was. *Who cares if it's a dead end and has zero chance of leading me towards Mickey? She's my fucking best friend. She should be there for me, right?*

Abby remembered three years ago when the two of them had shared a bottle of Malibu on the park swings. The guys had been at the pub watching the football, and the girls had decided to take a stroll, a slightly boozy stroll.

Nadia had tried her best to ask if Abby was alright. She knew it was that time of year and that it wasn't fair, especially not when it was piled on top of having to live in Belfry.

"I don't think I'm ever going to stop missing him," Abby had said. She knew the coconut rum was making her lips a bit looser than she'd like. She trusted Nadia, though. They were besties, stuck together through thick and thin.

"You shouldn't ever have to stop missing him. That's only natural. It's a good sign; it lets you know that the love is still there. If you still miss him, then you still love him, and I know it sounds corny, but he still loves you too."

Abby snorted, a drip leaking from her nose. She quickly wiped it away, but Nadia had already seen it and was failing miserably to hold in her laughter.

"I know, and yeah, it's corny. But I still feel him." She sighed, taking another large swig from the bottle. "I don't know. There's part of me that just wants it to be over, you know? The pain. I just want to move on. I'll always love him, I'll always miss him. But can it not be this big thing that swamps my head every year?"

Yeah, maybe Nadia was just trying to look out for me.

"Guys, hey, guys?" Troy said, chasing up to the group. The grey sky looming over them, clouds tumbling over one another. A sadistic audience wanting to watch the fray unfold. "Where are we going?"

"We're going to go back up to Lockwood," Abby said.

"Really?" Tom asked.

"Is that a wise idea?" Johnny seconded. Looking over his shoulder as a car flew past.

"We go up tonight. When it's dark. Before midnight, we stay sober. We look around with torches. We grab anything we find of interest and we take it back home. We look for anything that mentions owners, investors, landlords, any of that sort of shit. That place is filled with files and notes, we know that. There's got to be something in there for us to find."

"Why at night? Why not during the day when it's light?" Troy asked. Johnny and Tom flashed a thankful glance.

"We go up at night because it'll be easier to sneak in. Dougie will be on high alert after last night. Not to mention because his boss is around. Did you see how flustered he was?"

"Dude is easily scared, so what?" Tom hoped that they didn't have to go up to the asylum again. For all the machismo bravado he tried to cover up with, he was fooling nobody.

"So what do we do until then?" Johnny asked.

"I'm going to the library," Abby said, the three guys slowed their pace. Abby marched off down the street and turned onto the main street.

"The library?" Troy asked, "You guys have one in this weird little town?"

The Belfry Haunting

"Yeah," Johnny said, watching Abby disappear around the corner. The wind picking up and sending a chill through the boys. "Nobody uses it, though."

"So why is it still open?" Troy asked. He seemed to be handling the cold quite well now. Perhaps he was becoming acclimatised, or maybe he just didn't have any other room left in his brain to fathom it. Too many questions, concerns, fears and frustrations squeezing against one another, forming a confusing throbbing headache.

"Because this is a weird little town," Johnny said, his gaze still focused on the corner. "Come on. Let's head to the pub, there'll be Rugby on soon."

"Yeah. Just some old hag witch in that library anyway," Tom piped up, a warm comfort in following Johnny's footsteps. "We can show you what a real sport is, Yankee boy."

"Another witch?" Troy raised an eyebrow.

Tom slapped his lips. "Alright, sorry. A turn of phrase. Some old bitch runs the place. You coming or not?"

The Library was a place Abby hadn't seen herself in today, or this week, this month, this year. Hell, she hadn't seen herself ever going back there. She used to go when she was a little girl, excited to pick up another novel and escape into another world. While at school, she used the library to help her studies, the only person in the entire school to do so. She didn't care about getting called a nerd; she had only confided in Nadia and Johnny that she actually found learning new things interesting. Nadia shrugged it off while Johnny had teased her for a couple of weeks, telling her she'd need to get glasses. Before long, his teasing turned to requesting, telling her that glasses would look hot. She could be his hot librarian. Needless to say, Abby didn't get glasses.

    Still, she had fond memories of studying biology and chemistry at the library. Reading books of history, finding out about all of the crazy things that happened during wars. The battles that won and lost wars, the equipment and tactics that changed the course of history. Physics opened her eyes to space. Abby spent a year looking up into the sky after she passed her physics exam, watching as the twinkling celestial entities looked back at her. She'd considered asking for a telescope for Christmas, but before long, the idea left her head. Accepting that there was no need to look to the skies when she would be numbing her brain and senses each Friday night for the foreseeable future. Giving herself any glimmer of hope was only a recipe for depression and most likely suicide.

    As with anything, the good comes with the bad. Although her time studying at the library was pleasant to recall, the building was not. Nor the single librarian who ran the place. Miss Pendleton, formerly a Mrs, though the gang couldn't fathom how any man could love her. A woman that challenged everything life gave her. Nobody knew how she'd come to settle in Belfry. Rarely seen, rarely heard, only the library attendees would occasionally hear her strong posh English accent with its bitter taste of the upper class. Though she was tall, she would look down her nose at anyone. Not only did nobody know why she'd decided to settle in this quiet, decaying part of Scotland, nobody knew why she continued to stay. She seemed to have a strong distaste for the place, though the rumours were that she held an equally strong distaste for her home. From what Abby could tell, the woman had a strong distaste for many things: cats, dogs, children, teenagers, men, women, crisps, crumbs, mess, music, Scotland, England, Ireland, any other country, even herself. In the first few years she had lived in Belfry, people had asked about her husband. Some were trying to show a little sympathy; perhaps she was a bitter woman because her loved one had been taken from her.

"Oh heavens, I don't talk about Terrance. That wretched old man took decades from me," she almost spat at whoever asked her.

The only thing she would appear to have any affinity for was books. The best summation anyone could make to why she remained here was that she was so undeniably abhorrent to be around that she'd basically secured herself her own quiet lair. Most of the locals shared the same opinion: she stays in her dusty library, and we'll stay away from her. She can read her books until her eyes rot and fall out, good riddance.

"Miss Rennie." Her voice echoed through the Library as Abby entered the building. Beige was the colour and beige was the only choice. The shelving, the walls, the carpet, the children's area with one single child-sized chair, all of it differing shades of beige. The desk Miss Pendleton sat behind was situated at the back of the library. Not next to the entrance, as one might presume. It could only be guessed that the desk was at the back of the room to allow for the chance that someone might come in and Miss Pendleton might ignore them or hide, thus people would presume there was nobody to help and simply leave. Abby walked around the first couple of shelves enough to see Miss Pendleton leaning to her left at her desk. Her spectacles sitting at the edge of her nose, a gold chain connecting the legs glistened in the light, somehow also looking beige.

"Hello." Abby waved nervously, the familiar smell returning to her. The smell of the building, the smell of the books, the smell that could very well have been Miss Pendleton herself.

The Belfry Haunting

Stale sediment, the more you smelt it, the thicker it got. Coating your throat and clogging saliva.

"I thought it was you. I could tell by the way you opened the door," the old woman said. Abby wondered if the woman ever got up from her desk. *Have the two merged?* She doubted Miss Pendleton even got up to go to the bathroom. Probably hated the need to use the bathroom so much that she had scared her insides into not needing to go.

"The way I opened the door?" Abby quietly asked, turning back to see the door creep closed. A cackling squeak. She weaved between the shelves, recalling the quickest route to the desk and stood before the Queen of this domain.

"I believe you have penalties", Miss Pendleton said, a sharp eyebrow raising, so sharp her forehead wrinkled in pain.

"Pardon?"

"You still have one of my books. You were supposed to return it…" She flipped open a leather-bound binder and ran a single, bony finger down lines and lines of notes.

"September 3rd, 1971."

"That was three years ago," Abby said, a look of confused pleading spreading across her face.

"Exactly, quite a penalty shall have to be paid." Miss Pendleton said, her eyebrow stabbing back to its original place.

113

"Miss Pendleton, I'm sorry, I'll still have it in my room, I'm sure. I'm not here about that, I'm here because I need to use your microfiche machine."

The woman leaned back in her chair, a posture that looked unnatural for her. An eased spine and relaxed shoulders made her look even more inhuman than Abby could recall.

"And why would you want to use it?"

"I want to do some research on Lockwood." Abby regretted saying the sentence as soon as the words escaped her lips.

"Lockwood?" The old woman's eyes narrowed, Abby felt like the room was getting darker. "Have you been up in that building up to no good? It's not safe up there, girl."

"No. No. Not at all." Abby tried to snort off the comment as if it was a plain joke. Little old Abigail Rennie wouldn't dream of doing such a thing. "I've been here so long, and the nights are drawing in. I thought I'd give myself a little project to do. Find out more about the town I live in. You never know, I might be able to make it into something one of the Unis' nearby will take up."

"Why would a University want to know about an old abandoned asylum?" Miss Pendleton said, an accusation slapped across Abby's face. She was poking holes in the girl's story, Abby shrugged.

The Belfry Haunting

"I'm not sure at this stage. Won't know until I do the research and dig up something of interest." Abby moved towards the stairs. *Play it cool, act as if nothing is wrong.* "Is that alright then? If I use your Microfiche?"

The old woman stared at her, eyes widening now. As if tiny creatures hid behind her spotlight eyeballs, directing them to look into Abby, look through her skin, muscle and bone to her very core. Her head suddenly tilting to the side, Abby swore she could hear a click.

"Be careful what you dig into. History has a way of unpacking some unspeakable things. However, that said, knowing about one's home is a reasonable undertaking…this way." Miss Pendleton walked past Abby to the stairs, an arm motioning to follow.

It had been years since Abby had been in the library, the dusty thickness in the air beginning to feel almost normal again. It had been even longer since she'd been down the stairs and into the basement of the building. For all the old woman seemed to do to make the place as uninviting as she could, she'd clearly put in more work to make the basement feel like a comfortable place. Rumoured to have been an old bunker during the blitzkrieg, *something else you could look up on the Microfiche?* The solid stone walls hid their grey skin behind shelves full of colour. There was little beige down here in comparison to upstairs.

Miss Pendleton stiffened, if that was possible, as she led Abby to the far back wall, her footsteps stabbing Abby's ears while she followed. What would be sitting directly underneath the entrance? Why she felt the need to accompany Abby was unclear. Abby had been down in the basement many times when she'd been studying. All the best books were down there, the most prized, most insightful, most informative. Still, the old woman's spine straightened, almost bending back the wrong way as she walked. A creature nervous and unwanting to share its lair. Ready to defend it, unsheathe it's claws and tear the throat out of any threat…or prey.

"Here we are." Miss Pendleton spun as she reached the Microfiche machine, resting her hand on the top of it. "You remember how to use it?"

"Yes, thank you." Abby interlinked her fingers, feeling like she was being scolded.

"Normally I would charge three pounds for an hour's use," the woman said, her face appeared to crack. *Normally? Who's been in here in the past few years? Pfft. Normally.* Her wrinkles widening, her cheeks at the brink of their tension limits. *Is she smiling?* "But for you, I'll give a discount. Two pounds for an hour."

"Oh, you are too kind," Abby said.

Miss Pendleton cupped her hands together ."Of course, I'll add your late fee to the total once you're done," Her sharp eyebrow raised again.

"Oh, yes. Of course. Sorry again for that."

"The history of Belfry is bleak, Miss Rennie, Lockwood doubly so. You might find greater enjoyment looking into other topics." A silence dropped between the two of them. Abby smiled and raised her eyebrows. With a nod, the woman left Abby to it. There were no footsteps echoing through the basement as she left. Abby slowly sat down into the chair, looking over the microfiche, *how* do *I use this thing again?* She turned and looked back, seeing the old hag beginning to ascend the stairs. Eyes shooting at Abby from that distance. Abby knew that, even though the woman should be struggling to read at her age, her eyes could sharply make out Abby from that distance. An alert predator zeroing in, waiting for the moment to strike.

It took Abby, what she thought was maybe an hour or an hour and a half, to get what she was looking for. After dusting off the old machine, dusting off the chair and then having to dust off the desk, she stumbled across a binder with instructions on how to use the machine. Memories flooded back of looking up old newspaper articles about the war while studying history.

The bulk of her time was wasted looking for the file boxes that would hold what she was looking for. Sifting through article after article, month after month of papers containing any information about Belfry. Further and further back she went, past the "sheep invasion" of '66 when a nearby farmer's flock had decided to take a trip into town and clogged up everything. Passed "The great dump" when another farm had blocked the far side of town, headed south when his trailer full of manure had tipped over. The bulk of the Belfry headlines usually related to some fumble by the surrounding farmers.

It wasn't until she got to 1940 that she found anything mentioning Lockwood Asylum. A front page article with a picture of the front of the building and an old man standing out from of it. Two men dressed in doctors' coats framed him on either side.

LOCKWOOD LOCKED UP: ASYLUM CLOSES DOORS

The headline above the picture managed to catch Abby's eye before she zipped past it. The article provided further details further into the paper. She quickly shifted through to the necessary page, relieved to have found something just before she was going to give up hope.

The Belfry Haunting

The same picture was on page thirty-two of the paper, enlarged to show more detail. The old man's face was still firm and flat. Not an ounce of emotion shown.

"Viktor Dietrich standing in front of Lockwood asylum on the day it closed." Abby read the caption, feeling a chill down her spine. She rolled her shoulders to loosen up, looking over her shoulder, expecting to find Miss Pendleton breathing over her.

The man was the owner of the asylum, an institution that had been part of the family since it was founded in 1349. A Gunther Dietrich had started it with the intention to heal the overlooked and shunned. People who had been assumed to be of extremely low IQ, affected by some condition nobody knew about, or the more commonly diagnosed "affliction by demons". *Jesus, they were trying to cure possession?* Abby scoffed.

Through family lineage, Vitkor Dietrich was the man whom the facility had come to, and by the turn of several centuries, there was no obvious need for such a place. Medicine and psychology surpassed the archaic practices back then. There were no more patients in Lockwood, and so Viktor had taken the obvious decision to close its door. Of interest in the article, it did mention that Viktor still planned to hold onto the building, not stating what intention he had for the place.

"It is a place, near and dear to my heart and the family's. I would not pass it to another's hands," he was quoted as saying.

Who the hell was Viktor Dietrich? Abby thought. Fishing through previous articles, she could find only brief mentions of the family name in relation to Lockwood. Nothing on the old man, the occasional picture at most. His brow furrowing further and further as the years passed. His cheeks sagging more and more, his skin wilting as time took its toll. His eyes never faded, though, always holding the same concentrated focus. They looked alive in every photo Abby stumbled across, staring straight out of the article. Staring so strongly, the eyes felt like they had a voice.

I see you, I know who you are.

"Are you alright, Miss Rennie? Have you found what you were looking for?" Abby blinked, startled by the voice breaking her concentration. She'd been hypnotised by the photo of Dietrich in front of the asylum on the day it was closing. She didn't know how long she'd been staring at it. She felt as if the old man was going to reach out at any second and whisper something in her ear. Some secret he'd held onto for God knows how long, months, years, decades…centuries? *Lockwood is doing something to me.*

"Oh, Miss Pendleton. Sorry, yes, I found everything on Lockwood I was looking for."

Peering over Abby's shoulder, the old woman scanned the screen. Judgement pouring out of her. At Abby or at old Viktor Dietrich, who knew.

"If you are going to write anything about Lockwood, then you might want to consider looking into the history of its land" Pendleton's eyes didn't shift from the screen. Was she getting hypnotised by the old man as well?

"Oh?"

Pendleton's lips pursed, and she sighed; it was the most human Abby had ever seen her act. She didn't like it, wanted her to return to the creepy lizard woman she'd known before.

"Yes, Belfry has a long history; the land that the building sits on has seen a wealth of atrocities. A family that lived there left a mark…" Her voice trailed off. Slowly, her eyes travelled up and she turned. Her feet scuffing the floor as she slid off. *What is wrong with her?* Abby thought. She would never have let people scuff their feet like that when she was younger. You'd get a telling off, and if you persisted, a stiff ruler smack across the hands or back of the head.

"What do you mean, left a mark? Was it the Dietrich family? Did something happen to them there?" Abby rose from the chair, only taking a couple of steps in the direction Miss Pendleton appeared to be floating off in.

"Dietrich is only part of the story", the old woman murmured before turning at one of the shelves. Abby watched for a few seconds before hearing a door open and close.

Run!

Her fight or flight instinct kicked in. She grabbed her coat and bolted for the stairs. Peeking down every shelf unit she passed. Expecting to see Pendleton floating in the air, arms raising, head tilting back, eyes rolling into the back of her head. Skin peeling off, tearing and allowing the hidden monster beneath to emerge. All of those horror books Abby had read started to unfold in her memory. *Perfect, thanks.*

Reaching the bottom of the stairs, Abby took one last look behind her. She saw a door down one of the shelving units, as she tried to remember where it led to it clunked and began to creak open. Abby didn't want to stay and find out if those horror novels had actually been based on real events. Bolting up the stairs two at a time, she could feel the air lighten as she ascended. The musty, old smell is still present, but the beginnings of actual air are flourishing.

She rushed the front door, hearing the steps of Pendleton again. Sharp, piercing steps.

Rising.

Rising.

Closing.

Closer.

Closer.

Unable to stop her momentum, Abby collided with the front door. Flinging it open, surprised a scaly claw didn't slam it shut before she was away to get through.

"I'll come find you!" Pendleton's voice tore through the air, making a last grab for Abby as she bounced outside, stumbling over her own feet and tumbling to the concrete.

Staring at the front door, lungs heaving, heart pounding. She grew angry at herself for sitting there waiting for the old woman turned lizard to emerge and gobble her up. Had Pendleton said she'd come find her? Had she been changing into some monster? *Don't be daft, Abby. You've just got yourself worked up.* After what felt like an age had passed, she looked up to see the lamppost outside was on.

"Fuck."

It was dark.

14

How long had Abby been in the library? It had been what?...Just before lunch time, when she'd gone in. Granted, the days were shorter this time of year. It would get dark around half past five, but still. She'd only been reading for a couple of hours, right?

Had I been staring at the old creep Dietrich the whole time?

Pendleton is going to have a fucking field day with me and my late fees. Or she's going to literally tear me limb from limb and eat my brain.

Come on, Abby! Think! Get your head straight.

Lockwood!

The guys!

She peeled herself from the concrete. Dusting off the pebbles lodged in her hands, and looked around. Nobody around. That wasn't good. If it were only recently dark, then there would still be the odd person walking through the town. Folks off to the shop to grab some milk, folks heading round to their friends for a dinner party…maybe. Most likely, there would be punters headed to the pub.

She ran up the little road from the library to the high street.

Fuck!

It was dead as well. She ran down the high street towards the asylum. Slowing only when she passed the pub.

Fuck fuck!

The familiar rumble and boisterous vocals of Scottish folk music bounced in a muffled beat. *Oh god, everyone's three sheets to the wind. They've clearly been drinking for hours. What time is it?* A punter staggered out of the door to plant a hand against the wall and empty his stomach. The music clearing up. Abby did her best to peer in as she passed. Taking a couple of jumps to see in through the window and check if the guys were there.

The vomiting patron glanced up and frowned at Abby as she hopped and skipped past him in a panicked rush. Trying to figure out if the girl was a hallucination brought on by the drink. Abby's motions did little for the man's dignity, and he returned to emptying his insides on the wall.

All Abby could make out inside The Crying Witch were the usual patrons and a huddle of guys in the corner. The same guys that would turn up every Saturday with their fiddles and drums and would "tune up" to begin their evenings. Meaning they would drink down enough pints for their Dutch courage to blossom and their care for embarrassment to drown. *Not that the rest of the patrons weren't embarrassingly hammered.* Abby could still recall her first time seeing them, finding it humorous to think that you would expect them to play better while they were sober. Nope. As the alcohol filled the bellies of these old, wintered, and broken Scotsmen, they would begin to hold their tune better. The emotions of their songs would rise, images of vast landscapes, great mountains, winding rivers and stretching bodies of water. All of it was regaled with a fondness and ancestral memory. The tales normally turned towards these lands owned by the people, being taken from them. Not surprisingly, there were quite a few with some rather harsh opinions of the English.

The gang must be at Lockwood already, fuck!

"Abby?" A voice from down an alleyway snatched at her. She turned in time to see who it was, catching herself, hunching over, gasping for air.

"Mum?" Abby wheezed, her mother rushing to her in confused panic.

"Heavens, dear. Are you alright? What's happened?" Her mother wrapped an arm around her daughter to comfort her, to try and take some of the weight off her. Abby stood up, shrugging her mother's arm off her shoulders and feeling her spine crack in a loud sigh.

"I'm fine, Mom."

"Where have you been all day?" Her mother's eyes jumped across Abby's face for answers.

"I've been out with my friends, Mom. Nothing to worry about."

"Abby, you don't need to hide things from me. You can tell me. I saw you when you came in last night. I saw you this morning when you left. Something's not right, I can tell," She said. Abby didn't recall speaking with her mother when she got in. Only that she'd moped her way off to bed, it didn't seem out of the question that her mother might have heard her steps or the door close and checked to see if her daughter was in a new record drunk state. Abby couldn't remember seeing her mother that morning either. She'd made a conscious effort to slip out of the house before there was any conversation to navigate. Any questions about what happened the night before? There wasn't a chance Abby would have managed to concoct something that would put her parents' minds at rest.

"Mom, I'm fine. Honestly, I just had a bit too much and was struggling with a hangover. Johnny and Gary were going to be moving some stuff, and I was going to help Nadia look after her nephew." Abby zoned out, floating from her body and watching as this strange thing inside her painted an excuse.

"Mmhmm." Abby's mother's sardonic tone that she'd heard hundreds of times before. Abby knew the meaning; she could read the subtext. *I know you're lying to me, but I'm now at a mixture of not caring and accepting that you are an adult.* "Have you had dinner?"

"What?"

"Have you eaten? I put a plate out for dinner, but you never showed. So there's a plate of roast chicken, tatties and peas in the fridge for you. I assumed you'd eaten with Nadia or Johnny."

"No, I…" Abby considered explaining that she hadn't eaten, that she'd lost track of time, that she really needed to race to Lockwood to see the gang. "What time is it?"

Her mother scoffed, disgusted by how lackadaisical her daughter was acting.

"It's eleven twenty-six. Oh, by the way. I'm going to put some food in the freezer for you and your dad so you'll have food for the week while I'm away. Please make sure he doesn't try and have a chipper every night, will you?" Her mother's mouth curled at the edges. Bless the woman, she was excited for her new job starting on Monday.

"Shit."

"Abigail Rennie." Her mother's scolding falling on deaf ears. Abby started to shuffle backwards.

"I've got to go," she mumbled, turning on her feet and picking up her pace again. Her chest burning in revolt at having to work so hard again. All those years of sitting about, drinking, and smoking had done nothing to her already poor cardiovascular endurance. Her mother's voice chased her down the street, repeated calls of her name bouncing off walls and windows. Nobody would come out to see who was shouting. It was Belfry; nobody really cared. Everyone just assumed it would be somebody drunk and venting their frustrations, possibly because they lived in Belfry. It was a fair excuse.

Thumping into the side of the asylum entrance, Abby stopped to gather her breath. Just as her heart and lungs began to ease, she felt the warm tickling pressure of anxiety. Looking up at the old building, she second-guessed herself. Was this really such a great idea? Was it a great idea to bring the others into this? Would they act as a backup for her if anything went wrong? What did she even expect to find up here?

There's got to be some kind of answer. Mickey didn't just vanish without a trace.

Biting her lip and making her way up the road, she tried her best to convince herself that there was an answer. At the very least, she should pat herself on the back for finding something new to do. Something productive, if slightly risky.

Her legs flared with lactic acid as her pace slowed on the road. She considered taking a moment to properly rest on the grass. Before she could, the peak of the road gave way to reveal the reception entrance. Sitting outside the entrance was the black Rolls-Royce they'd seen the night before.

Abby threw herself at the grass, scurrying as quickly as she could into the treeline. She stared at the car for several minutes, checking in detail if she could see any movement in the driver's or passenger's seats. Nothing. No old hand waving orders in the back seat. No black suited man looking formidable in the driver's seat. Cautiously, Abby broke the tree line and crept towards the reception entrance. Her eyes still on the car, she waited for someone's head to pop up from the back seat. For the boot to open and a body to spill out. *God, I've got to stop watching all those fucked up horror movies.*

As she closed in, fifteen feet from the entrance, her vision was caught by a flicker of something in one of the reception windows. Too difficult to fully make out. Abby thought she could make out the vague outline of an upper torso. A person! She lowered herself, hoping she'd be out of line of sight of the person. If it were one of the Rolls-Royce crew, then she could be in trouble.

What if it's that strange person you saw in the corridor?

Her eyes widened, taking in as much light as possible. Fear bringing all different measure of ideas and hallucinations into her mind. She thought she saw movement from another window, another person. This time, she could make out movement for sure; it was more than one person. They weren't clad in black.

"Hey, Abby, over here." A rasping whisper escaped through the entrance. Abby nearly threw up in relief as she saw Tom's goofy face appear through the door. Johnny and Troy peeked out of a window nearby, waving like clowns.

"Quiet." Abby castigated. Pleading with them to keep their voices down.

"Why?" Tom blurted, spreading a wide smile across his face. A 'hey friend, I may have had four, no, five…maybe six joints' kind of smile.

"That's Dietrich's car," Abby said, pointing outside. Though she couldn't confirm that it was actually his car, there was no other explanation, right?

"Who the fuck is Dietrich?" asked Johnny, a playful smile unfurling on his face. Perhaps he'd joined Tom in those smokes.

"Viktor Dietrich, he's the guy that owns this place. It must be his car outside."

"There's a car outside?" Tom asked with panic.

"Yeah, dude. We saw it when we came up." Johnny giggled.

"Oh yeah. I totally forgot." Tom began cracking up. *Great, two stoned idiots to help me. I'm going to need to keep a closer eye on them than anything else.* Abby added a mental note to put Johnny through the ringer for the next coming week or two. No hand stuff, maybe even no kissing. *Maybe I'll wear low-cut tops and not even allow cuddling, stupid sod.*

Letting out a sigh to expel nerves and mostly frustration, she stepped further into the building. "So what have you guys found so far?"

"Huh, oh, nothing." Johnny stepped beside Abby, a little too close. The boy looked around like he'd forgotten where he was. "We, ugh, we got here and we waited for you. Figured if we went in looking around, then you'd never find us."

"Yeah, we'd get lost in that place, Abs." Tom concurred.

"Right, well, first off. Don't ever call me Abs. Second, we'll start with that corridor. That was where Troy screamed…or didn't scream, whatever. Wait, where is Troy?" Abby looked around.

"Here." A voice emerged from behind the reception desk. Troy's bulk pops up from underneath it like a stage show joke.

"What are you doing?" Abby asked, hoping that she wasn't going to have a third stoned mess to deal with.

"I was looking through these files," Troy said, motioning Abby to come over. She walked around the reception desk to find an arc of paper spread on the floor. Tom and Johnny held their position. Glancing foolishly around, either waiting for some instruction or enjoying colourful hallucinations. Troy sat back down, folding his legs and motioning for Abby to join him on the floor.

Scuffing some of the dust away, Abby regretfully joined him.

"Sorry, didn't mean to startle you. Those two were getting high, and I couldn't concentrate, so I sat behind here."

Abby could here Johnny and Tom whisper to each other, asking if they knew troy had been here the whole time and remembering that he'd been with them when they came here. Terribly trying to mask their giggles behind their hands.

"It's fine." Abby shook her head. "What have you got?"

"Nothing massive yet. Did I hear you mention about the owner?"

"Viktor Dietrich. Found an article on him at the library," Abby said with no intention of elaborating the mass of time that was now a blank to her, possibly staring at the old man's picture.

I see you. I know who you are.

"Ah, ok. There is mention of a Dietrich in a couple of documents. I thought he might have been a doctor. That explains a bit more."

"Oh?"

"Yeah, mostly I've got a mixture of patients' documents and staff complaints over here," Troy explained, motioning his hands over the two separations he'd been working through. He picked up one from the patient's side.

"Folks admitted here were mainly suffering from mental conditions, hallucinations, hysteria, post-traumatic stress type stuff." Troy skimmed his torch over the pages. Abby chuckled, thinking that her hallucinating boyfriend and bumbling friend could well be admitted in their current state.

"These, though, these are interesting." Troy picked up one of the staff complaints. "A lot of complaints from the nursing staff. Quite a few from the janitorial staff as well. Some of it is what you'd expect: having to deal with difficult patients, some violent guys attacking the female staff, and some of the staff getting caught getting off with each other. You know, normal HR shit." Abby nodded at the American like she knew exactly what he was on about. A seasoned expert in the investigation of these matters.

"There are a few mentions of the upkeep of the asylum, though."

"So? Big, creepy building with a bunch of nut jobs in it. I'd be surprised if people didn't complain about how the place was maintained," She chuckled. "Probably had the smell of patient's shit and piss soaked into the floorboards." Abby quickly curled her lips, upset with herself that she'd been so callous.

"Yeah, that's not a bad point. I wouldn't expect them to be along these lines, though." Troy focused the light on some paragraphs. "Orderly Jones complained of doors opening and closing of their own accord." Troy picked up another bit of paper "Nurse Cunningham complained of several voices coming from the storage cupboard. Upon inspection, there was no staff nor patient present" He picked up another piece of paper "Nurse Grant complained that she'd seen the shadow of a woman in the basement and subsequently heard a scream. She called for Orderly Jones to assist, and he confirmed there was no person present. Orderly Jones complained of finding blood on the floor where Nurse Grant had suggested a person had been. Weirdest one I read was some woman kept hearing someone whisper the name 'Cargill'."

The shadow of a woman? Was that the same thing I saw in the window? What the hell is going on here?

"Cargill?"

"You don't recognise the name?" Troy asked. Abby shook her head. *Great, another name I'll need to look up at the library. Fuck, I don't want to see that witch Pendleton again.*

"Okay, so if there are complaints, there must be some mention of an explanation, right?"

"Not really. That's what interests me," Troy said. "Every single complaint is simply a record of a happening. There's no action taken, or at least no mention of it. It's just a log. It's like, hmm, I don't know…" Abby could see the boy's eyes pinch; he was thinking. He had a theory, but he wasn't sure if he should share.

"It's like someone was taking notes just to make the staff happy? To make them feel like they were being heard?" Abby suggested.

"Exactly," Troy smiled.

"But that's a pretty normal HR thing to do. People always feel better about things when they get to explain it to people."

"True, but so many similarly strange things happening. Come on, that can't be a coincidence, right?"

"Yeah. If he was just trying to make them feel heard, what was he hiding from them?" Abby admitted. She didn't like the thought of it. It didn't feel right; something was wrong about this place. It shouldn't be surprising at all; this was an insane asylum after all. But it certainly didn't sit well in her stomach.

"So are we gonna snoop around or what?" Tom asked. Johnny nudged him, concerned by what he'd ask before starting to snigger. *Oh great, this is going to be seriously annoying if they've got the giggles.*

Abby looked to Troy, he shared the frustration.

"Alright, it's best we split up into two groups, I think," Abby said, rounding the reception desk and folding her arms. Troy followed, leaning on the counter.

"Cool, I pick Johnny. We'll go look around." Tom said, Johnny nodded, though his eyes remained on the floor.

"No. Johnny, come with me. Tom, you go with Troy," Abby said, motioning Johnny to come to her. At least if these two meat sacks were separated, they might be quieter, certainly more manageable. Troy gave Abby a glance; he didn't need to say a word. 'Thanks for giving me Tom' was understood by Abby. She gave a smirk back; she wasn't any better off. Johnny was her boyfriend as well. If he dropped the giggles, he could end up getting horny. There was *no way* she was going to get frisky with that boy, not in *this* building, not with *that* car outside and not with him in *that* condition.

"Alright, fine." Tom accepted the decision, patting Troy on the back.

"Let's meet back here in thirty minutes, alright? Remember, we're looking for anything that might mention my brother or my family. Mickey Rennie. You all go that?" Abby asked, glancing at Troy, who nodded, focused on the goal. Tom and Johnny stared into the middle distance while agreeing in unison. Abby shook her head; they'd just have to make do.

15

Abby half regretted choosing to head down the corridor that had caused them all such a scare last night. She knew it was her best bet for finding anything, though. Johnny, breathing heavily in her ear as he crept beside her, did nothing to help.

"Why are you hunched over?" She asked. Johnny responded by straightening his back and scratching his head.

"This place is creepy," he stated.

"No shit!" Abby sighed, taking the torch from Johnny, the boy had been simply pointing it straight ahead. It's cone highlighting doorways, their white outlines glistening portals into realms unknown. A stretcher was pressed up against the wall. Looked like it had been covered in some amount of dust.

"Hey, look." Johnny pointed a long arm at it, the outline of a single hand left in the dust.

"That's probably from some ghost or something. One that creeps through this place at night. Or some zombified patient, hell bent on finding some brains to eat. Abby, we aren't safe," the boy's voice quivered.

"Oh, settle down. It's probably just Tom's or Troy's hand when they came running back through here. Probably pushed the thing out of the way."

Johnny took in the argument for several seconds as Abby moved on, pointing the torch at things, squinting to analyse it further. "Oh, yeah, of course. That makes sense." And with that, Johnny scurried after his girlfriend, no longer paying the handprint any concern. Abby did think the size of it was a little off for Tom or Troy, but she wasn't going to tell Johnny that, though.

With the light now in her control, Abby leaned into some of the rooms as they passed. Swirling the torch around them to see if there was anything of note. From its appearance, Abby presumed the first room was a staff room. A couple of sofas surrounded a coffee table. An old TV in the corner. The floor is split into linoleum with a counter area holding a sink and a few cupboards. It would probably be of some interest to snoop around in those cupboards and see if there were any leftovers. That would be the case if the asylum didn't have a sinister breeze dancing through it.

Long fingers like touches of cold crawling up your spine.

A staff toilet was next to the staff room. Abby guessed they were staff toilets as the room that followed on from it was another bathroom, this one had no stalls for toilets, though. There were urinals against one wall, spaced quite far apart. The other side of this bathroom had a shower area.

"Men's bathroom." Johnny said, poking his head in the doorway. "This must be the women's then." he added, pointing to the doorway directly across from it. Abby flashed the torch quickly over it to confirm. Similar shower set, again no stalls but there were a few toilets standing very sadly.

"Why doesn't the mens have toilets? What would the male patients do if they had to shit?" Abby asked, regretting asking out loud as soon as Johnny picked up the words. His stoned mind going to work, concocting a plethora of different options. All stupider than the last.

"Maybe they didn't poop when they were here. Maybe they had some crazy disease that closed up their buttholes. Maybe they ate their poop." Johnny nearly tumbled into giggles again, managing to control it after seeing Abby's non-amused face.

Continuing to the next room, they finally met a closed door. All other doors had been open so far. This one was sturdy looking, a glass window on it, lines of security robustness crossing it. The number "1" glistened gold as Abby shone the torch at it. She squinted to see inside, but the glare from the dusty glass was too much. *I am not touching that dust,* she told herself.

She reached for the doorknob knob and Johnny swatted at her. Puckering his lips in frustration, mumbling in panic. She batted him away and grasped the doorknob. Cold. Far colder than she would have thought, even for it starting to turn winter. Not only was there a coldness, but there felt like there was an energy in it. As if the building had just been nudged from its slumber. An ancient beast coming to life.

SQUEAK!

The doorknob turned, Johnny and Abby's ears pierced by it, accepting its first visitor in years. The door opened, and just as the echo of the squeak came stabbing back up the corridor, a loud *CREEK* danced back towards it. The two remained frozen, eyes looking around, waiting for something to move. Something to emerge and welcome them, both of them hoped above all else that it would be a friendly welcome. *I wonder if Troy and Tom heard that?*

After a moment, Abby unfroze enough to scan the corridor with the torch, back the way they'd come, nothing. Further down the corridor, where they hadn't explored, nothing. Back into the room they had just opened. Abby slid into the room, Johnny remained outside balling his fists to cope with his fear. He nodded as if to say, "I'll stay here and keep lookout," but Abby knew he was too cowardly. *Another few points lost for you, Johnny. Going to have to step it up a good bit if you're hoping to get lucky.*

The room held little in it save for a very uncomfortable looking bed and a chair. Abby couldn't be sure the bed would have been uncomfortable in it's prime, time may have done a number on it. A cobweb draped off the leg of the chair, sparkling and beautiful from the moonlight pouring in the window.

Underneath the bed, Abby came across the answer to her earlier question. Pointing the torch at it, she smiled at Johnny.

"Buckets," she snorted. "Think you'd enjoy shitting in a bucket while locked in a padded room?"

"Pfft. Nope," Johnny said as if flexing his masculinity.

Abby stepped back into the corridor, painting it with light. The two of them continued further into the belly of the beast, passing by several individual rooms. Single beds missing matresses, rusted springs holding the beds together for dear life. A couple of rooms had mattresses, each covered with varying darknesses of stains.

They turned a corridor to find further doors, presumably all rooms, and a staircase at the end.

"Look." Johnny grabbed Abby's arm, the cone of light juddering.

"What?" Abby shrugged her boyfriend off.

"There, at the stairs. I saw a hand. It was on the ceiling."

Abby squinted down the corridor, pushing the torch out in front of her as if it might show more detail. "There's nothing there. How could you have seen a hand that far off in this light? It's like fifty feet away"

"I swear, I saw a hand," Johnny said, cuddling in next to her. She puffed in frustration and moved down the new corridor. Shining a light into each room, she quickly confirmed that there were no documents, only beds, chairs and buckets. The last two rooms of the corridor were larger, though. Keeping one eye fixed on the stairs, Abby opened the door to one of them. There were two beds in the room instead of one. No chair and worst of all, one bucket. This room held a stench that the others didn't. There was no cold and dusty odour, something, *there's some kind of physical matter in here.* She leaned her head in correcting herself; *some kind of physical matter had* been *in here.* High on the far wall, a streak of something black marked the wall up to the ceiling. Too high to be reached for and touched, thankfully. The mark did nothing for Abby's imagination as she realised that it ended in a handprint. A smeared hand up the wall. She quickly stepped back out of the room, preventing Johnny from seeing the same and flying into a panic.

"Hey, look here," Johnny said, his mood swinging again. He'd moved onto the second, larger room, also a room with two beds. These two squished together. No chair again, this time no bucket. *Phew*. Abby skimmed her eyes across the ceiling, no smeared hand mark either. *Double phew*.

"Look at this, they aren't that bad," Johnny said, circling the beds, pushing lightly on the mattresses. Abby had to admit, they did have very few stains on them by comparison. Perhaps it was less frequent for the patients to sleep in rooms together, and so these beds had only faced the decay of time. Johnny looked at the beds and then up to Abby, a dumb smile crossing his face. He sat down on one of them, the springs groaning as they took his weight. *Surprisingly little dust coming off them, hmm.*

"Come here," he said.

"Johnny, we shouldn't hang around." Abby pleaded.

"Come here," he said again, reaching his hand out. Abby stepped around to him, shining the light directly in his face. He blinked and slapped the torch away, laughing before wrapping his arms around Abby's waist and pulling her on top of him. The springs again squeeled in disapproval. Before Abby could feel certain the springs would hold, Johnny was placing his lips on her neck.

For the amount of time they'd been together, Abby had been telling herself time and time again that she needed to rethink this relationship. Sure, he was the most attractive boy there was in Belfry, but that wasn't why she was with him. It certainly wasn't anything to boast about. Belfry was slim pickings. Sure, he made her laugh and…she thought…made her happy. At this age, she'd come to realise that she had a list too long of the negatives of Johnny compared to the positives. Would she be better on her own? What about a different guy? Maybe one of the older guys would fit her better. Maybe she just needed to suck it up and move the hell away from Belfry already. Then she could not only find a better guy but also find a better life. Something more fruitful than getting hammered in a park most weekends. *I'd probably end up with a new group of friends getting drunk in a different park.* She half giggled as Johnny kissed her neck more. For all the faults she now felt, she couldn't deny that Johnny was a good kisser. The boy, full of testosterone, took the giggle as a playful invitation for more.

His hands crept across her back, an attempt to caress and feel her body. His lips working up her neck, over her chin and to her lips. Abby hated herself for allowing herself to enjoy a moment of making out. *Damnit, Abby, not the time, nor the place.*

"Cargill," a voice, slightly familiar, whispered past the door. Abby pulled her head from locking lips and peered out from where they'd come.

"Did you hear that?"

"What?" Johnny asked.

"Someone said something."

"Oh, come on. It was nothing. Why don't we have a little kinky fun while we're here? You said we had half an hour, that's plenty of time," Johnny said in his best ladies' man voice. It sickened Abby every time she heard it. "I'm scared too, but that makes it hot, right? A bit sexier?" He pleaded. Abby hopped off, dusting her shins off and moving slowly towards the doorway.

"Fuck's sake. What? Too dark or something? Too cold? Oh fuck, you're not on the blob, are you?" her boyfriend asked as he shuffled himself off the bed, the creaks and shreaks from the springs and bedframe sliced down the corridor.

"Fuck you," Abby shot back over her shoulder. Yes, she'd had plenty of excuses for not putting out, yes, she'd been too cold on more than one occasion, yes, they had been too drunk on another, just didn't feel like it on another. But fuck

Johnny, she had every right to allow intimacy or not. It didn't matter that he was, in fact, correct. She was on her period, and the boy would learn his lesson for pointing that out later, though. *Little horny shit.*

Poking her head out, Abby looked up the stairs. She didn't know how, but she knew the voice had come from up there. Johnny sulked to the doorway and looked up with her. At least he was being quiet now. His frustrated state of arousal dampening his stoned idiocy.

Abby didn't say anything, only moved off towards the stairs. She didn't look back over her shoulder to see Johnny confusedly following. The stairs absorbed Abby's attention for longer than they should. They were somehow immaculate, save for the expected dusting. Stunning wooden stairs, carefully crafted lips on each step. A sturdy bannister up the side with beautiful carvings on each pillar. Resting her foot on the first step, Abby eased her weight onto it. Hoping to God that they were as sturdy as they looked. No sounds came. *Thank God.*

She moved up the steps, carefully pressing her foot onto each one. The staircase turned on itself mid-way up. As Abby turned it, she saw Johnny cautiously ascending behind her. He shooed her to carry on, *lead the way into the potential danger, oh, apple of my eye that won't put out. Troy wouldn't leave me to walk into danger if he were my boyfriend,* Abby caught herself thinking. Scolding herself for being so bitchy. *Gary would, hell, Tom would as well, I bet.*

They reached the top of the stairs, and another corridor of stale linoleum rolled out in front of them. To their left, a corridor crossed through the middle of the building. A darker corridor, the doors looking slightly different. Not sturdy doors with hefty locks on them and security glass. These doors were regal, fine wood and etching. A few of them with plaques screwed into them. What little light crept down the corridor jumping back in reflection off the gold plates.

"Hey…Abby…where are you going?" Johnny rasped a whisper as Abby moved towards the darker corridor. Abby shot a glance back and a shushing gesture. Something stood out in the darkness, something that looked so out of place it drew her eye and held it with hypnotic control.

Abby's figure disappeared into the darkness from Johnny's point of view. He dared not continue any further. Trying another couple of whispered calls for her, he began to bob in place. Trying to muster his courage and go after her.

"Cargill," a cold breeze breathed past his ear. His eyes sharpened, widened and peered down the corridor. Though the end of the corridor was some fifty to sixty feet away, his vision zoomed in and saw. There…on the cold linoleum floor, just reaching out from behind the corner, was a hand. Johnny panicked. The hand he'd seen before! He wasn't going mad. It wasn't because he was stoned. If anything, seeing the hand on the ceiling had sobered him up. This hand was there, facing him, palm flat on the floor, fingers pointing…looking at him somehow.

Everything in Johnny's body told him to run, to get the hell out of this place. *What about Abby?* He asked himself. *Screw Abby, if she makes it out, then you can deal with that then. If she doesn't make it out…well…you just better make sure you do!*

As the voices battled in his mind, his feet frozen to the floor, spine stiff as rock, his heart pounded faster. A second hand emerged from behind the corner, this one wrapped its claw-like fingers on the wall. It took Johnny a second to realise that both hands were left hands. The voices in his head silencing to consider what that meant as seven more hands emerged from the corner, grasping their way up the wall until the final one rested on the ceiling. All of them knew Johnny was there, all of them waiting for their moment to pounce. To chase down their prey.

Abby shifted further into the darkness, towards the point of interest, a thin slit of light. Too difficult to make out the details around it until she closed further in.

A light on behind the door?

She squinted, as if her thoughts had been too loud and whoever was behind the door would rush out with a weapon. After a few moments, satisfied she had disturbed nobody, she proceeded to the door. A warm light pushed out through the slit in the door. A light that was old, a brown orange that had heat to it. Abby took a slow, deep breath in, holding it as she reached for the handle. Inches away, she halted, her eyes thrown open by a noise behind her.

An inhuman scream, filled with rage and spit and purpose, shuddered through her. She looked back over her shoulder to see if Johnny was there. *Damn pussy. Where is he?* She thought, only the slit of light from the door and the dimming moonlight from the corridor windows to assist her.

Johnny's face turned, his weeping baby face returning to him after years. The scream punched him; he felt his clothes jolt back in the pressure. The hands at the end of the corner began to move, to grip whatever surface they landed on. The floor, the wall, the ceiling, taking purchase and pulling themselves on.

"Fuck this!" Johnny finally managed to blurt, turning on his heels and running down the stairs, two steps at a time. Turning halfway to run down the final flight, his eyes looked up, hoping to dear God Almighty that whatever that thing was wasn't fast enough to catch him. His ankle rolled on the very last step, sending him sprawling across the floor. Trying to push himself to his feet and kick himself forward, his shoes scuffed the linoleum. Squeaking and crying for help. Another scream replied, something beastial, something horrifying, the scream grew louder, closer.

Johnny turned and pushed himself off the ground, bolting back down the corridor from whence he'd come. Looking back over his shoulder to ensure he was, at the very least, making distance from his pursuer. Reaching the corner, turning back to the reception, he took one last glance towards the stairs. The corridor was empty; his chest heaved as he desperately sucked in air.

A hand curled around the ceiling.

Johnny didn't wait any longer.

Abby frowned as she heard the scream, so pained, so angry. Shortly after that, she heard Johnny's "fuck this" exclamation followed by his feet on the stairs. She heard him fall and heard the scuffs of his shoes on the floor, but she didn't concentrate on it. She could hear something else. Some movement. Something large. Skin pawing and slapping on surfaces.

It's getting closer.

She turned towards the door, wrapped her hand around the doorknob knob and quickly thrust herself inside. Closing the door behind her as she did. Peeking through the last slit of the door before it sealed, she saw movement at the end of the corridor. Not clear enough to distinguish, but she could make out something.

It's large.

An animal?

A bear? You don't get bears in Scotland, do you?

Wait, it's not, it's covered in something else. Hair?

"Who are you?"

Abby turned, forgetting she'd entered the lit room. Her heart racing from whatever she'd just witnessed, she tried to fathom what she was looking at.

"Who are you?" The voice repeated.

Viktor Dietrich sat in a chair, a single wrinkled finger pointing at Abby.

16

The old man held his finger at Abby as if pointing a gun. Ready to pull the trigger and shoot her down.

"Who are you, young lady?" His voice rose.

"Wait, what? You're Viktor Dietrich." Abby turned her head. The old man's nostrils flared.

"And you are?" A command rather than a question.

"Abby…what are you doing here?" Abby closed the distance between them. Feeling a slight relief as she moved away from the door, away from whatever she'd seen move on the other side of it.

"How dare you ask me that. Everything around that you see is mine, I can do whatever I bloody well please with this place," the man harrumphed. He straightened his back slightly, pulling his shoulders back to puff his meagre chest.

It was strange, Abby thought, seeing this man before her. His image in the article she'd read

The Belfry Haunting

was intimidating, haunting, somehow alive. Sitting in his large leather chair before her now, he intimidated nothing. A small table with a glass of some presumably expensive alcohol in it. His suit was too big for him, not because he wore an oversized suit, but obviously due to his thin, frail frame contained inside. A body that once fit now dwindled remains. Still, his clothes were pristine, his tie shining with the pride of affluence.

How? Abby thought. He looked just like he did in the photo she'd seen him in, but without the dark mystique. There were no added wrinkles or increased sag to the ones he currently had. No new liver spots marking his skin. His hair, if anything, looked darker that it did in the photo but that could easily have been due to the in person effect, or the light, or dyeing.

That photo was some thirty years ago. He must have been in his seventies then.

"So old rich men like to take weekends in their abandoned asylums to drink whisky and think of the good ol'days, huh? That it?" Abby stepped behind the chair that faced him, its leather warm from the light. She glanced up at the bulb, large, twice the size she was used to seeing. The coil inside a burning snake. *How old is that light?*

"Men like me have things to do that girls like you cannot grasp nor should not be privy to." Dietrich raised an eyebrow. A warning.

A scream echoed through the walls and rattled the door. It seemed further away than the last one, Abby felt mild relief. She followed the noise as it swept like a wave through the room. *Still too close for comfort.*

"I see you've met her then," Dietrich grinned. Abby remained quiet. The old man looked to the corner of the room, in the small amount of darkness there hid a gramopahone. Abby noticed a record sitting on it already. *Geez, how much old crap is there in here? Bet it would sell for a good amount. Enough to get me out of here potentially.*

"My Amara." The old man gently spoke to the corner, remorse seeping through his words.

"Who is Amara? Don't tell me that's your wife." Abby said.

"My girl, you have some nerve coming into my building like this and demanding answers." Dietrich whipped his eyes back at her. Eyes that had held command over God knows how many people before. An experienced control and disrespect for those beneath him.

"I have some nerve? A teenage girl in a shithole town dares to go snoop around an abandoned building with her friends? It appears you have some naivety to you, sir!" Abby exclaimed the sir at the end, flaring her eyes. Eyes that had experienced enough authority in their life and thrown their middle finger up at it.

"You brought friends here? How many of you are there?" Dietrich's tone changed. Panic and concern flooding his voice.

"Why?"

"How many?"

"Three others," Abby shrugged. "My dumbass boyfriend, his best friend and a new American boy we met recently."

"American? Oh no." Dietrich shifted in his seat. Looking around for something to help him up out of the seat, some panic button, some megaphone to call an assistant to come help. Abby looked around and scoffed.

"You don't have anyone here, do you?"

The old man sighed. "My driver was meant to be back twenty minutes ago, now that you mention it." His fingers curled, gripping the leather arms of the chair. His teeth grinding together, hollow cheeks tightening as he flexed his jaw.

"Well, it doesn't seem like he's coming anytime soon." Abby walked towards the chair and leaned forward. Pinning her hands on the arms as the old man wretched inwards, disgusted by the young girls proximity. "So why don't you tell me who Amara is and what the hell that thing outside was?"

The old man looked into her eyes, fear-stricken across his face. Holding her gaze for what felt like several minutes his wrinkled skin unfolded around his cheeks and brow, his mouth relaxed back into it's normal contemptuous grimace. He let out a wrasping chuckle.

"My girl, your pretty young mind would struggle to comprehend the world you've clumsily walked into." He glanced over to the corner again.

"Believe me, Belfry is one of the most boring, strangest, fucked up places in the world, and I've lived my entire life here. I've been dealt the shit end of the stick, so just spill it, would you, Gramps? I'm not going anywhere soon, and neither are you."

Dietrich held his despising expression, his upper lip curling slightly more as he decided to submit.

"Don't you understand, you silly girl? That thing out there. It *is* Amara."

"What the fuck does that mean? I don't know what that thing is, you grumpy old shit." Abby struggled to contain her anger. *Get back on track, girl. Why are you here? Remember!*

"Don't talk to me that way."

"Mickey Rennie…name ring a bell?" Abby changed the subject. The old man squinted, searched the floor for answers before giving another quick glance to the corner.

"Father?" he asked.

"Brother. Disappeared here. Was that your fault? Did you find him here and decide you wanted to let your rich, creepy old man fantasies fly and chop him up in the basement?"

Viktor Dietrich leaned his head back and let out a cackle. The power swung back in his favour.

"My dear, I've never heard of your brother before. By the looks and sounds of you, I wouldn't have held much interest in him either. Trespassing on a man's property is not only unsightly but also verges into legal matters. But amuse me, you tell me, when did he disappear?"

"Nine years ago."

The old man shook his head. "What time of year?"

"Nine years ago, yesterday," Abby squinted. *How the hell is that relevant?*

The side of the old man's mouth rose. "Well, I can tell you this, young one. He won't have been chopped up in the basement...but that may well be where you'd find him."

"He's still here?" Abby stepped back from the chair.

"He may be. I don't know. Never met the boy."

"The basement, that where you keep Amara?"

"The less you know about Amara, the better." His grin faded. "You should thank me for trying to keep you away from her." He glanced at the gramophone in the corner.

"What is it with that?" Abby asked, marching to the corner. Looking around the device, checking if there was a walkie-talkie next to it or something. A hidden panic button that would alert Dietrich's goons to come and rescue him.

"Careful!" Dietrich commanded, pushing himself forward on his chair. Pressing white knuckles against his knees. Slowly rising, old bones creaking and clicking. Brittle yelps and pleads to return to his rested position.

Abby stared in part revulsion and part amusement as the old man eventually straightened out. *He's taller than I imagined,* she thought. He was taller than Abby, though not by much. In his prime, the man must have stood a good six feet four inches or so. His depressed skeleton and crooked lean left him at around six feet or so now.

"Please, be careful." He slid a foot forward, barely able to lift his gangly legs.

"What? Is this the gramophone that your one true love left you? The one person that didn't put a stick up your ass?" Abby leaned on the table that the gramophone sat on. Dietrich moaned in panic.

"Do not mention my wife."

"Does she know you're such a creep?"

"My wife died. She was the one who saved me from my father. I'll not have you slander her good memory."

"Your father? What? Another one of your family that grew up with a silver spoon in his mouth? All the way back to Gunther Dietrich. I'm sure he'd be turning in his grave to see you be such a fuck up." Abby didn't know where this energy had come from.

The old man sighed, his eyes dropping to the floor. "He would indeed roll in his grave if he saw me today. But my girl, you mistake my bloodline. There was no father, grandfather or father's lineage between me and Gunther Dietrich…"

"What?" Abby asked.

"Gunther Dietrich was my father."

17

Light glistened off tears, gradually building in Viktor Dietrich's eyes. The shadows in his wrinkles softening. Abby almost felt sorry for the man as he stood there, presenting the weakest of visages.

"That's impossible. Gunther Dietrich was born in like nineteen oatcake."

"1313 in fact."

"How?"

"For the amount of years my father and I have lived in this world, it would take longer to explain everything that brought us from that century to now. My father, though he disliked and despised most of my endeavours, managed to find relief from me in death. He died in a car crash seventy-five years ago"

"What? None of this makes sense."

"And yet here I stand. I told you that you don't know what you are getting into. I'm doing my best to keep you as safe as possible. I'm telling you some of the truth now only to bargain with you. Please, I beg of you. Leave that gramophone be. Leave this place. Never return"

Abby searched the middle distance for answers. Something that could explain what the man was saying. Was she somehow high? Had Tom slipped her something? Was the man simply trying to trick her with some scary story? Was he buying time?

"You're telling me that you are like six hundred years old?"

"I'm trying to keep that gramophone safe by any means, that is all. I believed some honesty might assist in that. If money is what you seek, then name your price and I'll write you a cheque this moment."

"Money? What the fuck?" Abby laughed and turned to face Viktor, her hip bumping the table. Dietrich shimmied forward a step and let out a wheeze, reaching out as if he would be able to dive the four feet in his crumbled old age in time to save it.

"What does it do?" Abby asked, resting a hand on the gramophone. The old man flexed his jaw, infuriated to see her touch it.

"It is the only thing to keep Amara at bay."

"Alright, now you're talking crazy. Some music makes the girl calm down from her tantrums."

"Girl, you cannot even fathom what a tantrum from Amara would look like."

"So what, you set this to play and then what?"

"Amara rests."

"Rests? What, she just curls up and has a little nap? That what happens?"

"Like I said, there's too much to explain!"

Another scream roared through the walls. This time closer. Both Dietrich and Abby stared at the wall. The noise of movement, footsteps? Hands? Something moved back up to the first floor.

"She's coming down the corridor," Dietrich said.

"What will she do to us?" Abby said, fear bubbling inside of her suddenly.

"You, she'll kill. Me? She'll eviscerate. Have you ever heard of such strange supernatural things happening in a world as this?"

"What? Some crazy girl ghost and a six-hundred-year-old man? No, can't say I have."

"Exactly. And you never will again. When things like this happen, there are deep-set links between such occurrences. Things that bind entities for eternity. Things that drive focus and purpose in the lives of those involved."

Abby and Dietrich turned their heads in line with the sounds as they moved down the corridor. The movement reaching the wall of their room.

"So what's her purpose?"

"Revenge."

"And yours?"

"Survival."

"Wait, are you telling me that you are the cause of Amara?"

"Not me."

"Your father, Gunther?"

"My great-grandfather. Colton Cargill."

The movement continued to the door. Battering it in what sounded like an army rampage. Abby pulled back, expecting the door to explode inward from such pressure.

The movement continued on, past the door, moving further down the corridor. Viktor sighed.

A scream again, piercing right into the brain. Abby threw up her arms to cover her ears. Slamming her wrist into the table and accidentally shoving it over.

The table toppled, the gramophone fell to the floor and crunched in on itself. The record on top of it bent for a split second between the floor and the horn before cracking, fine breaks webbing through it. Many years having made it brittle. The horn slid free, landing on top of it.

"What have you done?" The old man cried.

18

Panicked, Abby made a run for the door. Flinging it open and darting out towards the stairs. She heard a shift of something large behind her. She didn't look back until she reached the stairs.

A great mass of shadow hid in the darkness. In the centre of its mass, a head catching the faded light pouring out of the room, Dietrich was still in.

Amara?

A pale, grey face, no, not a face. An attempt at a face? It was hands, fingers, nails. All of it was constructed together to form what looked like a woman's face. Her eyes were the only clear, non-hand feature. Focused towards Abby, the eyes didn't move. The fingers comprising her face undulated. Four fingers, making up her mouth, opened slightly to reveal a real tongue, though it had turned black. There were sharp and haggard teeth surrounding the tongue. Teeth that had not been filed down, but teeth that had broken into shards, dark yellow and black shards glistening with spit.

A single hand moved from the shadow and into the light on the floor. The creature inhaled, smelling Abby's sweat, her scent, her fear. It screamed. Abby didn't wait, knowing what was coming. She'd seen feral creatures on television. She was prey, and the hunter was coming.

She raced down the stairs, thumping and pawing, booming behind her. *Fuck, I was hoping she'd go after Dietrich.*

Why me?
Why me?
Why me?

She raced down the first set of stairs, turning to go down to the ground floor. Glancing up she saw hands grip on the corners of the wall, too many hands. Taking two steps at a time, she jumped the last four stairs, nearly stumbling before she raced off down the corridor back towards reception.

Reaching the end of the corridor and turning to see the moonlight breaching into the reception area, Abby wondered why she hadn't heard the pounding chase after her more. Turning back to look at the stairs, she saw a small female figure standing at the last step. Hair draped over her shoulders, a gown-like garment dangling down to her shins. *That's not a patient's gown, something old, something odd.*

The woman reached a single arm out, faded pillars of moonlight rubbed against it. The arm looked marked. Burned? No, Abby thought, scarred maybe? Her head tilted to the side, eyes glistening a frozen blue.

Abby felt entranced as the woman's arm turned, her hand opening, motioning for Abby to return. The fingers flowing like string in the wind. The marks on her arms started to move, to shift, to squirm? Fingers dislodged from the elbow down to the wrist and across the palm. The woman screamed, the fingers stretching with her shriek.

"Abby!" a shout echoed from reception. Troy peaked his head down the corridor. Enough to free Abby from her trance, she bolted towards him as the cry of Amara chased after her.

Thumping into Troy, he picked Abby off the ground, catching her momentum and resting her gently on her feet in the middle of reception.

"Where were you?" Johnny gasped, still trying to catch his breath.

"What? Where were you?" Abby accused.

"Nevermind. What was that?" Troy asked, pointing in the direction of the scream.

"I told you," Johnny pushed himself up off the seating. "It's some fucking monster, some crazy thing they made in this madhouse."

"Monster? They wouldn't deal with animals here. It's an asylum, right? For treating patients?" Troy asked.

"Right, you're freaking out, Johnny. I told you this was a stronger bud, dude." Tom sniggered, toking on another joint.

"Fuck you, Tom. That was some creature. I'm telling you. Abby, you saw it, right?"

"Amara," Abby said.

"Right, it's an am…what?" Johnny frowned.

"Amara, it's a person… apparently…I'm not going to explain it all now. We've got to get the hell out of here." Abby looked to Troy for confirmation, and he nodded. He thrust the boys forward out of the doorway and into the cold night.

"Who the fuck is Amara?" Tom asked before gasping. He, like the rest of the group, heard whimpering. The pained sobbing of a female. Johnny focused on the reception, Abby joined him before realising the crying was coming from in front of them. Down the road, behind Dietrich's car.

The crying moved towards them with the noise of feet dragging through gravel.

"Nadia?" Abby said, moving around the Rolls-Royce to see her best friend hugging herself and walking towards her. Tears had clearly been running down her face for a while, her makeup lining her cheeks.

"Nadia, what's wrong? What happened?"

"It's Gary," she mumbled.

"Oh, fuck, don't tell me Gary's in there. Is he dead?" Johnny's panic escalated.

"Nadia, what happened to Gary?" Abby said as she hugged her.

Nadia sobbed into Abby's neck. Feeling something was very off, Abby guided her away from the boys. Looking over her shoulder and wafting them away with a hand signal.

"Nadia, it's ok, you're with me. I'm here. What happened?"

"It's just…it's Gary…"

"You can tell me", Abby felt that same urge to protect she'd felt in the playground years ago. This time, things weren't right, though. There wasn't a Craig to kick in the balls.

"He raped me."

19

Walking back down the road with a quickened pace. Abby held Nadia's shoulders as the girl continued to weep.

"What happened?" Johnny asked as Abby guided Nadia back over to the group. "Is Gary alive?"

"Yeah, he, uh. Yeah, he's fine," Abby said, biting her tongue. He's *not fine. He hurt my friend.*

"Oh, thank fuck. I thought he was dead." Johnny blurted. Abby slapped his shoulder hard. He glowered at her.

"Uh, Nadia isn't alright, guys. We need to get her home"

"No!" Nadia blurted, pushing away from Abby. Abigail's jaw rolled, desperately grabbing for words that could help. *What do I do? How do I help?*

"What happened? Are you alright, Nadia?" Troy asked.

"I'm fine, I just…I don't feel well. Gary…hurt me"

"He what? Did he hit you?" Troy frowned. Johnny looked from Nadia to Abby and back. Abby glowered back and nodded to Nadia.

"No, I…I don't want to talk about it"

"Alright, well yeah. Let's get you home," Johnny said, sensing Abby's concern.

"No, I don't want to go home!" Nadia shouted, folding in half as she sobbed again.

"Hey, hey. It's okay. You can stay with me tonight. Okay?"

Abby approached slowly. She couldn't protect her friend, and now she was even more scared than she was when she saw all the parents talking about getting police involved over a playground scuffle. *Do I tell her mom? What do I say to her? How can I help her?* Raising an arm and gently leading Nadia off towards her home. Nadia kept glancing at Abby's hands. Nadia looked up into Abby's eyes, weighing up if she had the strength to tell her best friend what happened. How would she explain it? Abby wouldn't believe her. She'd tell the boys, and they'd all make fun of her. The whole town would start calling her a slut.

"It's okay, Nads. It's me, Abby. I believe you, I'm on your side, I'm here for you. I swear," Abby said. Nadia's eyes flooded again, and she buried her head into Abby's shoulder for a few more sobs. Abby gave her time, let her gather strength. Peeking over her shoulder back at the asylum. Nothing chased them. *Thank Christ!* Abby stared at the reception, unsure if her eyes were playing tricks on her. The slight outline of a leg, arm and one eye spying from behind the wall.

"I was…I was with him when you left. You know, you went to the…Library," Nadia sniffled. Abby's attention returned to her friend.

"Shhh, it's okay. You don't have to tell me anything. Don't say anything right now. Let's just head to mine and relax. Sound good?" Abby

"Yeah", Nadia sighed. "Yeah, that sounds good."

They reached the end of the driveway to the asylum. Johnny directs the boys towards the main street. Troy gave a straight-faced nod and a wave. *I hope he knows how to deal with them.*

On the way to Abby's, Abby struggled to hold back thoughts. *Gary? Really? The one boy in Belfry who actually seemed to have his head screwed on, at least somewhat correctly? What happened that drove him to do that? Was he on some new drug? Was there some malevolent force controlling him?* They reached Abby's house quicker than she thought they would. Nadia curled into herself as Abby poked around the house, letting her mother know she was home and had her friend was with her.

"Oh, be sure and have your dinner, quine," her mother exclaimed. Abby nodded and took the plate from the fridge up to her room with Nadia in tow. They sat down on her bed, the plate between them, cold roast chicken dinner, some pale and sad potatoes and gravy that was growing a thicker and thicker skin. Neither of them feeling hunger in the slightest. Nadia picked a sliver of the chicken up and played with it in her fingers. *I can't think about why Gary did it right now; I need to help Nadia.*

"I don't know why Gary would think that I was into Troy."

"Oh, oh, right. Okay…" Abby flustered, they were going to talk about it, she guessed. *Don't force her to talk about anything she doesn't want ti. She's calmer now. Just let her talk?* "Do you think he might have misjudged the situation after seeing the two of you talking for so long and laughing?" As soon as the words left her mouth the sting of regret stabbed Abby in the stomach.

Nadia raised her eyes to Abby, a deep breath filling her lungs with shame and pain. As their eyes met, Nadia cowered away, returning to her piece of chicken, slowly tearing it, strand by strand.

"I wasn't flirting with him. I was just trying to be nice. He's a stranger here; he doesn't know what things are like. I've been there." Silence

The Belfry Haunting

lingered; Abby didn't want to break it. *Let the girl talk.*

"He wasn't even flirting with me," Nadia said. Abby parted her lips, ready to argue against the comment. Troy seemed more than happy to be chatting with this beautiful girl and giggling away with her. Finding mutual interests and building rapport. "He told me he likes *you*." Nadia kept her head down.

"What?" Abby asked.

"He thinks you're pretty. He actually said that Abby. Pretty…who says that anymore?" The poor girl forced a smile through tears.

"He likes me?" Abby asked, Nadia bobbed her head to confirm. "Why?" *Does it matter, Abby? Nadia needs help. Wait, maybe the distraction might help ease her mind?*

"He said he thought you were pretty and he liked your style. That you didn't seem to care or take shit from anyone, I told him you're with Johnny and you won't leave him." Nadia carefully set the torn chicken strands back on the plate, drowning them in the thick gravy, squelching through the layer of skin at the top. She picked another piece of chicken off and began to pick it apart. Looking up to her friend and sighing.

"Yeah, I wouldn't…I mean, I don't know…I mean…did you tell Gary?"

"Of course." Nadia flared her eyes, holding her hands up as if she was apologising to her mother. "He didn't believe me. Said that if that was the case, then why hadn't he been flirting with you? It's because he's nervous, like I said, he's not from here. He doesn't know how to go about that sort of thing with Scottish girls."

"So he was arguing with you about Troy, he attacked you because he was jealous? Sorry, you don't have to say anything. The facts can sometimes help, though," Abby reasoned, for herself more than for Nadia.

Nadia let out a long breath, a tear dripping from her nose onto her knee, soaking into her tights. "He said I'd been doing…stuff…with Troy. He pushed me onto my bed and kissed me, and then asked if he was a better kisser than Troy. I told him to get off of me. He kept forcing me down; he was hurting me. I told him he was, I told him I was in pain. He just…he didn't stop. It was like I wasn't there, like he was just seeing Troy and me talking, and he had to be on some winning side. He stuck his hands between my legs and asked if he was better than Troy. Then he put his hand over my mouth…" Nadia swallowed pain, Abby's eyes welled up, she could see in Nadia's eyes, she wasn't just remembering it. She was seeing it all again. Experiencing it all again. For a moment, Abby thought about stopping her, not wanting her friend to go through it all again.

"God, Nadia, I'm so sorry" Abby felt the tickle of a tear on her cheek.

"No, I need to…I don't know…" she sighed again. Abby restrained herself from changing the subject. *Does she need this? Does she need to let it out?*

"He put his hand over my mouth and then unzipped his trousers. I tried kicking him off, but he pressed down on my face; it was hurting. He was pressing down on me so hard I was struggling to breath. Then he…he…put it in me. He wouldn't stop saying it all the while. *Am I better than Troy? Am I better than Troy?* I couldn't do anything, I was struggling to breath so much I felt the strength going out of me. I couldn't even scream. I couldn't look anywhere else but his eyes; he was looking right back at me. This monster, not Gary, something evil looking back at me. Spit was dripping from his mouth. I don't know how long it all took, but it felt like a lifetime. When he was done, I can remember the feeling of coming back into myself, like I had just faded away into the back of my head. I was watching it all happen, pulled away from it. Watching this girl get used and raped like nothing, knowing that it was me and unable to do anything. That was when I felt the…the pain of him…of everything" Nadia inhaled a deep breath; she'd stopped crying. Seemed to almost be staring off into the middle distance, to be idling. *She's pulling away from it again right now.*

    Abby reached forward, pulling Nadia into a hug. Nadia didn't raise her arms to hug back, but Abby felt her adjust her head in the crook of her neck. She was back from zoning out.

    "I'm so sorry, Nadia," was all Abby could think to say. She heard Nadia begin to weep again, met with the salty taste of her own tears running down her face. She took the plate between them with one hand and moved it to the floor so that she could hug her friend better. To somehow protect her from everything she'd just said. To be supportive of her best friend. To protect *herself* from the words Nadia had just said. To rest in each other's protection while she figured out what the hell she was going to do.

    Gary raped Nadia.

    "I'm so sorry, Nadia."

20

Calling the police was the obvious thing that came to Abby's mind around dealing with the rape. *I need to get Nadia settled first.* Nadia had pulled away from the hug, explaining that she felt so tired, she just wanted to sleep. Abby insisted she had a shower before they went to bed.

"Feeling clean will help you feel better. You can borrow some of my clothes, no problem." Nadia nodded as if to say thank you and slid off the bed. She'd stayed over at Abby's house enough times to know where things were.

Hearing the shower knock on the other side of her bedroom wall, Abby let out a long, pained breath. She'd felt like she need to keep everything tight while she was speaking to Nadia. To hold everything together, to look like things were going to be alright. *Are they?*

She undressed herself, feeling like she needed to rid herself of the dirt of the day as well.

She pulled on some pyjamas, clothes she hadn't worn in years, surprised they still fit, she pulled some clothes from her drawers to offer Nadia and got into bed. The duvet and double mattress had never felt so welcoming. *I feel so exhausted...wait, don't be so selfish...imagine how Nadia feels!* Abby fought to stay awake, drifting off just as Nadia came back into the room with a towel around her. Jolting up, Abby pointed to the clothes.

"Pick whatever you want."

"Thanks." Nadia looked through the selection, picking out a top and some shorts.

"There's pyjamas there too." Abby pointed to another pile, and Nadia pulled on the first set she saw.

"They are a little big," Nadia snuffed a laugh. Looking herself over, the arms and legs hanging off her. She looked up and saw Abby, unsure how to react, before the two of them awkwardly laughed. Nadia crawled into bed next to Abby.

"I don't know what to do, Abby."

"I know, it's alright. You don't need to figure everything out right now. We'll figure this all out together."

"I don't know if I should talk with Gary or break up with him," Nadia said.

Oh god. She is broken.

The Belfry Haunting

Abby cuddled her friend close, stroking her hair.
"Just go to sleep for now, alright?"
"Yeah...alright."

Little was spoken of the event the next morning.
"Nadia, you stayed over? Oh, Abby, you should have told me. I'd have cooked her up breakfast as well," Abby's mother said as they came down to the kitchen.
"Sorry". Abby brushed the comment away. Abby's mother huffed, bringing another plate to the table and swiping half of the sausages, beans and eggs from Abby's plate onto it, offering it to Nadia.
"Thank you," Nadia said in a frail voice.
"You alright, darling? Want some coffee or tea?" Abby's mother looked in the girl's face for something.
"No, thanks. I'm alright, just a bit tired is all"
"Ah!" the woman laughed. "Two-day hangover, eh? I remember those. They never get any easier, I'm telling you!" she returned to the sink, washing up her dishes.
"Where's dad?" Abby asked.
"Gone off to watch the football at the pub," her mother spoke over her shoulder.
"Game isn't on until one thirty, I thought"

"Aye, you know your dad, though," her mother said over washing the dishes.

Abby gave it no thought; her dad was rarely in the house. Spent more time out and about, probably trying to find someone to drink with him. *At least he's a sociable person,* she snuffed. Looking down at her plate, she assembled a hearty forkful of food. Before shovelling it into her mouth, she noticed Nadia looking at her clasped hands in her lap.

"Hey, it's alright. Have some food, and then we can catch some fresh air and think this all over."

Nadia didn't nod, didn't look up, didn't acknowledge Abby, but she picked up her knife and fork and cut off a small bite of sausage.

Who the hell can we speak to? Abby thought. The police? Obviously, but they already knew Abby and Nadia. They knew the whole gang; it wasn't like there were a lot of people in Belfry for the police to remember. They weren't exactly Scotland Yard either. Bill and Norman, officers Reid and Ward, respectively, were two boys who had grown up locally. They'd had the sense to spot the hole that Belfry was missing and capitalise on it. Getting trained in Glasgow and returning home to man the "precinct". Less of an official local HQ and more an unused room at the back of the antique shop on the high street, conveniently across the road from the Crying Witch. There was no other police authority in town. All other resources were either "stretched" or "reprioritised" to bigger towns and cities.

Bill and Norman were in their mid-twenties and, like mid-twenty-year-old boys will, spent most of their time sitting about doing nothing. The difference these boys had was they were getting paid for it.

Abby ruled out asking them for help. They'd probably just tell her to fuck off like the other thousand times they already had. They knew Abby and the gang had been underage drinking, they knew that they were "loiterers" and trouble-causers. In any other more respecting place, the police would have scared them with threats of cell time or informing their parents. Bill and Norman knew better than that, though. They understood that involving the parents in things meant they'd get called out by their elders for slacking on the job. No, they kept to themselves and returned almost every penny they earned to the local pub. Which of course meant they had a deal with the landlord.

Tell the parents? No, that idea was bad. The parents would freak out, they'd drag all of them through the streets, they'd embarrass Nadia by putting her up in front of the whole town. They'd destroy Gary's life by hanging him. No, no parents.

You haven't heard Gary's side of the story yet. Abby heard from the back of her mind. It was true, she hadn't, she didn't know if she could. To be able to see that boy who she'd trusted for so many years. To know that he'd defiled her best friend. Left physical and mental scars that would probably never heal. Things like that never healed in a place like this.

Wait, hang on. What the fuck was that thing last night?

Memories flooded back over Abby. The thing in the asylum, the old man, those blood-curdling screams. Johnny was scared out of his wits. All of it drenched Abby's brain, washing away the thought of Nadia's rape.

I need to speak to the boys.

Finishing their breakfast, Nadia followed Abby as she returned upstairs and the two of them got dressed. Abby told Nadia they needed to go to the park so that they could speak to the boys and agree upon what to do.

"Really? What if Gary's there?"

"I'll check and see if he's there first; if he is, I'll tell him to leave." *If he is, I'll tear his head off.*

"Do I have to tell the rest of them what happened?"

"No, you don't have to say a thing. I'll handle that," Abby lied. She had no intention of going over that with the boys. She needed to talk to them, to see if her memory was right or if she hadn't concocted some bizarre, elaborate story in her subconscious to blur over Nadia's rape.

Mickey, I might find Mickey?

But Nadia's life has literally cracked; she's falling apart!

Her chest ached, pushing her to make a decision. She felt her lips try to explain that it wasn't that simple. As if replying, she saw her brother's eyes looking back at her.

Mickey!

If there was a chance she could track down Mickey, she had to throw herself at it. For the time being, this had to be her focus.

Sorry Nadia.

The park was empty save for the boys, as Abby expected it would be. Gary was not there, *thank god.* Nadia hid behind Abby's shoulder as they approached the roundabout. Troy lay on his back as it spun. Johnny sat in the centre, Tom sat on the edge, gently nudging them round and round.

"Abby!" Johnny gasped, jumping up to see his girlfriend. It was the most concerned he'd looked for her safety she'd seen yet. He spotted Nadia hiding behind her and slowed his run to her.

"Nadia, hey. I'm sorry about last night. I was an asshole. I'm so sorry. Are you alright?" he asked. Nadia sidled further behind Abby.

"Leave her alone!" Abby commanded Johnny, shoving him out of the way.

"Where's Gary?" she asked as Troy sat up.

"We, uh, haven't seen him."

"Good. I'd crack that boy's skull off the ground if he was," Abby said. Nadia flashed her eyes up to meet her.

"We know where he is, though," Johnny said. Pulling a note out of his pocket.

"What?"

"He left a note on his back gate. It's for us. Said he had done something stupid and that he was going to look for us at the asylum. Guess he must have gone up there looking for us. Maybe last night, maybe this morning?" Johnny said, handing the note over to Abby. She scanned it to make sure Johnny hadn't adlibbed the words. He was right.

"He wasn't at his house?" Abby asked.

"His parents haven't seen him. We thought he might have tried to apologise to Nadia or something."

"Wait, last night. Johnny. You saw something, right?" Abby pointed a finger at him.

"He was high and scared. He doesn't know," Troy said.

"Shut up!" Abby shouted. "Johnny, answer the question. You saw something, right?"

"Y-yes."

"It was something with hands, right? Lots of hands?"

"I-I think so. I'm not sure."

"It was big?"

"Yeah. What are you getting at, Abby?"

"I saw the same thing. I saw a woman as well."

"Amara?" Tom asked with a sarcastic tone. "Please don't tell me we're going over this again"

"Yes, Amara."

"Abby, look, we were all a bit scared. A bit tired from drinking. Some of us were a bit high. It was dark. It's a creepy place. We don't know what we saw."

"Shut up, I said." Abby scolded, and Tom stepped behind Troy. Clearly, he'd picked his new leader.

"Who is Amara?" Johnny asked.

"Never mind. If that thing is still in the asylum and Gary went to try and meet us there, then god knows what's happened to him." *Why do I care what's happened to him?*

"What if he's dead?" Nadia cried.

21

The last person the gang expected to show such pain for Gary was Nadia, and yet here she was crying at the thought of his possible demise. The gang stared at her in disbelief, awkward silence filled the space.

"I don't know." Nadia's cheeks began to turn red, her brow pinching, wells beginning to gather in her eyes.

Mickey!

"It's okay. Look, we have to go and find him. I'm sorry, but we do. You can go home or go back to mine if you want. Guys, we need to go looking for him at the asylum"

"Right," Troy said.

"Right." Johnny puffed his chest up and stepped next to Troy. Laughably small by comparison.

"Right." Tom stepped to the other side of Troy. The boys had no idea how ridiculous they looked.

"It's fine. I'll come. I need to know," Nadia said. Abby nodded at her friends, her fellowship, her band of brothers. *God, why do we keep having to go back to that fucking place?* she thought as they made their way to Lockwood.

In the daylight, Lockwood normally looked far less creepy. An abandoned building that only held a weight due to its sordid past. Now, the building looked like it welcomed the gang as they wound their way up the driveway. A finger extended to them, teasing them to come inside if they dare. *My my my, what beautiful skin you all have.*

"What do we do? Split up again?" Troy asked as they reached the reception. Abby's eyes locked onto the Rolls-Royce, still parked outside.

"Why is Dietrich's car still here? Did he stay here all night?"

"Who's Dee…what is that German or something? Deetree?" Tom snorted.

"Dietrich. He's the guy who owns the place. I saw him last night, spoke to him inside the building."

"What?" asked Nadia.

"The old guy that was in the car? He was like ninety or something, right?" Johnny added.

"He was on the first floor, hiding in some room, an old office or something, I think. He knew Amara, or that thing we saw, whatever it is. It's going to sound crazy, guys, but he's actually like six hundred years old." The gang stopped in their tracks, turning to Abby before joining her in staring at the black car.

"Six hundred? That's impossible," Troy stated.

"I know, I said it'd sound crazy."

"Must be some old man lying and playing tricks on you, Abby. Don't believe him," Johnny suggested.

"No, it was weird. I wouldn't have believed him, but something about the way he said it and that thing outside the door, Amara. He said that they were like…linked or something."

"Like some kind of spiritual bond?" asked Nadia.

"I don't know, maybe. We need to be careful in there, though. We don't know what happened to Gary or Dietrich. If Amara is still in there, then we need to be careful. Let's stay together as a group, not split up. Hopefully we'll be safer that way."

"I don't even know if I want to go inside now," Tom said soberly.

"Agreed," Abby said before leading the group into reception. Watchfully stepping deeper inside, each member of the gang carefully placed their feet so as not to make any noise whatsoever, and they quietly floated down the corridor Tom and Troy had ventured down.

"We didn't find much when we were looking down here," Troy whispered as he shuffled next to Abby.

"Yeah, all we found were weird treatment rooms. Oh yeah…and they have a basement here," Tom added.

"A basement? Dietrich mentioned that last night. We should start there," Abby said.

"Why?"

"Fuck if I know, this whole place is a mind fuck. Let's just start there, alright? Get it out of the way," Abby said. The boys shrugged their acceptance. They turned a corner in the corridor, and Abby saw what Troy and Tom had mentioned.

"What kind of treatments did they do here?" Nadia asked.

"Looks like it was all weird stuff. Sounds kind of like torture to me. I presume nobody does it these days. Cold water submersion therapy, locking people in cold water tanks. Trephination, where they'd basically drill holes into the brain to see what happened. Look in there." Troy pointed to one room that had a large cross table in the centre. The arms and bottom of the cross had large cogs attached to them, leather straps lying on their surfaces. "I don't know what they called it, but I guess they stretched people in there. There's a steel chair in the next one, where I think they used to do lobotomies. I didn't see any of the rooms, but there was mention of 'detachment rooms' and 'deprivation chambers' where it sounds like they locked up the craziest people and would just try different things on them."

"Different things? Do I want to know?" Nadia asked.

"They'd raise the temperature of the room really high or make it super cold. They'd blast loud music or noises into them. They'd blast light into them or leave them in darkness. They'd expose them to their fears. Some had phobias of spiders that were left in the rooms with tarantulas and stuff. It's fucked up. Doesn't sound like it was much of a treatment as much as it was experimenting on people."

"So no then. I don't want to know." Nadia sighed. Troy looked back at her "Thanks!" She said. Abby didn't like the topic much either, but at least it seemed to be taking Nadia's mind off of Gary.

"Look," Tom said, pointing to the floor. It's pristine linoleum pointing to a single red dot. Highlighted by the daylight coming in the corridor window. Trying to move quicker, they shuffled towards it, a few light scuffs making noises that they scolded each other for.

"Fuck," Johnny said.

"Yeah, fuck indeed," Tom added.

"Blood…fuck!" Abby said, her voice raising. The boys quickly looked down either end of the corridor, waiting for a scream to come booming after them.

"Is it Gary's?" said Troy.

"How the fuck are we supposed to know that?" Johnny blurted, seizing his chance to put the big, handsome American down.

"Look, over there." Abby pointed. More red dots, growing slightly larger the further they went. She began to follow after them, the gang falling in line.

"Oh, fuck. Really?" Tom huffed.

"What?" Abby asked.

"They are going down into the basement." he said, pointing further down the corridor. He was right, the blood spots danced down the linoleum until they reached a doorway. A sign above it, somehow still clinging to the wall though it was cracked in several places, stated 'Basement level' with a downward pointing arrow.

"Alright, I guess that's a big fuck no to going down there then, right?" Johnny tried to mask his plea with a chuckle.

"We've got to go. If someone's down there, we need to help them." Abby said to the gang.

"Really? Do we?" Tom said. "We could just leave here right now. Get the fuck out of here and not find anyone down there. Not get in any trouble. Not get killed! Fuck, let's get the police in to look at it, the fucking army!" he said, his throat drying up in dread.

"What if it's Gary?" Abby said.

"If it's him, then by the looks of it, he's lost a lot of blood, so he's probably dead. I'm sorry, buddy. I hope you find peace in Heaven and all that, but I don't want to die. Especially not to try and get the corpse of some rapist!" Tom spoke upwards to the ceiling. Abby didn't want to comment that Gary would probably be going to hell for raping someone. *No need to open that can of worms.*

Down they went, Abby leading the way, torch pointed in front of her, an orb of light revealing step after step. They weren't the pristine wood of the stairs Abby had climbed the day before; these were stone, cold and void of colour. As they descended, the temperature dropped. How the place could be getting any colder, Abby didn't want to venture.

At the bottom, Abby stopped. The gang huddled behind her on the last few steps. She scanned the area, a similar corridor layout as the floor above, but without the linoleum floor and

The Belfry Haunting

faded blue walls. There was no sanitised feeling here. This was not for patient's eyes. Grey stone floor, walls and ceiling. The outside wall bubbled with brick texture. There were several doors in the corridors. The same standard wooden doors with brass handles. Each one marked simply. Storage room 1, Storage room 2, Storage room 3. Abby approached the first one and turned the handle, but it didn't budge. She tried the second one, finding it more agreeable. Pushing the door open, the gang peeked in. Bed frames were propped up against one side of the room, buckets on the other side next to some chairs and cushions.

"Creepy," Tom said. They moved on, trying a number of other doors, changing from Storage room 10 to Equipment room 1. The door opened, larger than the storage rooms. This room held shelving. Gause, hypodermic needles, leather restraints, straight jackets, empty jars. Beyond the shelves at the back of the room, there were rolling stretchers, scalpels and various metal tools with varying sharp and blunt ends. Saws, clamps, spikes, cutters, spreaders, gougers, graters, slicers, gutters, snappers, breakers, what looked like a psychotic surgeon's dream.

"Why would they need all this stuff?" Nadia asked.

"My guess?" Troy said, picking up a scalpel, gently pressing the tip of his finger on the point of the blade. His finger instantly withdrew, a bead of blood forming. He shook it, splattering blood on the floor before sucking his fingertip. "They probably did post-mortems on their patients. If they were experimenting on them, then they no doubt opened them up to see what happened to them"

"What do you mean? They died is what happened to them," said Tom.

"What he means," Abby interjected as she scanned the instruments. "Is that if they experimented on someone by depriving them of something, it might have had a biological effect on them. It may even have had a psychological effect on them that changed their brain in some way. Being able to see that might provide enough understanding to help reduce or negate those symptoms in other patients." Abby looked over to Troy, Tom watched as the American nodded.

"Bit fucked up though, right? Screw with someone so that you can cut them open and see what you've done to them?" said Johnny.

"Very fucked up," Abby agreed. "And you wouldn't just do it with one patient. You'd do it with many so that you had a better pool of information to confirm or deny your hypothesis."

"They cut open lots of people?" Nadia asked, a lump in her throat, acidic burn of bile tickling the back of her tongue.

"Probably, this place was open for centuries. God knows how many people came in here with unknown conditions only to get sliced up." Troy shifted past Abby, a slight grin on his face. Abby clocked it, smiling back. *Damn it, Abby. Don't start falling for the boy yet.*

"Come on, let's look further," Johnny said, motioning everyone out into the corridor again.

"Where did the blood trail go anyway?" Nadia asked, gulping down her disgust.

"It stopped on the last step", Abby said, turning back the way they'd come. She gasped as she realised she'd been holding the torch pointing downwards the entire time they'd been in the basement. She panned the light up to the ceiling.

"Oh my god!" Nadia exclaimed.

Following them down the corridor, ceiling from the stairs was a long, dark red smudge. It travelled all the way up the corridor and over their heads. Turning, Abby pointed the light in the path it took. Following it down the corridor until it opened up into a wider area.

"How did the blood get up there like that?" Tom asked with clear concern.

"Something dragged something or someone along the ceiling," Abby said, unable to expound further.

"You mean Gary?" Nadia asked again. Nobody challenged her on her concern this time.

Abby halted as they emerged from the corridor into the more open area. Pillars of concrete shooting down into the floor in odd places. No consistency or conformity to them.

"Could be Gary…could be that guy," Abby said. The gang looked over her shoulder.

Beyond a few of the pillars, the outline of a body could be seen. Ten feet away from it, behind another pillar, a hand reached out on the floor.

22

Taking three cautious steps towards the nearest body, Abby looked back to see the gang stood in place. She frowned at them. Nadia stared back, her jaw quivering. Tom gawked with a 'fuck that, I'm not moving' kind of look. Troy scanned the area before beginning to move. Johnny shoved him out of the way and joined Abby.

"Is that Gary?" he asked.

"I don't know," she whispered back, trying to quieten her boyfriend. "I also don't know who or what *that* is." She pointed the light to the hand. Johnny pursed his lips, a silent attempt to apologise. Abby flexed her jaw at him and returned to her approach. Moving closer, closer, closer, Troy and Johnny staying close behind her, hiding behind the barrier of the cone of light.

As she got closer to the nearest body, she could make out more details. She presumed it was a male; he didn't have long hair, and every female that Abby could remember in Belfry had at least shoulder-length hair. He was white, no big shock there, Nadia and her family were the only people of colour in town. His jumper, and the flesh of his back beneath it, had been shredded. Long bloody gouges leaked onto the floor. It wasn't until Abby had moved around a little that she could see the trousers on the body. She took in a sharp breath. She knew who it was. She pressed back into Johnny and Troy, pressing a finger to her lips. They both looked to her, understood the command and then took in what she'd realised.

It's Gary.

Her friend, former friend, she should say, lay on the cold floor. Blood pouring for countless wounds on his back, his legs and arms. A puddle of blood formed around his front, his face concealed by it. Approaching closer, Abby realised that the puddle in front of Gary was not just blood but also his innards. His rib cage had been pulled open, and his organs spilt out in front of him. She tried her best to control her breathing, knowing that she was looking at someone she used to know, now dead before her. Someone she'd had lengthy conversations with, someone she'd laughed with, someone she'd seen cry when he'd had too many drinks and told her about his plans with Nadia to marry her and move to Edinburgh. Someone she used to respect so much. Someone who had raped her best friend.

Don't throw up.
Don't throw up.
Don't throw up.

"What about that?" Troy pointed to the hand ten feet away behind the pillar. Letting out a slow breath, trying to push the lump in her throat back down only to hear Troy and Johnny similarly making their best attempt at controlling their heart own rates, she turned the light away from Gary's corpse to the hand. Moving closer, she glanced back towards the corridor. Tom and Nadia's heads were just visible, still peering over at them.

"Did it just move?" Johnny asked. Abby's attention snapped back to the hand. She didn't see any motion.

"You're just scared," Troy said.

"I'm not scared", Johnny retorted.

"It's okay, man. I'm scared too."

"Both of you, quiet," Abby instructed.

Circling slightly to get a better angle, Abby noticed a pool of red gathering further up the arm. Torn and shredded material wrapped around the arm, further up, nearer to the shoulder. A stained red shirt and black suit coated the rest of a body. Abby sighed.

"What? Is it Amara?" Troy asked.

"No, it's Dietrich's driver, I think," she said.

"Oh, thank God", Johnny exhaled. Troy nudged him. "What? I don't know that guy. I'm glad it's a dead guy and not some crazy ghost thing coming to get us."

"Quiet," Abby hissed. She motioned to Tom and Nadia to come over. They edged out from behind the wall, two gazelles straying into the open, checking every direction for hiding lions. Abby knelt down at the driver, looking over his body. His face was missing, a torn open mess of blood and musculature. His lidless eyes staring in stunned disbelief. He hadn't been maniacally gutted like Gary had. Scanning the light down, Abby discovered that the poor driver's lower body was no longer attached. A pool of blood and a trail led towards his lower extremities. His stomach wound through the path to connect them. One of his legs had been violently broken, his shin bone stabbing out through his calf.

"Oh my god," Nadia said as she saw the gore.

"Please, guys, I know it's a fucking mess, but be quiet," Abby said.

"Okay, but tell me. Is it Gary over there?" Nadia asked. Abby shone the light back at Gary's body and nodded. Nadia's chin quivered, a stammered breath escaping her lips. She leaned into Tom, the boy startled by her touch, before propping her up.

The Belfry Haunting

"Amara did this?" Troy asked.

"I guess so?" Abby said, standing from the body. She shone the light around the room. The pillars getting confusing, it felt like they were moving. Edging closer and swooning away, waves of stone approaching and backing off. Testing how close they could get. A wild pack of predators closing in on their cornered prey. It was difficult to remember where they had come from. The corridor was in the corner, right? But there seemed to be only walled, closed-off corners now. The gang didn't say a word as they all followed the beam of the torch. The tension growing, breathing getting heavier, heartbeats racing again.

"There." Troy pointed as the light swooped over a dark rectangle. Abby swooped back, a corridor-shaped rectangle of darkness.

"What do we do?" Johnny asked. Abby waited…hoped that somebody else would answer or suggest something. The repetitive in and out of their breaths confusing their brains. She quickly whipped the torch around again; the original corridor they'd come down was definitely gone. All that was left was the new corridor in front of them.

"We go down there", she said.

Tom snorted, "Fuck that. Haven't you seen horror movies? You don't go down the spooky corridor."

"Yeah, you also don't go into the spooky asylum building, and you definitely don't go in at night, and you most certainly don't go speaking to creepy old man hiding inside it and fuck me if you decide to go down into the dark, creepy basement," Abby said. Tom sighed. "Besides, where else are we going to go?"

"Ugh, guys?" Johnny said, Abby turned the light on him, he held up his hand, squinting through blindness. "Where did the bodies go?"

"What?" Abby said, slapping the light on the floor. He was right. There was no blood, no bodies lying with their innards spilt or bodies split in half. There wasn't even the faint, odd smell of sweetness in the air. The coppery sweet, almost acidic tinge the blood had given the air around them, gone.

"Come on," said Abby, leading the way towards the corridor. The torchlight pouring down it, solid cold stone walls, flat, lifeless, featureless. Nothing of interest about them. The asylum come to life and allowing its prey to venture deeper into its hidden bowel catacomb, its fingers closing in around them. The gang fumbled after Abby, fearing getting left in pitch black darkness. As they proceeded further, the corridor felt like it was getting smaller. The ceiling getting lower, the walls closing in. Nadia and Tom marched along at the back, shoulder to shoulder, quickly having to move to single file as things closed in. Nadia gave Tom a terrified look, and he submitted to her to move in front, leaving him at the back. Troy squeezed through the corridor behind Abby, much to the rest of the gang's frustration. His large figure held back what little excess light managed to reach back and provided solace to them.

"See anything?" Johnny asked over Troy's shoulder.

"Nothing. It just keeps going," Abby replied. They continued on, walking for what felt like twenty minutes. Abby tried to figure it out in her head how far they must have travelled. There was no way they could have gone so far. They'd be nearly a mile out underground, too far away from the asylum. There would be no point to have something this long to lead to any kind of bunker, surely. You'd just build it deep enough and put a big, thick metal door on it, right?

"Ssssh," Abby whispered back over her shoulder as something grabbed her attention. She wasn't sure how she knew, but something had changed.

"What is it?" Johnny asked, Abby shushed again, turning her ear down the corridor. Listening, squinting to concentrate, leaning her head forward. There was something, very small, ever so slight. A sound, something wiping, something shifting. Something moving.

"You guys hear that?" she asked. Pulling the light onto the wall so it lit up her friends' faces.

"Hear what?" Tom asked from the back.

"That sound," she said. Everyone squinted and looked into the middle distance as they attuned their ears. They looked forward down the corridor. Tom looked back.

"AAGH!" he screamed, grasping at his chest and pushing into Nadia. He gasped for air.

"What is it?" Nadia asked.

"Shit. Shit, fucking shit. I thought I saw something back the way we came. On the ground, I thought I saw something. I don't know. Maybe it was a rat or something?" Tom calmed himself.

A rat? Down here? There's no food. Why would a rat come down here? Abby thought. She didn't want to challenge the boy, though.

"There it is again," she said, hearing the shift, the pushing, the scratching?

"I hear it too," Troy confirmed. He looked back down the corridor in front of them. Abby moved the light in that direction again. The noise begins to rise, the movement edging closer.

"Wait, do you see that?" Johnny said, his eyes nearly closed with how far he was squinting.

"What?" Abby asked, bobbing her head around to see what Johnny was seeing.

"There." Johnny pointed, his finger dead centre into the darkness of the corridor. The rest of the gang couldn't make out any detail. Still, the sound moved closer.

Shuffling.
Scratching.
Clawing.
Crawling.
Closer.

It sounded as if whatever was making the sound was right on top of them now. Like many limbs working their way towards them. Elbows, wrists, fingers, palms, knees, toes, shins, shoulders, all pressing into the concrete to get closer to the gang. Abby tried to control her breathing, felt beads of sweat running down her face.

A hand burst from the light, larger than any hand Abby had ever seen. It pounded into the floor, the fingertips digging in. Shorn, cracked nails digging into the concrete.

"Run!" Abby screamed, turning, and the gang followed suit. Moving as best they could back down the corridor. Troy scuffed his shoulders off the walls as he waded back down the corridor. *It's fine, it'll open back up again, and he'll move faster, that or I can get around him. What was that saying? You don't need to outrun a bear, you just need to outrun the other person?* As her chest began to burn, her lungs aching and lactic acid starting to take over, Abby realised the corridor wasn't opening back out.

"What's happening?" Nadia screamed.

"Just keep running!" Johnny shouted.

"We can't!" Tom shouted back. Abby raised the torch as best she could to give Tom enough room to see where he was running.

"Why not?" Troy shouted. None of them looked back over their shoulder; it didn't matter. Whatever was connected to that hand could fuck off back to where it came from.

Tom thumped into a door. Nadia into him. Johnny into her. Troy into him. Abby bounced off Troy. It was a door, a door unlike any door they'd seen so far in the asylum. A door that looked like the door to a house.

A red door.

23

Abby wasted no time in pointing the torch back the way they'd come. Her head pounded from running. *Haven't run that much in years. You are seriously unfit, girl.* Kept rolling over in her head before she realised that she couldn't hear the sound anymore. The shifting, the movement, the thing chasing them, all silent. Just the gasping breaths of her friends.

"What is this door?" Tom moaned, running his hand along the frame. Nadia leaned over him to get a better look.

"Where does it go?" she asked.

"Does it matter?" Johnny whined while looking down the dark corridor.

"Nadia?" A voice came from the darkness. Everybody froze. Nadia and Tom slowly turned to face back into the dark.

"What was that?" Troy asked.

"Nadia?" The voice came again. Pained, near whimpering. It inched closer, repeating the name.

"Gary?" Nadia instinctively replied.

"It can't be Gary, we saw him, right? He's dead. That thing…Amara…whatever, it killed him, right?" Johnny asked. His question following Troy's earlier question into nothingness.

"Nadia, please," the voice pleaded again. Abby's muscles tightened. *Nadia's right, that's Gary's voice.*

"Gary, are you there? A-are you alright?" Nadia asked, returning glances at each of the gang. Nobody questioned why she was replying; all of them wished she wasn't.

"Nadia, I need you." The voice took form. Gary's face, distant, hidden behind a veil of black of shadow. His eyes blinked; his nose and brow could be made out. His lips and teeth. An almost blurred mess of Gary's face, too far to make out clearly.

"Gary, you hurt me," Nadia sniffled.

"I need you, baby. Why won't you come to me?"

"Gary, stop. I saw you. Y-you were dead."

"I'm not dead, baby. I'm better." The head tilted, smiling, the eyes not matching the expression. Staring, cold, an intention behind them that was far from welcoming.

"You're better?" Nadia asked, feeling the hypnosis of Gary in front of her draw her forward. She pressed into Troy. He frowned and shifted, allowing her to pass.

"Yes, I'm better. I need you...I need you to tell me..."

"Tell you what, Gary? Tell you what?" she begged as her body squashed against the wall, struggling to get around Troy's mass.

"I need you to tell me..." The face moved closer. The eyes blinking, brow twitching, pain spreading across Gary's face. Abby focused and thought that his face looked strange. Like, there were markings across his cheeks and forehead. The more she looked, the more she could make out the markings moving.

No.

Not markings.

Fingers. Dozens of fingers comprising a face that looked near exactly like Gary's face.

"To tell me I'm better than Troy." Gary's eyes flared. His face pushed closer into the light, the finger construction of his face beginning to move quicker. His face extended further, revealing a long neck, too long to be human, no, not a neck, an arm? An extension of hands, hand upon hand upon hand.

Gary smiled. Dozens of other hands moved from the darkness, smothering across every surface of the corridor. Floors, walls and ceiling, digits scuttling like spider legs, pulling Gary's face towards the gang.

"Go, go, GO!" Abby shouted. Johnny screamed and pushed Troy back, he didn't budge; now wedged against Nadia's body. Tom threw himself against the door with his shoulder.

"Fuck!" He shouted, grabbing the handle and turning it. The door flung open as Tom threw another shoulder at it. Troy managed to rip Nadia out from wedging him in and throw her through the door before grabbing Johnny and Abby and pulling them back with him.

They collapsed onto something soft that gave off a light crunch sound. Abby landed on Troy's stomach, firm. She could feel his abs flex in pain against her thumping on him. She didn't wait to feel how defined they were, though, pushing herself back to her feet so she could turn a quick one-eighty and slam the door closed. Gary's face turned as it edged further down the corridor. That same grin with vibrant eyes, eyes that wanted to kill. His head turning, turning too much, turning a full circle. The door slammed shut. Abby turned the handle and heard a click, unsure if the door had just fallen back into its lock or if she had secured it. She pressed her back against the door.

"Troy, help!" she shouted. Troy was already off the ground and threw himself next to her, planting his feet firmly.

Johnny, Tom and Nadia pulled themselves to a sitting position and stared at Troy and Abby. Watching them eagerly, praying that they had enough weight and strength to hold the door closed. Abby stared at the floor, not picking up anything, not thinking of anything apart from making sure the door didn't budge.

"Wow." Troy's silly American accent tickled her ear. His eyes dancing around, taking in all that he saw before him.

Seconds passed, Abby held her stance strong, eventually deciding that the Gary thing wasn't trying to get through the door. She allowed her pulse to calm, her focus to ease. Her eyesight to take in what she'd been staring at. *Leaves?* She nearly said it out loud. No need, the gang would be seeing the exact same thing as her, right?

Crisp leaves covered the ground, so many leaves that Abby wondered if she'd ever walked on ground covered so entirely. They didn't have that warming orange and brown colour to them, the colour that you knew meant cold weather outside, but somehow made your heart feel a little bit warm. These leaves were red, Abby wondered if they were stained red, a specific type of leaf from a tree that only blossomed the bloodiest red coloured leaves. She raised her head slowly, taking in the scenery in the same way Troy had been and still appeared to be.

Those leaves weren't red due to soaking or some special tree. Abby saw it now, it was the sky, a blood red sky, clouds angrily looking down at them. Pouring beams of red light onto everything around. Tree surrounded them mostly, their dry wood looked black in the light. A sea of black trunks with an ocean of darkness behind them.

"Look," Troy said, pointing in front of him as he pushed off the door, apparently also convinced the door would not open. His finger pointed to a house some hundred feet away. A wooden cabin it looked like. Old, Abby guessed, not having the typical frame structure you'd imagine. Not the door, windows and roof every child drew when asked to draw a house in their formative years. There were walls, sure. Logs lay one on top of the other to create them, smeared with mud, Abby wondered? There was a roof of sorts, moss, straw, twigs, whatever could have been gathered from the surrounding area, presumably.

A window and door were present as well but the window was far from technical. A hole in the wall, exposing a black square to the interior. The door at least had a little more detail and work put into it. Several planks of wood strapped and boarded together. Unsurprisingly, no number marked the door, no letterbox, no path down a front garden. Only a stretch of compressed mud in front of the house.

"Where the fuck are we?" Johnny rose to his feet.

"Fuck if I know." Tom got up. Abby walked over and helped Nadia to her feet.

"Are you alright?" she asked.

"Yeah, I, ugh. Yeah. I'm okay," Nadia replied, blinking frequently, giving her head a quick shake.

"Are you sure?" Abby asked.

"Yeah, I just, I don't know, I couldn't hold myself back. It was like I was looking back at the Gary I'd known, the one who was, you know? Alive. Like he was the Gary who hadn't done anything to me, who hadn't…"

"Okay, look at me. It's alright. We're going to be alright." Abby nodded at Nadia, she nodded back.

"Are we?" Troy asked. He'd been turning around, looking for any other details he could find. He nodded his head back at the door, to the side of it. Abby stepped away from Nadia and circled the door, expecting to see the long concrete corridor stretching back into the depths of the forest around them. For there to be a crack in the wall, a crack that was growing, Gary trying to break through.

"What the fuck?" She expelled her thoughts as she circled the door.

There was only the door.

A door standing in the ground and nothing else.

"I don't like this," Tom said, shifting his gaze from the door to the house and back. "How do we get back home?" His breath faltered "I just want to be back home", he began to whine.

"I…ugh…I, I don't know," Johnny said as if he was still the leader of the group. His old tendencies returning. Resorting back to a time where he had control and felt comfortable.

"This is fucked," Troy said, panic seeping into his body. He slapped the door frame, slapped it again. Punched it, thumped his hands on the door. Utilising his most basic instinct and strength to power through any problem in his way.

"Stop, everyone. Just stop," Abby said. She'd moved away from the door, towards the house. Something drew her towards it. She saw no point in fighting with the door; it was where they had come from after all. Leaving it well alone was probably the best choice. The gang gathered behind her, unwilling to cross the invisible line in the ground before them.

"Listen," Abby said, raising a finger as if to help their ears focus. "Do you hear the singing?"

"What the fuck, Abby?" Tom blurted.

"Abby, I don't hear anyth-" Johnny was nearly finished before he cut himself off. Looking around, confused. "Yeah, I hear it".

Before anyone else could question them, they all began hearing it. A soft voice, a calm melody, a female voice in the distance. Coming from the cabin. Abby walked closer to the door, the singing growing, the gang began to follow.

It was pleasing, the melody conjured images of sitting in a field of flowers, caressing winds rolling over your skin, walking between the flowers and feeling the soft touch of the petals, the aromas filling your lungs. A mothering melody used to help children drift off to sleep, into a realm of happiness and safety where nothing could hurt you. A warm hug from a loving parent when you'd woken up on a beautiful summer's day, ready to go out on your brand new bicycle and have fun.

"Who is it?" Johnny asked, his voice settled. Abby didn't answer as she reached the door, resting a hand against it and lightly pressing. The door gave no resistance, creaking open.

The inside was far from welcoming, not to the gang's standards anyway. The floor a mixture of wooden boards and mud. A single table that looked like it might fall apart at any second. A stone hearth on the far wall nuzzled a crackling fire. There were four thatched beds on the other side of the room. Weeping cloth hanging in the middle of them, they did not look comfortable or clean. All of this washed over the gang as they looked in, not a care for the details; it was the woman they looked at.

The woman who hunched down in the corner of the house, the firelight dancing on her back. Her hair poured over her gown. *Is that a gown?* Abby thought. It was too dirty to be a dress; there was no design on it, on the back at least. It looked like it had been made hundreds of years ago and served only the purposes of covering the body and protecting it against the elements, pure practicality.

"H-hello," Abby said as the gang moved inside. The woman gently rocked back and forth, her hair covering her face, her fingers rolling strands of her hair. It was the woman that was singing, the origin of that hypnotising lullaby that pirouetted across the room to their ears.

"Hello?" Abby asked again, stepping forward from her friends. She noticed that though she was closer to the fire, she felt no heat from it.

"Hello, are you Amara?" Abby asked. The woman's head jolted up, hair still hiding her features. She halted the melody. The room filling with the sound of her breath, long inhales and exhales.

"Amara?" Abby reached her hand forward slowly, meaning to gently touch the woman's shoulders. Before she could, the woman's head snapped in her direction, her hair whipping out in a fan. Abby retracted her hand, stumbling back a few steps into Johnny and Troy. They buffered her in their hands.

The woman's eyes seemed to pierce through from behind her hair, pupils dilated until they almost filled her eyes. Lips trembling, they appeared to be whispering a message, almost, trying to conjure someone to help her. The lips calmed, flattening out before spreading wide to reveal brown and black stained teeth. She stood up from the corner. Abby's memory flashed back to running down the asylum corridor from the stairs, looking back and seeing a woman standing at the bottom of them. This same woman.

She screamed.

The gang's heads fogged, the piercing noise ripping at their eardrums, burrowing into their brains and shredding at whatever it could. Raising her arms, the woman's scream rose in pitch, disabling the gang from moving. Troy fought to gain an inch of purchase in his limbs but felt burning pain sear through his body. The rest of the gang stood no chance by comparison, submitting to the petrifying cry. The woman's arms rose above her, her scream morphing into a manic laugh. The gang's vision started to warp, to bounce in and out. Abby could feel her stomach turning.

Before the bile taste in her throat was chased by the contents of her stomach, the woman exploded. Hands spilling from her form, hundreds, *thousands?* Varying in size and skin colour, they tumbled onto the floor of the cabin. Scurrying over each other like a plague of rats. Finding their territory before switching to their need to feed. They scampered at the gang. Abby snapped out of the trance quick enough to grab her friends and shove them out of the door. She slammed the door on the house and planted her back on it. Between the holes in the door, pushing through the edges, fingers emerged. Prodding and probing for human flesh.

"Come on!" Troy shouted back as the gang raced towards the door. Abby couldn't do it, couldn't let her friends be taken. She looked at the door standing in the ground, alone and mysterious. She prayed that it would lead them back home, to safety, to peace. As she thought it, the door opened, vague light snuck around pillars of stone. As she realised she was looking at the room they'd seen the driver's and Gary's bodies, hands spilled out of the window next to her. A river of palms and fingers poured onto the ground next to her. Hands crawled out of the edges and began to cover the wall of the cabin. Abby shot off the door, running after her friends. They'd reached the door already by the time her feet hit the leaves. Her prayers changed when she heard the scuffle and rustle of leaves behind her. Masses of hands chasing after her. *Oh god, please don't let these things kill me.*

"Come on, Abby, come on!" Johnny shouted from the door. His arm reached out, Tom, Nadia and Troy holding him back as if the door was pulling him back in.

Abby's legs felt like they were sinking into the leaves, having to wade through thicker and thicker masses, burning as she pushed to move forward. The scuttling behind her grew louder and louder; she dared not look back to see a wave of fingers about to crash down on her.

A sudden grasp at her ankle made her gasp. Fingers wrapping around her leg, more wrapping around her other foot. She didn't stop, *keep moving, keep moving, keep moving.* She was a few feet away from the door as she felt the vibrations of the hands behind her. Felt more hands grabbing onto her legs beneath the leaves. The leaves parting to show the collection of digits fiddling and trying to hold her. One hand crept over the other hands, up her leg, up her spine and onto her shoulder. Digging its fingers in. She screamed in pain and reached out as far as she could. Johnny leaned out, his fingers scuffing off of Abby's. He tried again, managing to interlock his fingers with hers. He pulled her closer, wrapping his hand around her wrist. Tom, Troy and Nadia pulling with all of their strength. The hands around her legs pulling back. Forming a gigantic limb stretching all the way back to the house.

"Pull!" Troy shouted. Abby felt the fingers clamp around her legs, feeling like her skin was going to tear, her bones going to break. She looked into Johnny's eyes, terror mixed with determination marking his face. Kicking her legs as best she could, Abby found a slight growing purchase. She could feel herself inch closer to the door.

"Pull!" Troy repeated, a coxswain commanding the rhythm. Abby kicked harder, a few fingers slipped their grasp. Clicking and cracking pierced everyone's ears. Abby felt the vibrations through her legs. Assuming it was more hands coming to bolster the grip on her. She kicked, harder, harder, harder.

Click.

Crack.

CRACK!

Looking down, she saw that several hands were falling off her, deformed and misshapen. They hadn't been losing grip. Those cracks were bones breaking.

"Pull!" Abby screamed to her friends. With one final yank, her legs broke free. Her body tumbling through the door, the gang falling on top of each other in a pile. Abby rolled off the top of the gang and clattered to the floor. Tom riggled free and slammed the door closed.

"Abby, Abby, are you alright?" Johnny pleaded, scraping himself from between Nadia and

Troy and over to Abby. She clutched at her throat, facing away from the gang.

"Abby, Abby", Johnny called to her again as he realised the hand on her shoulder had come through with her. It had scuttled around to her throat and was clamped tightly around it. Abby silently failing to take in air. Scratching at the hand to release it.

Abby's vision went black, her eyes rolling into the back of her head. A figure shifted in her vision, something trying to reach her. It shifted closer, turning and swaying in the shadows. Details occasionally flashing, a face she hadn't seen in so many years.

Mickey?

"Help, guys, help," Johnny said. Troy and Johnny scrambled to their knees on either side of her, flipping her onto her back. Both of them trying to pull the hand off.

"Here," Tom said, pulling his lighter out of his pocket and tossing it to them as he held his body against the door. A thunderous rain was battering against the door. Nadia leapt to her feet and helped him hold the door closed. Johnny quickly flicked the lighter open, trying to light it. "Damnit, damnit. I've used this thing a thousand times," he said. Taking a quick breath before giving a last attempt.

The darkness around them gave way to the lick of light from the flame. Johnny held it for a moment, letting it grow before holding the flame to the base of the hand. The part where a wrist would connect to a forearm, but now was only a grey stump. The hand twitched as the flame burned the skin. Troy managed to get his fingers under two of the severed hand's fingers. Johnny managed to pull the thumb free. As they pulled the hand away as best they could, it dug nails into Abby's neck. The pulled hand gouged four lines down Abby's chest.

    Johnny and Troy stood, both grasping the hand. They glanced at each other before throwing the hand off the nearest pillar. The hand flopped onto the ground on its back. The fingers curling inwards like a dying spider's legs. Just before it looked like it was going to give up and die, the finger snapped open, it flipped over and scuttled towards Abby again. Troy lifted his leg and slammed down his boot on top of it. A squelch and several cracks echoed around the room. Troy lifted his leg again, the hand giving a slight twitch. The American stamped on the hand again, again, again. Kept stamping until it felt like his foot was landing on concrete. Lifting his leg, he expected to see a blood splattered mess, to find chunks of flesh and blood on the underside of his boot.

    There was nothing. Only cold concrete with the vague outline of a boot from the dust that had been moved.

    "Where did it go?" Troy asked.

"Abby, are you alright?" Johnny asked, helping her sit up. She coughed and spluttered, gasping for air. Feeling her vision return.

"Where are we?" She said, her voice hoarse.

It was at that point that the gang looked around. They were back in the large room with the pillars.

"This is where we saw Gary and that driver guy, right?" Tom said, realising the battering on the door had stopped.

"Yeah, their bodies aren't here now," Nadia said, scanning the floor.

"There's the corridor we came down, right?" Johnny said, pointing to the corner that he and Nadia had hidden behind while they watched the others check out the dead bodies, what felt like a lifetime ago.

"Right. But there wasn't a door when we came in here first, right?" Abby said, turning back to look behind Tom. Tom turned around, nodding, raising a hand to slap the wood. His hand landed on stone.

There was no door there anymore.

"What the fuck's going on?" Troy asked.

"I don't know. Let's get the fuck out of here," said Johnny.

24

The basement corridor felt like a welcome return after the terrors the gang had come from. The doors into storage areas flying past as they ran to get to the stairs.

How did we come right back into that room? There was a corridor, right? A corridor that kept getting smaller? Abby thought as their footsteps boomed through the basement.

"Come on," Johnny said, leading the way up the stairs. The cold linoleum leaving a chittering feeling down their spines as they raced towards reception. A roar emanated from behind them, further down the corridor. Only Abby looked back.

"Fuck, run!" she shouted as she heard a man's voice roar at them. Hands pouring out of the corridor, pulling a man's head towards them. A man's head too large to be real, surely. The height of a grown man, but clearly distinguishable as a man's head. Abby wondered if it might have been the driver. The gang forced everything they had to outrun the voice behind them. Not realising that hands making up the lips of the man's face parted, sharp digits chomped hollow clicks as it gained on them. They turned the final corner to reception, seeing the doors that led into the waiting room. Abby looked back over her shoulder, the hands morphing, rippling like a wave, crashing into each other. Hair blossoming from the crawling mass.

A woman emerged.

"Amara," Abby said to herself, looking the woman dead in the eyes. The roar turned to a piercing death scream. Troy covered his ears as they burst into the reception.

"Hey, I told you kids not to come up here!" Dougie shouted, pointing an accusing finger at the kids as they crashed into him. Splashing on either side of him to the floor. Somehow, Dougie managed to keep his footing. Turning to the gang, biting his lip to hold his fury. "What the fuck is wrong with you lot? Why do you insist on coming in here and fucking aro-" His voice cut short as hands wrapped around his head. More grasping his shoulders, more working their way down his body to hold him in place. His scream of resistance heightened as the hands tilted his head to the side. Amara's face was hidden behind a swaying cloud of black hair. Dougie's eyes winced as pain and pressure took over. With a violent turn, his neck snapped. Abby's eyes involuntarily blinked at the disgusting sharpness of the sound. Amara continued to twist his head, hands around his neck, digging in talon nails. Severing flesh, severing muscle, severing veins until, with a prolonged shlop, his neck parted, and his head was tossed to the ground. Raising the body above her head, Amara's hand minions bent his limbs in the wrong direction. Her eyes savoured the revulsion in everyone else's eyes as they heard bones break.

"Cargill," the words crept from her mouth, a chilling whisper. What felt like a warning. She threw the body down, landing in front of the gang. They screamed and scrambled to their feet, hopping out of the door. The stones of the parking area outside like shattering marbles as the gang grasped and huddled at each other. Swarming to a stop and looking back in the reception.

"She can't get us," Tom said.

"What?" frowned Abby.

"It's the rules, right? Monsters, ghosts and shit. They are confined to a place, a building, right? That's what all the horror movies taught us? Right?...RIGHT?" Tom turned to the gang.

Amara floated to the door, halting at the doorway.

"Cargill," she hissed again.

"See. She can't come out," Tom said, laughing through fear. Abby stretched her arms out around the rest of the group, edging them backwards.

Amara floated past the threshold, silently moving into the moonlight. The white bathed the hands, turning the abomination a lighter grey. The hair on her head still swaying, not affected by the light breeze.

"Tom, come here," Johnny said. Tom laughed, turning manic. As the group shifted back another six feet, Tom stepped forward two.

"Tom, fucking move it!" Nadia rasped.

"No, it's alright. We just have to burn the fucking place down, right?" Tom said, pulling his lighter from his pocket.

"We can't burn it down," Gary replied. Tom halted, thumb flicking at the lighter, whimpering sparks flashing no fire. Slowly, he turned to see Amara floating, towering over him.

"What?" his body instinctively replied.

"We can't burn the building down. This whole place has to burn, burn everyone." Amara spoke, but it was Gary's voice they heard.

"Tom, run!" Abby shouted. Tom's feet slid through the stones as he tried to make a leap away. A single hand wrapping around his throat before he escaped.

"No, Amara, please!" Abby begged as she watched her dumb, stoner friend lifted off his feet. His hands scratching at his neck trying to free some room for air. His legs kicking violently. Amara's gaze shifted to meet Abby's, no remorse or care present on her face.

The arm latched around his neck gripped tighter, muffled hucks of spit forming on Tom's lips. At Amara's elbow, a bulge seemed to gather, moving down the forearm until more fingers burst out at the wrist. They slide up the hand around the throat and dug into Tom's face, tearing at his flesh. Two of the fingers, what looked like thumbs, dug into his eyes. Pushing deep into Tom's skull, for how grey the skin was, Abby could still make out the whitening of flesh as pressure was applied. Tom's throat spasmed, allowing him to gasp a breath of air and wretch a blood-curdling scream.

"No!" Tom screamed. Abby wanted to run to her silly, stoner friend to help in some way. *But how?* More fingers slipped out of the wrist, these coming from the bottom. Latching onto Tom's screaming jaw. His cries of pain muffled by the fingers in his mouth. The fingers pulled at his jaw, stretching his cheeks until they started to split. His tongue flopping around in a desperate panic, a hysterical animal unsure if it should retract into safety inside or part ways and flee. Before it could make a choice, Tom's jaw clicked and tore his cheeks in half, the jaw used as a handle to tear the boy's neck open. Blood poured down Tom's body, his arms and legs as they went limp.

Fuck, he's dead. Fucking Tom's dead. You stupid fucking stoner, Tom. Why? Why?

The fingers released the jaw, it slapped against his belly and dangled, glistening dark red in the moonlight, a coppery tang starting to gather in the air.

"Come on," Troy said, grabbing the gang as Amara watched them flee. She released Tom's body, and gravity dropped it to the stones. Falling into a pile of what once was a person known for dick jokes and a supply of illegal substances. A boy who had always wanted to be the leader of the pack. A boy who had always wanted his friends to have a laugh and to party. A boy who'd struggled making friends growing up. A boy who would have defended his friends until the end. A boy who had met his end without being able to defend it.

Racing across the grass and down the hill to the driveway, Abby could hear Amara's voice still in her head.

Cargill.

"Where do we go?" Johnny said as they reached the entrance to Lockwood.

"We need help," Abby admitted.

"Where do we get that?" Troy asked.

"Only place where we can get anyone in Belfry," Abby said.

She led the gang to the pub.

25

Sunday wasn't a day you'd normally find pubs packed to the gills. For most of Scotland, it would be the lucky few people who didn't have work the next day and could enjoy a drink or two. Of course, Belfry wasn't very normal now, was it?

Huffing and puffing, the gang, now two less, arrived at The Crying Witch. Lights still on and a healthy noise of chattering, laughing and jostling going on inside. It was safe to assume that the majority of the remaining population of Belfry was inside. Safe to assume that they held no care for anything that was going on outside. Safe to assume everyone inside was pickled senseless. Safe to assume none of them knew of the terrors that had happened at Lockwood.

"Come on," Abby said, leaning against the door. It jostled ajar, the noise bloomed, spilling into the darkness. A beacon call, the gang looking back up the road from where they'd come, *hope that can't be heard at Lockwood*. It was loud enough to deafen them but not as deafening as Amara's screams had been. They rushed inside to close the door again, to dampen any possible giveaway of their location.

"Oi, you lot. You better not be in here to cause any shite," Big Ronnie bellowed from the bar. No matter how noisy it got in the pub, his voice would always cut through.

"Ronnie, we need your help!" Abby shouted as best she could. She hadn't mastered the art of throwing her voice like the landlord had. She pushed through the crowds of people, neighbours, family members of friends, people she'd seen and spoken to countless times over the years. The gang huddled in behind her, weaving towards the bar. Ronnie held his frown at them as they got to the bar. Abby repeated herself.

"Help? Aye, I've known that for years. Now what can I get you?"

"Pint of Tennants, pal," Johnny said. Abby halted her words and turned to Johnny, slapping him on the shoulder.

"We need help, we need the police!" Abby shouted, leaning over the bar. A few of the punters holding up the bar squinted and smirked. They'd seen and heard of enough things going on around town. No secrets were sacred in this town. *Apart from the six-hundred-year-old man and a killer monster, pfft.* Tilting back over their drinks, a couple joked that kids these days didn't know how to cope with hard times.

"Oh fuck off, you kids *are* here to cause shite. What have you done then? Set fire to a bin? Knicked a car and crashed it into someone's house?" Ronnie raised an eyebrow. His eyes quickly counting the group, realising they were 2 less than usual. "Aw fuck. Don't tell me one of your bloody junky mates has OD'd."

"Ronnie, please, are the police here?" Abby asked.

"Aye, usual spot. Now fuck off and keep your shite away from the pub." Ronnie shooed the gang away, sidestepping down the bar as far as he could to take an order.

Abby turned, stepping on tiptoes to see over the heads of the patrons. Right enough, as Ronnie had said, over in their usual corner were the local Belfry authority. Officers Reid and Ward sat at a table, *their* table, their feet up on the two other chairs at their table, pints in their hands. If any of the other patrons asked if they could take the free chairs, the young coppers would kick up a fuss. Wax lyrical about how much of a service they provided the town, the security they never got thanked for. There were never other friendly guests at their table. The boys had their spot, they didn't invite anyone to join, and nobody wanted to join them; enough said. Even when Reid or Ward would get up to get another round in, nobody tried to swoop in to take the seats. It wasn't worth the hassle.

Shoving through the crowd, Abby tried to peek out of the window, but blackness sheeted what she could see. Something moved, not clear enough to make out. As she shouldered round Johnny's cousin, she realised that it was the outline of a tree shifting in the wind. *Thank god.*

"Ward, Reid!" She rasped as she broke free of the crowd and into the corner. Johnny and Nadia popped out behind her. Troy, with his arms tucked into his centre, emerged with locals giving him a shocked look, amazed by his size.

"Fuck off, not tonight, Abby," Ward said, not even lifting his eyes from his pint.

"We need your help."

"Aye, what have you little cunts broken now?" Reid said.

"Just fucking listen, would you?" Johnny shot at them. Both of them rested their pints and shot scowls back.

"Young Mr McCintosh, you'd best hold your tongue with that kind of language. We might be forced to react to hostility with punitive force."

"Punitive force?" Nadia questioned.

"You can't chuck that shit out here, and you know that", Abby said. "You both know if you tried to exercise the law, then you'd both be at risk of losing your jobs because you've been drinking." She folded her arms. The officers sighed; they hated having to deal with Abby. The rest of the gang were easy enough to deal with; a threat of arrest would settle them down. Abby was whipsmart enough to challenge them on most occasions, though. Mainly because she still saw them as the pathetic, creepy, horny boys who'd tried to hit on her a few New Year eve's Eves ago and she'd shamed them when they'd told her she'd love "a proper police double teaming".

"Right, well you just hush your shite then Johnny or I'll tell your mum about us catching you with weed."

"When?" Johnny refuted.

"Three weeks ago?" Ward said.

"A month and a half ago?" Reid added.

"That weekend we caught you four times," Ward chuckled. Johnny's shoulders dropped. If he'd had any wherewithal about him, he'd have pointed out that the main reason they kept catching him was because both he and Tom had been their suppliers.

"Look, just listen, we need your help-"

"Oh, aye? Finally come round, have you?" Reid grinned, elbowing Ward.

"Fancy some of the good stuff, do you?" Ward leaned back, grabbing his crotch in one hand and shaking it. Nadia let out a gag.

"Are you two fucking mad? People have been killed," Troy said, his voice seemed to carry more weight thought Abby. He'd maybe even give Ronnie a run for his money.

"Oh aye, and who the fuck are you, Yankie doodle?" Reid puffed his chest out.

"Big fucker, aren't you?" Ward said, standing from his chair. The officer's head only meeting Troy's collar bone.

"Listen to what he said. People are dead?" Abby pleaded.

"Aye? That right? Notice your young stoner pal Tom ain't here? He finally had his fill and OD'd? Fuck, Reid, that'll make our lives a bit easier, eh?" laughed Ward.

"Aye, and where's your lad then?" Reid nodded to Nadia. "Or have you had enough of him finally. You want some action too?" he winked.

"Actually," Nadia stammered ", He…he… he's dead." Nadia glanced at Abby, unable to tell the whole truth. *It's okay, Nads. Don't worry.*

"Well fuck me sideways. You kids must have been on something wild tonight, eh? People have been killed, and this merry band of fuckwits has decided to come down to the local pub and tell the po-po all about your adventures? What is it?

Absinthe? Meth? Coke? How much do you have and how much will we slip in the back of our pockets?" the young officer chuckled and held a mischievous grin. Proud of his corruption.

A sudden scream hushed the pub. Animalistic and brutal, it shredded through the windows and walls. Tearing through the ears of the inebriated Belfry locals.

"What the fuck was that?" Ronnie scoffed from behind the bar, looking over the hushed crowd, expecting it to have been caused by some ruckus. "You kids, aye, you, Rennie! Was that you and your mad crowd setting that shit off?"

"No!" Troy shouted back.

"A Yankee?" a random punter exclaimed, shocked by the accent.

"Yes, a fucking Yankee. I'm American. What the fuck does that matter? What matters is that fucking thing outside." Troy pleaded the masses to act more concerned.

Two loud clangs echoed through the building as something slammed into the wall and roof.

"Rennie, do you know what that thing is?" Ward asked. Abby glanced a side eye at him and nodded. The lights cut out, drowning the pub and everyone inside in darkness. Everyone blinked as their eyes adjusted, a few of the more inebriated locals stumbled slightly. The moonlight coming in the thin windows highlighted the eye lines of everyone. Shifting, uneasy gazes danced around the room.

"Cargill." That piercing whisper crept into the room, the locals nearest the windows jolted and stepped back. Those nearest the door shifted gently, closer into a huddle at the centre of the room.

"Who is that?" One of the old men near the bathroom asked. Nobody replied; all eyes scanned the windows and halted on the front door.

"Calm down, calm down," Ronnie said, shifting his mass to the end of the bar and lifting the gate. He shimmied through, sucking in his belly. "It's probably just some trick of the wind. You lot are all pished to kingdom come," Ronnie said as he pulled a set of keys from his belt, fishing through them to find the right one and then locking the door.

"If you're not worried, then why'd you lock the door, Ron?" Reid asked. Even in fear, the boy couldn't hold back his sarcasm.

Ronnie turned to the huddle, sighed and flexed his jaw. Locking eyes with Reid.

"Boy, you give me much more of your sass, and I'll ban you from this place. I don't care if you're the local bobbies, you know as well as I do that I hold the sceptre around these pa-" The door ripped open as Ronnie lifted a pointed finger at Reid. Hands smothered around Ronnie. Fingers seeming to grip around every edge of him. Before

Ronnie could react, he was sucked out of the doorway.

The huddle gasped, holding silence in hopes that it would hide them all. A deep bellowed yelp of shock rung through the door followed by an even deeper cry of agony. Everyone's ears ached as they heard the noises of flesh tearing, bones breaking, pained screams. Splatters of blood marked the window, little paths of red running down them as the landlord was brutalised above them.

"What the fuck do we do?" Ward whispered.

"Fuck if I know, that thing just pulled big Ron out and tore him apart," Reid hushed back.

"Well, you guys are the fucking police; we need your help," Abby rasped at them. Faces turned to scold the three talking and revealing their position.

Crackles and squelches could be heard above as Ronnie's attacker moved across the roof of the building. Eyes focused on the centre of the movement as it travelled down the roof, then back, then down again before stopping.

"Cargill," the whisper returned.

"We don't know who Cargill is, and he isn't here!" Reid shouted. Everyone shot him a look. *Why the fuck did you say that?* The young officer shrugged and tried to chuckle off his mistake. From the roof came another deafening scream that turned to laughter. The laughing coming from many different voices. Nadia thought she could make out Gary's laugh amongst them. Abby's ears deceived her; *was that Mickey's childlike laughter as well?*

"Look," one of the patrons said, pointing to the window on the far side of the room. The shadow of fingers could be made through a stained glass window. A unicorn no longer up on it's hind legs in white, stained dark by searching fingers on the other side. Hands started to raise, pointing at the other windows, more fingers emerging into sight. Gently pawing at the windows, feeling them, testing them.

"Oh fuck," Abby said.

"What?" Troy glanced at her.

"We've got to get out of here." Abby said, only the gang heard her.

Smash!

The windows imploded as hands poured. Too many to count, they scurried up onto the ceiling, down the walls and flopped onto the floor. Abby turned and hurled herself at Troy. He wrapped his arms around her waist as he fell back and through the door to the mens bathroom. Nadia and Johnny lept in after them.

The mass of hands quickly wrapped around the nearest patrons they could find. Swarming over them, their faces screaming as they disappeared under hands and digits. Blood poured from between the fingers, squelching and cracking, filling the room along with screams of terror. The first five people swarmed by hands were squashed to bloody, broken piles of mess in seconds.

Tumbling over each other and forming their own mass of limbs and panic, the patrons tried to pull away from the hands. Fleeing to the corner of the room.

"Help!" they screamed as a female figure slowly stepped in the door. Amara staring out through her hair, draped over her face, her eyes flickering an evil orange.

Nadia covered her ears, pushing one of the stall doors open. Johnny jumped into the one next to her. Troy threw the bathroom door closed and thumped himself against it. Abby joined him, pressing her weight against it. *We've got to stop bumping into each other like this.* With no resistance, she realised Amara may not have seen them. Or at least she was going to have her way with all of the local punters before she came after them. *Gives us a little time, I guess.*

"Look, there's a window. We could get out there," Troy said, nodding at the thin window high above one of the stalls. Abby frowned at him.

"You won't make it through that thing. You're too big."

"Shut up, shut up, shut up. You'll let her know we're here," Johnny cried.

"It's alright. You guys get out through there, I'll make a run for it and jump out one of the windows while she's distracted ki...killing everyone else." Troy gulped down vomit at the thought of what was happening on the other side of the door.

"Shut up, please, shut up," Johnny cried again.

"Johnny, will you shut the fuck up, *please?*...you know what? I'm fucking done with you," Abby bit at the poor boy crying in the stall. *Oh god, get a hold of things, Abby.*

"He's right, stop talking," Nadia said from her stall. Abby bit her lip and left Nadia be.

"You can't do that. She'll kill you." Abby turned back to Troy.

"I'm pretty fast", Troy chuckled. "Remember, I'm a quarterback. Gotta have fast reactions."

A thump made them both jump as a leg was thrown at the bathroom door. The number of living patrons reducing and the number of pieces of patrons increasing fast. A trickle of blood crept under the bathroom door. Abby watched it gather into a little puddle.

"Troy, stop. We'll figure something else out."

"Fuck you, Abby. Shut the fuck up." Johnny spat, putting his feet against the stall door.

"Fuck you, Johnny. You're fucking useless. At least Troy is trying to help."

"Yeah? Well, why don't you fuck him then!" Johnny shouted like a petulant child. Abby sighed and turned back to Troy.

"I heard you thought I liked Nadia," Troy said softly. From the sobs of both stalls, it seemed neither Nadia nor Johnny heard him.

"Yeah, so?" Abby said.

"It's…I li-…I like you." Troy stumbled over the words.

"Troy, this isn't exactly the fucking time for this."

"I know, I just. Y'know, if I'm never going to see you again, then I wanted you to know."

"Fuck off. You Americans are so dramatic." Abby blushed.

Amara screamed a gleeful cackle as she ripped and tore the patrons apart. There were no more screams, no more blood-curdling cries, only wet noises of innards spilling out and the cracking of bones.

Fuck, she's done with them. She's killed them all.

Abby and Troy gently pressed their ears to the door. Their breathing getting heavier as they felt it through the wood.

Scratching.
Scurrying.
Squelching.
Thumps.

Cracks.

"Cargill," Amara spoke to the room. Abby could imagine her hovering over the remains of the locals, analysing their remains to confirm if one of them was the person she seeked.

Why does she even want this Cargill guy?

A whack shuddered Abby and Troy's heads back. Abby exhaled frustration as her ear throbbed from the noise. Something had tried to push the bathroom door open.

"Quick, hold it," Troy whispered.

"What do you think I'm doing?" Abby snapped back. Another whack silenced them both. Nadia peered over the top of the toilet stall, tiptoeing on the toilet seat. Another whack, this time followed by a deeper one. Nadia shrank back into the stall to hide.

WHOMPF!

Both Abby and Troy were pushed back a foot, their weight slamming the door closed again.

"Cargill," Amara's voice spoke louder, breaking that piercing whisper. Vocal chords expressing an immortal need. Abby wondered if that was Amara's real voice or one of the others she'd used. *Is she using the voices of her victims? Consuming them when she kills them?*

Another smash against the door, this time, Abby and Troy were thrown back further; still, their body weight pressed the door back closed.

"I don't think we're going to last much longer," Troy whimpered.

"Alright, fuck it. We go with your plan, then," Abby said. "Johnny, Nadia, you guys try and open that little window and squeeze through. Troy and I will throw the door open, he'll make a break past Amara in the confusion, and I'll jump out the window as well."

"I don't like that plan," Johnny sniffled.

"Not much fucking choice unless you've got a better idea?" Abby said.

"Fuck you," Johnny said through tears.

"Didn't think so." Abby turned to Troy.

"Are we sure?" he asked.

"Sure, we're going to survive against that fucking hand monster woman thing out there? Fuck no. At least we'll be trying, though." Her words bounced around Troy's head before he nodded his acceptance.

"Alright, you ready?" Abby said.

"Wait," Troy said.

"Cargill."

The door blew open.

26

Abby and Troy flew across the bathroom. Thudding against the stall doors. Nadia and Johnny both juddered in shock, pulling their knees in close to their faces. Troy looked unscathed, though his back burned with pain. Abby yelped and fell to her side, gripping her shoulder, the earlier pain of the hand ringing strong again. *Feels like my shoulder's dislocated.*

A few hands crawled into the room, slow, cautious. Behind them, the soft slap of Amara's feet on tiles echoed. Once she'd crossed the threshold, the walls turned dark grey as hundreds of hands poured into the room from the doorway.

"Cargill," she said, her eyes switching between Abby and Troy.

"We aren't Cargill," Troy pleaded.

"Amara, we aren't who you are after. I don't even know why you are after him. What did he do, Amara? Did you lose him? Did he hurt you?" Abby spoke through pain. Amara focused on Abby, her eyes seeming to soften. As if hearing her own name was restoring some sense of humanity in her. She stepped closer to Abby, slowly kneeling in front of her.

"Amara, that's your name, remember? You were a person once I'm sure. You had a family, right? A mother, a father? Maybe some brothers or sisters?" said Abby. Amara leaned forward slightly, lifting an arm to her. Troy sneered at the arm, noticing all the fingers interlinked to form the limb.

"Maybe you had a husband? Did you have children? Amara, you don't have to hurt anyone, it's okay," Abby said. Amara's glance faltered, searching a middle distance for a second.

"Cargill," she said.

"Cargill, right, you're looking for Cargill, we can help you find him," said Abby, her smile twitching.

"Cargill."

"Was he your husband?" Abby asked. Amara's rageful gaze returned, her eyes blossoming a darker orange.

"Abby, run!" Troy shouted, he threw a fist at Amara, aiming directly at her head.

"No!" Abby shouted. Before she could do anything Amara whipped her head out of the way. Turning her gaze to Troy and screaming. The young American tried to throw another punch, this time landing it on her jaw. His fist didn't shake her head, nor did it cause any sign of pain. Instead his hand seemed to be half consumed by Amara's face. Abby took a second to notice that the fingers comprising Amara's face had opened up and were gripping Troy's hand.

"Amara no!" Abby begged. Amara was already rising though, showing no signs of struggling to lift Troy from the ground. He scrambled his legs to get balance. Huffing through the pain of the grip on his hand.

"Cargill," Amara spoke.

"Fuck Cargill and fuck you!" Troy growled jumping, his hand still held, and kicking Amara in the ribs. He stopped in mid air, his foot now consumed in the woman's stomach. Amara's hair began to dance, an invisibile wind shifting it up around her head. She grabbed Troy's arm and pulled the elbow inwards. The mass of Troy hanging from the little girl as she snapped his arm inwards was both terrifying and impressive.

His scream of pain didn't break Abby's trance as she watched the boy who liked her try and kick with his free leg. Amara caught it, grabbing his head and forcing him to look into her eyes as it looked like she crunched down her jaw. The stump remains of a hand pulled free from her face, blood dribbling out. Troy gasped in shock looking at the end of his arm where his hand had been. A hand he'd thrown a hundred touchdowns with. A hand he'd written his homework with. A hand he'd put down Chelsea Van Bacht's pants one night a year ago. No more.

Amara's face imploded, fingers and hands spilling out of it. Her body wrapping around Troy's, fingers tearing at his flesh, the unwelcome familiar sound of a stream of blood pouring from the victim held within the hands. Abby pushed herself away from the growing puddle of blood. *I have to do something* she thought.

Standing she took a stride towards Amara, or the Amara thing now wrapped around Troy crushing and tearing him apart.

"Amara, stop now!" she shouted. *Great, I'm sure telling her off is going to help.*

Amara's head emerged from the mass, staring at Abby. Abby's spine tingled as she felt, not heard, the sound of Troy's bones breaking, hollow cracks. With each crack more of Amara appeared, less of Troy to deal with. Eventually, the woman stood in front of Abby in full form. Troy's compressed face lying atop his squashed body.

The remaining hands continued to scamper around the room, covering all the walls, the floor and working outwards from Amara. As they moved over the ceiling, Nadia looked up and saw the swarm above her. She screamed, without thinking, she kicked the door open. The floor teamed and squirmed with hands. She screamed again. Kicking at the hands in front of her and lunging out of the stall into a run.

"Nadia!" Abby called. Amara frowned at the blur of Nadia running past her, awkwardly stamping on hands. She whipped her gaze back to Abby and screamed.

"Cargill!" The words almost consumed Abby. She could only make out the muffled roar of Johnny kicking the stall door open to run out as well. She felt the pressure of hands working their way up her body. Vice like grips squeezing her feet, legs, waist, abdomen, chest, arms. Fingers crawled up her face, her vision nearly gone when she saw Johnny stop in the doorway and look back. She tried to scream, muffled by a palm over her mouth, fingers worked at her lips. Parting them before shoving themselves deep into her throat.

Johnny stamped on a few of the hands, kicking some away to make a path to Abby. Moving three feet into the sea of hands at his feet. He reached into the mass, consuming Abby. Punching his fist in and finding her hand. He screamed as he pulled with everything he had. Unable to make any progress, he didn't notice the hands crawling up his back. Five of them wrapping around his head, one perching on the top. It dug its nails into his forehead, two fingers scratching at his eyelids as the other snapped his neck. His body went limp and fell into the sea of hands before his limbs were torn from his body.

Abby felt the warm blush of tears build; she wanted to scream, but could feel the air tighten in her throat. She didn't want to breath too deep for fear the fingers would crawl deeper inside her. The room went dark, covered by hands. Then, in the darkness, two orange eyes stared into her. *Amara, please let me be.*

Two hands emerged from the darkness as well, not comprised of many different hands, real hands, attached to real arms. They rested on Abby's cheeks, and she realised she felt like she was floating in black.

"Abby, I've missed you." The orange eyes came forward.

"Mickey?"

27

It was a light day, clouded over, but light. Abby could feel a calm chill against her skin. She lifted herself from leaves. She was lying in the back garden of her home. *How did I get here?*

Looking around for someone, something to give a clue, she rose to her feet. The grass felt softer than she remembered. Like it wouldn't scuff your jeans green if you did running knee slides. Something Abby and Mickey used to challenge each other to see who could slide the furthest. Much to their mother's dismay, at the increased volume of washing they created.

Abby looked in the back window, not enough light pouring in to see anyone. Just the black outline of furniture. She opened the door and stepped inside.

"Hello?...Mum?...Dad?" She called. The perfect silence was unsettling. There was never silence in the Rennie household, let alone this kind of silence that Abby was experiencing. There was nothing, no sound of her feet as she walked, no sound of her breath, no gentle noise of wind or air. No fizzing and popping of her mother cooking food, no rambles of commentators and fans on the television. No snoring from her dad asleep in front of the television. No laughter of children playing in the street or cars driving past. There was nothing.

"Hello?" She called again, her voice trickled off, as if all sound was being swallowed up, circling a whirlpool into nothingness. She moved through the house, hoping to see her father in his most common spot. He wasn't sitting watching football on TV. Maybe he'd gone out to the pub. *Oh god, was Dad at the pub when Amara attacked? I didn't see him…no, he can't have been.*

Running upstairs, Abby searched in a sweat trying to find one of her parents. She stopped when she stepped into the spare bedroom that had long since become a dumping ground for gifts and purchases no longer used.

"Mickey?" Abby asked. The name and thought pained her; it had cropped up so much in the past few days. So much more than she'd expected. So much more than she thought she could handle.

Before her, there was no pile of clothes her dad had "thrown out". They weren't resting on top of the cycling machine he'd bought so that they could all get fit at home. There were no boxes sitting on the old bed, filled with their old teddies and toys. The old, broken television wasn't propped up in the corner of the room.

It was Mickey's room.

His bed was there, the old bed, but it looked like he'd not long gotten out of it. The covers flipped over, their mother would shout at him if she saw he hadn't made his bed. The drawers had his stuff on top of it. His trophy from being the top goal scorer on the school football team, a feat he was overly proud of. There wasn't exactly a catalogue of talent in any nearby town to compete with, let alone any real competition from within his own team. A box Abby knew contained all the different Spirograph pieces he collected. A poster on the wall of Ursula Andress emerging from the water in Dr No. Ever since Mickey had seen it, he'd started showing signs of becoming a more 'typical' boy.

Everything in the room looked just as Abby could remember when Mickey was still alive, *no, still around.* The bed, the posters, the trophies, the pile of clothes, that faint smell of her brother, like pine and coffee, Abby had always thought. For all the resemblance it bore, Abby still couldn't understand. She stepped into the room, running her fingers over the surface of the set of drawers, over the trophy. Those familiar textures and surfaces bring back all those memories. Too many memories. *I wish his room still looked like this, still smelled like this. Do mum and dad still miss him? They cried for so long. Am I weaker than them because they've moved on? Have they even really moved on? Mickey, I miss you so much.*

Dusting her hand over the bed cover, she felt a tear run down her cheek. She lifted the corner of the cover back into its place and tucked it down as their mother expected them to do. Lifting her eyes to the window, she thought she heard a sudden giggle. Kneeling on the bed she'd just made to her mother's standards, she looked out the window.

There, running around in circles with his arms outstretched like he was a plane, was Mickey. The same goofy-faced, early-acned boy Abby had grown up with. He continued in circles a few more times before stopping and looking up at the window.

"Mickey!" Abby shouted. Her brother smiled and giggled before waving for her to come join him. Abby bounced off the bed, leaving her indent in the covers, not caring as she raced down the stairs. Nearly tearing the front door off its hinges, she pounced out the door to where she assumed she'd see Mickey.

"Where are you?" She called, spinning in circles. A teenage giggle caught her attention, and she turned to see Mickey again. Standing some fifteen feet away down the road.

The Belfry Haunting

"Mickey, wait for me," she said as he waved for her to come to him again. He turned and started to run. *He was always faster than me,* Abby thought. Even though he was still his young teenage self, and she was now nearly a fully grown woman. It seemed like she could not make any ground on the running teen.

"Come on, Abby. I've got something to show you," his voice rang back, though the boy didn't look back or show any signs of stopping. He ran up the street and turned, weaving through lanes Abby remembered like the back of her hand but hadn't looked up at them for years. She'd kept her head down when travelling these lanes, either because it was dark and she felt hiding her face would be safer or because she was drunk and hiding herself might save her from being noticed.

They broke from one of the lanes, Abby still racing to catch up, running through the park. The swings and roundabout gleamed bright painted colours. Colours that had long faded as far as Abby could remember. Still, Mickey ran, and Abby felt her chest begin to tighten.

She followed him as best she could out of the park, round the corner and up onto the high street. She'd seen the street empty a hundred times, but something about this seemed even more barren. All the buildings sighed a desolate emptiness as she ran past them after her brother. Mickey turned at the end of the high street, and Abby saw where he could only be heading.

Lockwood. The building still looming over Belfry, still the exact same building Abby remembered, the windows dark, a couple boarded up.

"Fuck," she said as she turned the corner and saw Mickey's feet disappear in through the entrance to the grounds. By the time she'd caught up to the entrance, she could see him running halfway up the driveway.

"Abby, come on. You need to see this," his excited voice beckoned. Reluctantly, her feet moved forward, her brain unable to pull focus from Mickey. *I need to see him, his face, to speak to him, to know what happened to him.*

Reaching the top of the driveway, her feet scuffling in the stones of the car park outside the reception, Abby stopped. Mickey stood in the reception doorway, five other teenagers around him. *Those are the same assholes that used to bully me. What were their names again? Freddie, James, Peter, Richard and…oh, it started with a G…Gregory, that was it.* Abby noticed that each of the boys looked exactly like she remembered. Their young complexions, Freddie with his signature cowslick, Gregory always had a lollipop in his mouth as if it made him look cool. James and Peter were brothers, though they couldn't have looked more different. As for Richard, Abby never got around to telling Mickey that she had a crush on him for months. She never built up the confidence to tell Richard either. Not long after Mickey disappeared, all of his friends left Belfry. Or, at least, that's what Abby had been told. She'd never questioned it; she was secretly happy that her bullies were no more. She never had to build up the strength to ask out the cute boy. Instead, she'd grown strength through intelligence, and boys had come to her.

"Come on, Mickey. It's cool in there, I swear," Richard said.

"I don't know, guys, why don't we just play football on the grass over there?" Mickey said.

"Fuck Mickey, you're such a pussy," Gregory said, the leader of their little group of miscreants. "Why don't you show us how tough you are for once?"

"Why? I don't have to prove anything to you," Mickey reasoned. Abby admired his lack of care for this kind of childish behaviour. It's probably why the boys had him in their gang. A tough-witted, savvy kid to make the rest of them look hard.

"Fine, if you don't come in, then Richard will fuck your sister", Gregory laughed. James and Peter nudged each other. Richard flashed that smile that made Abby and other girls her age flutter.

"What?" Mickey stepped toward Gregory. Abby wasn't sure if Mickey had ever beaten any of them up, but he certainly didn't seem scared to step up to them.

"Oh come on, you've seen it. We've all seen it. She fucking fancies Richard. *Oh, Richie, do you need any help with your chemistry homework? I've been studying it really hard this year,*" Gregory raised a high-pitched voice, a terrible impression of Abby. *Fucking prick!*

"She's never said anything like that to him," Mickey snorted.

"She's said close enough. Honestly, mate, she's constantly looking at me when we're in the school dinner hall." Richard said, folding his arms.

"So? You are actually going to fuck my sister if I don't come in? You realise I'd kick the fuck out of you for that. She wouldn't actually be that stupid to fall for that. You'd be raping my sister. I'll fucking kill you if you do that." Mickey's voice rose; he was tired of this game. A fist balled in his hand as he stared down Richard.

"Alright, alright, settle down", Richard laughed.

"No, he'll fuck your sister, and we'll kick the shit out of her friends too." Gregory piped up again. Trying to regain control. He only really led the group because Mickey didn't have a care for organising the boys and because Gregory had a lighter from his older brother that had moved to Australia. A large Zippo emblazoned with a skull with a dagger through it. Looking cool and tough was all it took to lead. Actually being cool and tough, that didn't matter in Belfry.

"Oh yeah? Why don't you go in there? Go down to the basement, Gregory. In the dark, you go down there, go on! Don't call me a pussy, you fuckhead. And don't talk about my sister like that, or I'll break your arm" Mickey had stepped right up to Gregory. The boy pulled out his lighter, flicked the lid open and closed a few times while he looked up into Mickey's eyes.

"I've been in-"

"You haven't been in there. You've told a bunch of people you have and everyone you told that bullshit story to you said I was with you" Mickey smiled. "You go in there, down to the basement in the dark. Fuck it. I'll even come with you. Then your story will be true." Mickey rounded Gregory inside the reception area. Gregory held a stare, trying to call Mickey's bluff. He flicked the lighter open and closed a few more times, holding his thumb on it and flicking a flame loose.

"Fuck it!" Gregory said, whipping the lighter lid closed. He marched into the reception area and glanced over his shoulder at the rest of the group. Abby caught a glint of panic in the boy's eyes as he followed after Mickey.

Oh shit! He did have something to show me. He's showing me exactly how it happened, isn't he?

Abby raced into the building, past James, Freddie, Peter and Richard. They didn't notice her; the wind she pushed past them as she entered the building didn't shift a hair on their heads.

Chasing after Mickey again, this time running alongside Gregory, Abby cursed the realisation of what she was heading towards.

"Mickey, don't go into the basement," she called out, knowing full well that her brother couldn't hear her. She looked to her side, the young teenage Gregory running next to her. His eyes gradually filling with more and more fear. His gaze mopping up the wall, across the ceiling and down the other wall. Peering into rooms as he passed. At one point his eyes seemed to lock with Abby's and she felt a chill shoot through her whole body.

"Mickey, wait up," Gregory called as Mickey reached the top of the stairs to the basement. Her brother looked back and exhaled in frustration at the boy before disappearing down the stairs. Gregory and Abby reached the bottom of the stairs at the same time. Gregory pulled his lighter out of his pocket and lit the flame. For being the biggest asshole of the group, Abby was thankful he had the lighter to shine some light. It felt darker than when she'd been down here with her friends. No long cone of light from a torch to provide a

sense of safety. Only a small orb of light
surrounding them, crushing them in.

Abby shook with a slight scare as Gregory
ran after the vague outline of Mickey. She hadn't
seen him but she followed, not wanting to be left in
the dark. The young teenager skipped through the
corridor, slowing at each door to peer in. Holding
his arm out in front of him to see where he was
going. Trying to catch Mickey up. The vague
outline just out of reach. Constantly pulling them
further and further, deeper into the basement. Closer
to where Abby knew she didn't want to be heading.

"Boo!" Mickey's face appeared out of
nowhere, from behind Gregory. He'd been hiding in
one of the rooms. Gregory panicked, flicking the
lighter in the air and managing to catch it. Adjusting
it back to it's normal position before he burned his
fingers.

"Jesus fucking christ. You scared the shit
out of me Mickey!"

"Yeah, that gets you back for saying that
shit about my sister. I'm serious, leave her the hell
alone."

"Yeah, yeah. Alright," Gregory agreed, his
eyes continuing to look down the corridor, his mind
focussed on other things. "Did you see that?" He
pointed after the vague outline he'd seen.

"See what?" Mickey smirked, sure that he
was about to be fed some lies again.

"There was something there."

"Aye, alright. Fuck you, stop messing around will you?"

"I'm not lying. I saw something."

"What did you see?" Mickey folded his arms. Abby wanted to lean in and tell him Gregory wasn't lying; she'd seen it too.

"There was someone leading us down here. I thought it was you at first. Come on," Gregory said, stepping in the direction of the outline. Holding his pace just enough so that Mickey had to come with him and be a couple of steps in front. Abby marched alongside Mickey, trying to think of anyway that she could stop this happening.

"I lost you on this day." Mickey's voice bounced around the corridor. His lips didn't move, though. The voice was coming from everywhere. "I never saw you again until you came down to the basement with your friends. I've missed you so much, Abby." The three of them reached the end of the corridor, where it opened up into the large room with pillars situated at odd places. It wasn't empty now; there were random pieces of furniture sitting around. Sofas, chairs, coffee tables. Filing cabinets rusting away, old bed frames with cobweb-ridden springs.

"Over there," Gregory said, pointing to a stack of cardboard boxes containing napkins and paper cups. At the edge of it, a hand slid out of view.

"Yeah, I see it," Mickey said, leaning at angles to see if he could make out any more details.

"You see, I'm not crazy," Gregory said.

"Yeah, yeah. You're still the dick that said he was going to get my sister raped."

"I didn't mean he would *actually* rape her. I was just fucking with you that she fancies Richard," said Gregory. Abby felt her cheeks warm.

"Cargill." Abby shuddered as she heard that familiar whisper weave its way through the air and slither into her ears.

"What the fuck was that?" Gregory stood up straight.

"Quiet," Mickey hushed, putting his index finger to his lips as he lowered down and moved towards the cardboard boxes.

"No, no. Don't do this," Abby pleaded.

"This was the day that I died, Abby. You have to accept that." The universal Mickey's voice returned. Abby refused to move any further; she closed her eyes, refusing to watch what happened.

"You have to watch," Mickey's voice said, feeling fingers pry at her eyelids, pulling them apart.

Gregory and Mickey shuffled closer and closer until they reached the cardboard boxes. Mickey looked back at Gregory and held up three fingers, counting down silently. Three. Two. One. He jumped around the boxes and shouted, expecting to find either Richard, Freddie, James or Peter hiding down here. There was nobody there, though. He inhaled a deep breath, ready to turn back to Gregory and find all of his friends sniggering away at the "clever trick" they'd played on him.

Instead, turning back, Mickey found Gregory standing perfectly straight, his lighter held up next to his face. Breathing heavily, he couldn't push out more than a mumble. A large hand grasped his mouth closed. Seeping into the light, Amara's face appeared, all the quivering unhumanness of the fingers making up her face trembling with rage. Mickey's jaw opened in utter disbelief. That was all Amara needed. An arm thrust forward, hands upon hands, diving into his mouth and down his throat. Gregory watched, trying to scream through the hand, tears running down his face as he watched Mickey's body spasm and enlarge, his throat bloating. His chest expanding and his stomach ballooning. Details of fingers could be made in his throat and his distending belly. Abby tried desperately to close her eyes.

"This was me dying, Abby. I felt so much pain that day. I knew that I was never going to be able to see you again. Never going to be able to look after you anymore."

No, I don't want to see this. Make it stop!

"She wants you to see"

More hands gripped around Gregory's arms and legs, spreading them and lifting him up as he and Abby were forced to continue watching Mickey's torture. His stomach, now some three times the size it normally was, finally ruptured. Bloodied hands poured out of the maw, crawling back up the body and tearing flesh away. Pulling at him to reveal yellowy red fat, scarlet muscle and white bone. His stomach acid poured out of him and spattered on the floor. Mickey, of course, had long since died from the sheer shock and pain. Gregory whimpered into the hand covering his mouth. The hands on Mickey gathered at the neck, some squeezing, others clawing. The neck separating in seconds, getting pulled upwards, Mickey's still connected spine came with his head.

Mickey, no! I can't see this.

"She says you must share the pain"

Finally, Gregory's whimpers turned to screams, and Abby watched as hands gathered at his neck; within seconds, Gregory was dead. His head and spine were also removed. Amara's hands brought the two together, facing each other.

"It's alright, Abby. We're together again. I can see you now. I can spend time with you. I can keep you safe." Mickey's voice tickled her ears. Amara looked back into Abby's eyes and smiled before she smashed the heads together. In an instant, she'd covered the gap between her killings and where Abby had refused to move from. Darkness swamped Abby's vision. Again, Mickey's face revealed itself in a pale moonlight, eyes a trancing orange.

"You can be with me now, Abby. We can bring everyone to us. Mum and Dad. We can be happy, we can be a family again."

"How, you haven't brought me here?" Abby said while crying.

"Amara has."

"Amara killed you."

"Amara saved me. She has helped me see how things can be better."

"Killing everyone won't make it better"

The voice growled. Angry at Abby's challenge.

"People in this world don't deserve what they want. They spit on what they have and expect riches even though they've earned nothing." The voice changed to a female, raspy tone.

"Amara?" Abby asked.

"You will come to understand the pain that humanity brings itself. I deserve peace. We deserve happiness. The world deserves pain."

28

How had this happened? Nadia kept asking herself. How had she escaped? How had Amara not noticed her? How had none of those horrible, disgusting hands not felt her stamp on them as she fled the pub? How did Troy not manage to escape? Where was Johnny?

Though the questions kept coming, she knew the answer to them. Answers she wished she didn't know. Troy had been caught by Amara; she'd heard him getting crushed to death. Johnny was dead as well; he'd tried to save Abby. *Bloody fool. Why did he think he was stronger than that…that thing?*

Worst of all, the answer that she didn't want to accept. Abby was dead. She'd been swarmed by Amara. Nadia had screamed as she'd heard her best friend snap and tear. Abby hadn't screamed in pain at all; oddly, everyone else had unleashed their agony, but she had remained quiet. Had Amara torn out her throat? Her lungs? Had she killed Abby so quickly, there was no chance for her to scream?

Standing outside the pub, hearing the scuttling of inside, Nadia didn't know what to do. All she could think about was that she was now completely alone. She didn't have any friends anymore. They were all dead, all obliterated by that thing inside the pub. She'd never get rid of the images of all that violence. Puddles of blood that the hands were pattering through. Viscera, shards of bone, splats of fat, shredded organs all mopped up the walls. Drips falling from the ceiling confirmed the utter destruction of everyone who was inside. The smell of death still lingered. Who was even left in Belfry now but Nadia?

"Cargill." Amara's voice crept out of the doorway. Nadia felt a breeze tumble down the main street. One single light flickered on inside the pub, enough to highlight shadows inside through the window. Nadia noticed curtains of hands pulling down from the window, various pieces of human remains still stuck in place. Between it all, a head moved through the pub. Towards the entrance.

Nadia turned on her heels and ran. *Where am I going to go?* She thought. There was no time to think. Amara stepped out of the pub, almost floating on a wave of hands. She stood in the middle of the road, hands making a mound underneath her. Looking upwards, Amara cursed the skies with a scream. More a command than anything else. Rain began to speck on the few cars parked on the street. Growing quickly until a thick downpour surrounded her. Nadia had to squint to see through the rain as she ran down the street. Amara turned her head, somehow hearing the fleeing footsteps through the noise of the rain. Raising her arms, her hair began to dance again and morphing into a mass of shadow and fingers, she gave chase.

Turning down the first alley she could, Nadia hoped that Amara wouldn't be able to fit down the alley in her current form. *Why would that matter?* Her brain argued. Right enough, Amara seeped into the alley as Nadia popped out the other side. *Where am I going?* She asked again, hoping something inside her would discover the perfect answer. She ran, running was all she had. Everything inside her knew she just had to keep herself away from Amara.

"Nadia, wait." Abby's voice called from inside the mass. Nadia blubbered a sob between breaths as she listened to her friend.

"You're not Abby," she called back.

"It's me, Nadia, it's me. It really is. I'm your best friend. Remember when we were younger? We used to sleep over all the time. Remember?"

"Fuck you!"

"Oh, Nadia. You don't remember how we used to play, do you? How we used to dream up fantasies of escaping this place? How we used to make shadow puppets on the wall when our parents had gone to bed. We should have been asleep, but we were having too much fun, weren't we?"

Nadia hopped the fence to the park and made for the swings. Amara was closing in, with every breath Nadia struggled with, with every step she slowed, Amara gained.

"Leave me alone," Nadia prayed.

"You remember how you got scared of the shadow puppets I made? You couldn't make your fingers move like I could. You hated when I made a big spider shadow puppet. It's alright, I won't scare you like that again." Abby's voice spoke from Amara's mass, a playful tone to it.

"No!" Nadia screamed, she weaved through the swings, hoping Amara might get entangled in them somehow. She hopped over the roundabout and turned to give it a single solid shove. Lifting her eyes, she screamed in terror. Amara had shifted from her form of a ball of darkness and fingers. A gigantic spider now stepped across the park. It's eight legs flexing hands. Its eyes on stalks of palms. Large mandibles shook in excitement at a potential meal. Nadia gawked for a moment, the spider Amara twitched its legs, moving too fast to follow and nearly pounced on Nadia. Jumping out of the way just in time, she rolled across the mud and pushed herself to her feet. Picking up her pace again and hopping the gate at the other end of the park.

Fuck, where do I go?
Where do I go?
Where do I go?
Nobody is alive. Where do I go?

She turned down onto one of the smaller streets. A couple of hairdressers the only shops on it. It was at that moment that Nadia saw something that stood out.

The library.

The lights are on?

Nadia had been past the Library too many times to remember. The lights were rarely ever on, and certainly not at a time like this. It seemed like the only option in her mind. Running towards the door, she could hear the disturbing scurry of Amara behind her. Nadia struck the door, happy to accept the throb of pain in her arm as the door opened. She turned and slammed the door closed. Spider Amara raced towards her, eyes flaring brighter. Stepping back and opening the inner door, Nadia slammed it closed, and the sight of Amara disappeared.

"Excuse me! Who is that?" Pendleton's outraged voice tore across the library.

29

Catching her breath as best she could. Nadia stepped back from the door. Fully expecting to see hands start pouring in through it. The windows to smash. The roof to get torn off like a can of tuna. Amara reaching in to seize her prey. The sound of Nadia's gasping breath and her feet clumsily moving her back did nothing to ease her concern.

"Who is that?" Pendleton's voice repeated, moving closer. Nadia kept her eyes on the door as she moved between the bookshelves.

"Miss Hussain. What in the devil do you think you are doing here? And at this hour?" Pendleton emerged from behind a bookshelf. Expression pointed, lips trembling with anger.

"I...I...I was running from...I...I had to...please, Miss Pendleton, please help me." Nadia turned, nearly falling into the old woman's arms. She caught herself before she collided with her.

The Belfry Haunting

Pendleton held her hands behind her back, staring down her nose at the young girl.

"Help you? Help you with what?"

"There's a woman. No. A monster…a *thing* outside! It's killed everyone in Belfry, and it's right outside." Nadia rounded Pendleton, moving to the reception desk. Looking around for any place she could hide herself. Pendleton stood in place, turning to follow the girl.

"A monster? Dear heavens, girl. You've got yourself in a right state. Please don't tell me you've been indulging in illegal substances? You aren't drunk, are you?"

"Please!" Nadia shouted, tired of hearing that same line. "I'm not drunk, I'm not high, I'm fucking terrified is what I am. My friends are dead, so is everyone in Belfry. I need help. Do you have a phone so we can call the police?"

"Oh, I don't believe those two boys that call themselves the police around here would be much help if there have been murders." Pendleton's mouth raised at one side, an unnatural grin.

"No, they are dead too. We need *real* police. We need an army."

"An army? We are not at war, my dear."

"To kill that fucking thing, we'll need an army", Nadia pointed to the door. Pendleton held a moment of silence, turning to the door and frowning.

"Miss Hussain, I urge you to refrain from using such vulgar language. Now, there is nobody trying to kill you outside. Heavens, if they were, they wouldn't be waiting outside so politely." She moved towards the front door.

"No, no. Please don't go. You'll be killed," Nadia pleaded, but Pendleton ignored her. Walking her sharp heels to the front door, pushing open the inner door, followed by the outer door and stepping outside.

"Miss Hussain, there is nobody here," Nadia heard the old woman call from outside. Her voice was muffled but clear enough to understand. From the far side of the library, it should have been easy to hear Amara pounding on the door, scaling the roof, pouring into masses of hands crawling in whatever gaps they could find, a brain-shredding scream shattering through the windows.

The door opened and clunked closed again. Nadia leaned to the side to see Pendleton walking back towards her. *Oh, thank god.*

"Now, young girl, I do not know what you have taken or what has caused you to be in such hysteria. But I must insist that you leave."

"Leave?"

"Yes. This is no place for a girl to be at this time of the night. Please return home, and I suggest you go to your bed and try to sleep off whatever troubles you. Feel comforted to know that I shall not inform your parents of this episode, but if it happens again, I shall be hesitant to keep such a secret." Pendleton interlocked her fingers. An attempt to look reasonable and consoling that fell flat.

"I'm not leaving. That thing. Amara, she's out there. She'll kill me," Nadia said.

Pendleton's chest deflated, her eyes widening.

"What did you say?"

"I said, I'm not leaving. I'm staying here until we can contact someone to come and kill that thing."

Pendleton stepped forward and grabbed Nadia by her shoulders. "No, dear girl, what name did you say?"

"Amara?"

"Amara…she's here." The woman's eyes drifted up, her brain working hard to process what she'd just heard.

"You know her? Then you know how royally fucked we are. She chased me here after she tore everyone to shreds in the pub, including Abby. She killed my best friend," Nadia blubbered. She watched Pendleton drift around the reception desk and sit down, the chair yelping a dull creek.

"She killed everyone? Amara, I mean?" Pendleton asked, her mind on another matter.

"Yes. She killed my best friend, Abby. Like I said. You remember Abby. She spent loads of time here," Nadia shouted. The bitterness of her loss stung her throat.

"Miss Rennie…yes…she frequented here quite a lot. She was here recently, one of the better ones in this god forsaken town." Pendleton's eyes floated down to her hands, lying flat on the reception desk.

"Hey…hey. Pendleton. Do you understand now? We need to call someone to help to come and kill that bitch and get us the hell out of here. Some big, bulky guys with big, bulky guns…and rockets…*please*!" Nadia's words echoed around the library. Pendleton nodded her head ever so gently.

"No…no…no. Amara must not be harmed. I didn't think it would ever happen. We can finally do it now." She smiled, raising her head to Nadia.

"What? What do you mean?"

"Oh, my dear girl. You've brought me great news. Amara is my seven times great-grandmother."

"What?"

"She is family." Pendleton stood.

30

Backing away from the reception desk and the grinning old woman, Nadia felt a sour tickle on her tongue. Her lungs tightened a grip on her throat. Pendleton's eyes were nearly popping out of her head. Her fingers twitched in excitement. Her cheeks looked ready to crack from stretching.

"Family? What does that mean? You're going to kill me? Please don't kill me." Nadia tried not to burst into tears while she stepped back. Prey slinking back into the shadows to avoid the eyes of the predator.

Pendleton laughed, "You think I would kill you?" Her cackle tangled in Nadia's ribs. "I mean no harm to anyone. My purpose is not to give you to Amara for sacrifice, Miss Hussain. I intend to help he.r"

"Help her?"

Pendleton nodded. "Indeed. My poor ancestor has been locked in darkness for centuries, and she needs to be set free."

"Set free?"

"Released from her eternal bondage, yes. Allowed to move onto the next plane to rest."

"Mmhmm, alright. Cool. Can I not be a part of that?" Nadia hugged close to one of the bookshelves, still expecting Pendleton to contort and hunch over onto all fours, to gallop after her.

"My dear girl." Pendleton's eyes calmed. "You are already a part of this", she said, walking towards Nadia, drifting past her and to the door.

"Come with me, I'll keep you safe," Pendleton said. Her voice had morphed, somehow loosening, dropping that harsh hatred Nadia had always known her to have.

"Where are we going?" Nadia asked, everything was so strange, her mind hypnotised by confusion, tickled by intrigue and tainted with scepticism.

"Come, come." Pendleton wrapped an arm around Nadia's shoulders as she walked them out of the library.

The moon sat high in the curtain of night. The rain was still battering down. Both women instantly drenched as they walked down the library path to the road. Pendleton looked around, a curious glee spread across her face.

The Belfry Haunting

It didn't take long for them to walk to the main street. All the while, Pendleton's arm held against Nadia's shoulders. Moving her along. When they finally turned a corner and Lockwood filled their line of sight, Pendleton stopped.

"Amara, oh, how long it's been," the old woman spoke to the world.

"I don't understand," Nadia asked the woman, but got no reply. The sky sighed, and the rain eased, no longer battering the ground and bouncing back up. A light spit now tickled the earth.

"There." Nadia pointed, seeing a shadow move behind the walls of the Lockwood grounds. Pendleton released her grip of Nadia and stepped forward.

"Yes, is that you? Please. My dear ancestor. I've spent my life hoping that I could bring resolution to you. Let me help." Pendleton raised her open hands, rain gathering in them.

Slinking over the wall and pouring into the street in front of Pendleton. Amara emerged. Her movements slow, careful, controlled. She moved closer, into the moonlight. Slipping out of the mass of hands and stepping onto the concrete. Pendleton sniffed back tears as Amara looked up at her.

"Cargill," said Amara.

"Yes, I know. He's here." Pendleton said.

"What?" Nadia watched in disbelief. It was as if Amara recognised the old woman. Not a family member, not an estranged descendant. More like an emperor looking upon a peasant.

"She's been bound. Viktor Dietrich has a hold over dear Amara," Pendleton said, her eyes caressing the shape of Amara. The spirit patiently waiting, understanding the woman before her. "His lineage, like mine, is seeped into the very soil of Belfry. As I am a descendant of Amara. Viktor Dietrich is a descendant of Colton Cargill."

"Cargill." Amara's back straightened, a flare in her energy.

"What? I don't understand" Nadia stepped closer, an instinct more than command. Her eyes shifted from Pendleton to Amara, and she stepped back.

"Cargill held control over Amara; it gave him prolonged life. When he passed on, he gave his gift to his son-in-law, Gunther Dietrich, who married his daughter. Adopting the young German boy as his own flesh and blood. Gunther promised to continue the family legacy. He lived, as his father had, a life too long; it twisted and contorted him, made him greedy, and poisoned his soul. His only true gift was to pass Amara on to *his* son, Viktor Dietrich. The man that lords over Lockwood has lived for centuries. He must be stopped. His intentions are derelict, evil. He holds Amara captive."

"So what? That doesn't make sense. How do we free her?"

"Cargill," Amara whispered, her patience running thin. Her lips begin to curl.

"We end the lineage of Cargill. We kill Dietrich!" Pendleton turned to Nadia, Amara following suit.

"We? Fuck that. I'm not a murderer."

"You are entwined in this story now, like I said, young Miss Hussain. Death is all around. What better than to end this line of destruction than to destroy the one who causes it?"

"No. I can't. I won't." Nadia stepped back, her feet turning of their own accord.

"Dear girl, please. Think on what you are doing. Amara has bared too much punishment. If you do not assist us, then she will see you as no better than Dietrich," Pendleton reasoned. Amara's brow pinched, sensing the taste of adversary.

"No. Leave me alone. I can't do that. I can't kill someone. I don't care if you say he's evil. It can't be true." Nadia's shuffled turned into a jog. *I have to get away from this. I just need to get away.*

"Cargill", Amara's voice chased after her.

"No, Amara. No. She is innocent!" Pendleton shouted at her ancestor. Nadia didn't look back but heard the thump of movement. "No, leave her be. Show mercy!" Pendlton cried. The movement continued. Nadia reached the corner of another alley; she couldn't remember where it led. She stopped, hugging the corner and looking back. Amara moved towards her. A purpose in her steps. Her head low, hair raising to reveal her orange eyes.

"Run!" Pendleton shouted.

Nadia bolted, hearing the sudden increase in pace of Amara. She didn't realise the alley she'd chosen was a dead end. Heading round the back of a shop and to a ten-foot-high brick wall. Nadia frowned at the wall, blurted a sob in the hope that the wall would show sympathy and allow her to get over. Better yet, encase her and protect her from Amara.

"Cargill," the voice came, trickling down the alley. Amara's face hovering in the shadows and mass of hands.

"Please," Nadia sniffled. Holding her arms up in defence, how she could defend herself was not a thought that crossed her mind. Amara crept closer, closer, closer. Within reach of her, she stopped.

"Car-gill", she said, drawing out the word. Its meaning lost. A language only Amara understood.

"I'm sorry. It wasn't me. I have nothing to do with Dietrich…or Cargill," begged Nadia. Amara raised a hand, fingers outlining the definition of her biceps, her forearm, tiny fingers, baby fingers marked her knuckles. As her hand raised to Nadia, the fingers around her arms retracted. A single, pale fleshed limb revealed. The skin almost shining in the moonlight. Nadia sniffed back tears as Amara raised her true hand, brushing Nadia's cheek before she furrowed her brow. Taking hold of Nadia's neck and screaming. The hands swarming around her.

    Nadia could only think one thing before darkness engulfed her.

    I'm sorry.

31

To say Nadia opened her eyes would be blurring the truth. To her, it was closer to suddenly being awake. An awareness took over her, and she could see light again.

It was not daytime in Belfry. She was not in the alleyway she last remembered. There were no walls, no concrete, nor was there even the sound of footsteps, cars or business. No terrifying creature poured over her with festering hands ready to tear her to shreds.

It was a field. Grass, leaning to the side from the gusts of wind over open land. A forest in the distance. Hills and further off, munros. One hill looked more familiar than all the rest, as if something was missing from it. Standing on top of it, you could very easily lord over the lands below you.

Nadia tried to look around, but she couldn't look down and see what she was wearing, unsure if she was still in the sweat-drenched clothes she'd had on before. It was then she realised she couldn't feel the breeze she noticed moving the grass and brushing through the branches of the forest.

Movement, all too unsettling, Nadia began to move towards the forest. How she did not know, without any ability to look around or feel anything around her, she settled into the understanding that she was not in control.

The forest swept over Nadia like entering a tunnel. Light still peeked between the branches, enough to see clearly. Little ruts of grass and moss-covered stones bunched up between the trees. Nadia noticed little critters shifting within the fauna. Mice, rabbits and insects, all scurrying into hiding. Still, she moved deeper into the forest.

Trickling water tickled Nadia's ears and before long she could see a stream curving it's way between the trees. Settled upon a large rock next to the stream was a woman. Dressed in a long brown robe, a belt made of string or grass, similar bindings fitted around the woman's shoulders and tied boots to her feet.

Amara? Nadia thought, relieved that she was still able to hold her own conscience. To recognise the woman before her. The woman kicked water and smiled at the forest. Animals seemed welcoming of her and approached regularly. When they would catch her attention, the woman would flick her long black hair over her shoulder and pull a morsel of food from a pocket. Tossing it to the animals and whispering some message to them.

Moving closer to the woman, Nadia was able to distinguish her clearly. It was indeed Amara, not draped in the white dress she'd seen before. Not with dancing black hair, not with orange fiery eyes. Calm blue eyes sat in the skull of this Amara. Her skin smooth, easy to tell that it would have the softest feel if you were to touch her. Her lips a healthy ripe pink, she was beautiful.

Without warning, the image before Nadia snapped. Before her was now a cabin. A wooden cabin that she'd seen before. Leaves surrounding the building. *This is Amara's home.* The door opened, and Nadia found herself thrust inside. Amara was present, shuffling and preparing food in a wooden bowl. A man entered behind Nadia. Tall and thick-framed. He carried a deer on his shoulder, on his other he strung a bow. Resting on his hip a quiver of arrows. Hanging the deer up on the far side of the cabin near the fire, the man approached Amara. Hugging her close, the two embraced each other, rocking from side to side. From silence came a humming tune. A soft tone, a female voice. Amara's voice. She sung a song, at times words teased appearance, though they were words Nadia didn't understand. A language far older than she knew.

Why am I seeing this?

Again. The image snapped. Now, still inside the cabin. Amara sat at the table, a litany of small bowls spread out across it. Different herbs, plants and mushrooms displayed in an extensive collection. A different woman sat at the table. Dressed far better than Amara. A long dress, details of patterns on her corset. She spoke to Amara, explaining things Nadia could not hear. Leaning back, the woman's arms rested on her belly, large and rotund. Amara smiled and gave a gentle nod. Grabbing a small pouch, she began to fill it with different amounts of the contents of the bowls in front of her. She brought the pouch over to the fire and crossed her legs in front of it. Mumbling and rocking back and, lifting one hand, she made a request of the well-dressed woman. The woman, in turn, rose from the table, gave a tug on a hair to pull a single strand and pulled a pouch containing something unclear. She gave both to Amara, who tossed them both into the fire. The flames bloomed for a moment and calmed back down. Amara took in a long breath before reaching into the fire, her hands unfazed by the heat. Not expressing any pain, she removed her hand, a small black orb resting in her palm. She dropped the orb into the pouch and opened her eyes. The pouch was given to the woman.

How did she do that?

Snap! Again, the image changed. Outside the cabin now, men on horses and men on foot. All dressed in resplendent armour. Two men with swords drawn held hands up to Amara's partner. The tall man screaming anger as he held his place in the cabin doorway.

Arms grasped around Amara's shoulders, she kicked and screamed, tears running down her face as the men dragged her through the mud. Two men covered in dark cloth shackled her arms and legs. A design of a belltower displayed on all the mens' chests.

Snap! Now Amara stands atop a stage in a town center, no longer dressed in her brown garb. The buildings look old, no roads link them, only paths of heavily trodden mud. Straw thatched roofs, grubby windows, moss creeping up the building's walls. A white dress floats around Amara's body, draping over her shoulders and breasts, hiding her shape. An audience of cloth and rag-covered people watch with disgust on their faces, speckles of mud stain their clothing. A man walks up a staircase to the stage, his scarlet cloak arching off his back into the thick slick on the ground. He doesn't wear armour, but he looks far more glorious than the armoured gathering of men behind the stage. A barrier of guards holds back the audience as they hurl insults, spittle of anger fluttering from their lips. The glamorous man pulls a scroll from his

The Belfry Haunting

cloak and hushes the crowd. For the first time, Nadia hears someone's voice.

"Hush now, hush my people. I know you have gathered to see justice take it's course but I must have order." The man nods at the guards forming a barrier. They reach to their sheathed swords. The audience takes a step back and quiets down.

"Today we are gathered not to celebrate justice take its course, though it shall. We are gathered to see an end to a vile evil that has befallen our good people of Belfry." The man stepped forward, clearly in ecstasy at his power and performance.

"Before us, we have our guilty party. You, Amara Quinn, have been accused and found guilty of witchcraft and blasphemy." Amara wailed vowels through her gag as two men held her in place. Her shackles still binding her hands and feet. "You have not only partaken, but have been critical in the termination of seven gifts from God. Countless more, no doubt, destroyed by your hands. There is no place in this world for those who stand against the word of God, and there is no place in Belfry for the evils of black magic." The man turned to face her.

"Thus, as judge over these lands. I, Colton Cargill, sentence you to be executed. Being that your actions have affected several women directly and their partners. You shall be laid upon this table and be stripped over your womb. For the additional lives your actions have affected, that being the entire town of Belfry, no less, our audience shall take their lump of flesh from you. For your blasphemy against God, you shall finally be removed from this mortal coil. What say you?" Colton lifted his head. Amara threw cries and reason in muffled sobs.

"Dare not speak any more, we shall not give you the chance to cast your wicked words upon us. Your only choice is to ask for forgiveness. But…you cannot ask forgiveness from us. Not now, after you have turned your back on God and given your ways to the Devil. Trust in you will see the devastation of our way of life. I command our executioner. Begin the sentence." Colton stepped back, making way for a black hooded man. He was not large, nor showing the bulk of strength as Nadia had been led to believe from newspaper comic strips. Simply, a black hood gave him the authority to orchestrate Amara's demise.

Instructing the men holding Amara, the hooded man had her laid on top of the table. Her shackles unlocked, and her arms and legs bound to the corners of the table. Her gag remained tight, her eyes bursting with terror, her chest heaving in panic. The executioner walked out of her view, returning shortly after with a device in hand. Gripping the collar of the white dress she'd been clothed in, the man lifts the device, a sharp blade, and slices the dress with ease. He tosses either side of the dress away to reveal Amara's naked body. The audience cheers, hungry for blood.

The executioner's gaze laps at her flesh before drifting over Amara's eyes. She sees no sympathy in them, no mercy or humanity looking back. Working his fingers down in calculating measurements from her neck, his hands drift over her breasts, down her stomach and to her belly button. He presses, feeling for his target. Doing similar measurements from hip bone to hip bone, he then carries out similar measurements from her groin back to her belly button. He looks to Colton and, after receiving a nod, places the blade over Amara's abdomen. The audience erupts in glee as the blade enters her. A quick trickle of blood draws down her side. Halted gasps bubble through Amara's gag as she is cut open. Once she is severed from hip to hip, the hooded man thrusts his hands inside her. Pulling and stretching the wound further as he searches her insides. He shows no recognition of violating something living. Only frustrated that he struggles in his search.

As the waves of pain curl through Amara's body and mind, the hooded man grips her insides in one hand and slices through it with the other. Pulling globs of fat and tissues from inside her, he finally pulls out his target, her womb. A dripping mass of red laced with veins. He holds it aloft, his back to the audience; they roar and cheer. He steps away, bringing the uterus down and cradling it before tossing it into a bucket.

"As you have taken children from our people, we have taken the capability for you to bear a child from you. Now you shall pay your debt to the people of Belfry," Colton said, the guards shifting away from the stage. Colton himself quickly hurried down the steps and burrowed behind several guards holding shields, two horses whinny in proud challenge to the audience, their masters mounted with spears. "My good people, take your lump of flesh from this wretched witch."

Roars of greed explode from the crowd. Some of them rush up the stairs, others fall on top of each other as they try to climb up onto it.

Amara looks up as best she can, seeing Colton retiring away from the scene. A smirk across his face, knowing full well the gathered mass are going to tear the woman to shreds. She fixes her eyes on him, holding her gaze even as people surround her, blocking her from seeing her judge.

"Filthy witch! You'll pay," a woman screeches, slapping the naked and gutted Amara. More slaps break her concentration, and she looks up to the sky, trying to block out the pain.

Scratching and tearing at her skin, the rabble of insults morphs into a cacophony of hateful noise. A man mounts the table and looks at Amara with rage as he slips his trousers down. Forcing himself inside her as people cheer him on.

"Defile the witch! Defile the defiler!" people scream. The man punches her as he has his way with her. Amara's lip bursts, the copper taste lapping at her tongue. Moments later, he is spent. Hopping off, he is quickly replaced by another man. Amara prays for a numb safe space to hide her mind. She closes her eyes to contract inside herself. Alas, the crowd grabs at her hair, pulling it and tearing it out, latching her eyelids and holding them open.

Blades are drawn and repeatedly plunged into her flesh. Her shoulders, her chest, her side, her legs, all while man after man rapes her. A small man mounts her and snarls at her, staring her in the eye as he violates her. Wrapping his hands around her throat and smiling to his fellow oppressors. They join him, hand upon hand, squeezing, pressing, forcing her throat closed. Amara begs for it all to step, to be released. No longer wanting her body, they can have it, just let her soul fly off to whatever beyond there might be. The hands constrict and press, harder and harder until…crunch! Amara's throat caves inwards.

Nadia tries to scream in horror, to somehow force the audience off her. A flash brings her to see what Amara sees. Hands, fingers, grips of hatred, squashing her neck. The man on top of her thrusting spits at her. Suddenly, he changes, Gary grins a sadistic grin, pinning her down.

"Am I better?" Gary's voice cuts through the thunder of the crowd. He leans in, leans back, once again the smaller man humping away, spit dripping from his lips.

"Die Witch!" The man shouts.

"Am I better?" Gary's face returns.

"Die, die, die!" The crowd chants.

"Am I better than Troy?" Gary shouts.

"No!" Nadia's voice breaks through.

All goes black.

32

Nadia's eyes burn as she opens them. A pained exhaustion floats through her body. Throbbing in nauseating waves, she feels a lump growing in her throat, sour and bile tasting. She pushes against the ground, sitting up and looking around.

Where am I?

Moments pass as her heavy eyelids ease open further. *The alley. I'm in the alley*. Memories float and drift past her. In front of her, she realises there is a person standing. Nadia raises her head to the person. Blurry and shaped in a feminine form.

"Pendleton?" She asks. Reaching out, hoping for a hand to help her to her feet. Receiving no assistance, she blinks to clear her eyes a few times.

"Amara?" Nadia realises. The woman looks down at her, her eyes faded, grey, the orange fire gone. Her chin quivers ever so slightly. Tears trickle down her cheeks.

"Wh-what happened? Did you do that to me?" Nadia asks, managing to press on her knee to stand up. Amara doesn't answer. She steps back. Nadia realises that she isn't surrounded by hands either. Her face and body aren't an abomination of interlaced fingers and hands. Her chest and throat are heavily bruised, hand marks and fingerprints stain her skin.

She steps back again.

"No, Amara. Please. Wait." Nadia reaches out. Amara jolts away from her hand.

"Cargill," she says, her voice soft, pleading. She turns her head, a blurt of a sob escaping her lips. Amara's hair floats up, and from beneath her skin, the hands return. Pushing free and swarming her body. The mass flurries down the alley and disappears out of sight.

"Nadia?" Pendleton's voice echoes. Nadia blinks and follows the voice.

"I'm here", Nadia says, slowly walking out of the alley, checking all directions to see where Amara has gone.

"Dear heavens, girl. Are you alright?" Pendleton turns the entrance to the alley. Grabbing Nadia and wrapping her arms around her.

"Yes, I'm-I'm fine."

The Belfry Haunting

"Good, good. I'm so glad she didn't get you." Pendleton carries Nadia down the street. Nadia's feet follow the woman's control, unable to make a conscious decision of her own.

She did get me. Nadia doesn't tell the old woman. Partly unable to, partly not wanting to.

"Let's get you home, shall we?"

"No. I have to-" Nadia shakes, freeing herself from Pendleton's graps.

"What's wrong, Miss Hussain?" Pendleton asks, but Nadia ignores her. Her thoughts still fighting to form into something coherent. She looks around, remembering the decimation she'd witnessed. Gary getting killed, Johnny getting killed, Troy getting killed. *Abby is dead.* The blood-soaked pub sends a shock through her spine.

"Come on. It's alright, I'll look after you," Pendleton urges Nadia to come back to her arms. Nadia swings her vision left and right as it all returns to her.

Lockwood.

Her eyes stop on the building in the distance. Peeking over the shops and houses, watching Nadia come back to this world. She runs towards it. Chasing after what she knows is her goal.

"Where are you going?" Pendleton calls after her. Unable to move as fast as the young girl, she makes her best attempt to rush after her, sharp clops bounce after them as the old woman's heels move as fast as they can.

Tears roll down Nadia's cheeks as her jaw tightens, she picks up speed, breaking into a sprint. All the while keeping her eyes fixed on Lockwood. The driveway shouts panic as her feet race, slamming up the tarmacadam. The gravel stones of the parking area nearly trip her over. She slides through them and grabs onto the doorframe of the entrance, flinging herself inside.

"Amara?" She calls, hoping that the woman will appear, that she'll be able to hug her close and apologise for the evil that was cast upon her. She looks behind the reception desk, hoping she'll see the woman hugging her knees close. The cold linoleum peaks back between the littered papers from patient files.

Running off down the corridor, Nadia feels a weight build in her chest. A tension pulling her forward. She turns the corner of the corridor and sees the staircase Abby and Johnny had raced down, what felt like years ago now. Not looking into any of the rooms she passes as she runs down the corridor, somehow knowing exactly where to go, she reaches the bottom of the stairs.

"Amara? Please, come to me," she cries, ascending the stairs. A wind whistles past her ears, a breath, entrancing, alluring, it pulls her up the stairs and down a dark corridor. Peaking out of a door in the corridor, a pillar of light paints the opposite wall. Shapes twist and shift through the pillar, a shadow teasing Nadia to come closer.

She reaches the door and reaches a hand out to the handle. *What am I doing? This is insane,* her brain argues with her, frustration fighting the inability to prevent her movements. Her hand grips the cold doorknob, pushing it lightly. She doesn't enter, but waits for the door to creak open and reveal the room.

"Who are you?" an old man shouts from the floor. *Who is that?* Nadia steps inside, her left hand paws at the door, leaving it just ajar.

"Who are you? What are you doing in here? Are you alright?" Nadia asks of her own volition. Her body feeling heavier as she regains control.

"My dear, help me. Please, you must help me," the old man whines. A spindly arm outstretched, wrapped in a suit far too big for his diminished frame. His legs look like dead tendrils attached to his torso, no strength, no movement in them.

"What are you doing here?" Nadia leans her head back, the shadow from the man's arm swiping at her face.

"I-I own this place. Please, I am an old man who needs assistance. Would you leave a dying old man in such need? Help me, damn it!" Spit froths at his mouth as his brow begins to furrow.

"You're Dietrich! Viktor Dietrich!" Nadia exclaims, she looks around the room, waiting for a pat on the back. A mess in the corner grabs her eyes, some table toppled over. *Was the old bugger trying to get to it? Did he make that mess?*

"Yes, and what of it?" The old man's patience begins to wear thin.

"Did you hurt yourself on that table?" Nadia asks. The old man turns his head to look back at the mess, his eyes roll around in his head for a moment.

"Yes, yes. I was trying to use my old gramophone and took a tumble. I fear I have done some serious injury to myself. Would you please help me? I may need to go to the hospital," he pleads. Nadia continues surveying the scene.

"Cargill!" she blurts. A momentary wave of nausea hits her, a voice speaking the name in her head, moving her lips. Dietrich's feigned eyes of begging expand, replaced with an immortal terror.

"What did you say?"

"You are the old bastard that's imprisoning her," says Nadia, recalling Pendleton's explanation. The history of the Cargill family, the vision Amara shared with her.

"Her? Who is she?" The old man tests, rolling onto the back of his shoulder, edging himself away from Nadia.

"Amara"

"No!" Dietrich cries. Nadia breaths deeper, she feels a raw energy in her chest, her eyes beginning to burn. Dietrich shies away from her, seeing an orange tinge behind her eyes.

The whisper of wind tickles Nadia's ears again, her vision drawn to the door. She steps to it and whips it open.

"Amara, come to me!" she shouts. Dietrich gasps, his bottom lip quivering as it drips saliva onto his tie. Whistling gusts float through the corridor, hollow silence holds the pauses between them.

"Amara! Please, come to me!" Nadia shouts again. The whistles hush, Nadia looks over her shoulder and smiles at Dietrich.

A scream, pure and infernal, shakes the room. The vibrations turning to tremors. The whole building seeming to tremble in an earthquake. The candles atop the fireplace shift off, smashing to the ground. The brass firepoker clangs onto the floor. Nadia steps to the side of the door, holding it open.

"No. Please no!" Dietrich cries to her, pleading for mercy.

Amidst the cacophony of apocalypse, a rumble draws closer, clearly distinguishable amongst the rest. It tears through the corridors of the building, racing up the stairs and slams into the doorway.

Hands grasp around the doorframe, knuckles gripping into the wood. Splitting the frame in places, cracking their nails in others. The hands pull with all their strength, pulling a black darkness into the room. The darkness blossoms and bubbles as a smoke, breaching further into the room. Slowly blacking out the view of the corridor.

A grey naked foot emerges from the darkness, fingers wrapping a calf, thumbs forming toes, palms forming feet. It gently rests on the floor, pulling a leg from the darkness, a torso, arms and a head. All fingers and hands, a shell of dread. Casting terror into it's witnesses and protecting it's host. The hands gripping the door frame ease their grip, lightly uncurling and rolling back into the corridor. The darkness fades away. The hands encasing Amara open, peeling away from her and revealing her in the light. The hands and fingers ripple back through her skin and consume behind her spine. Nadia feels a shiver run through her as she sees the last few knuckles sink into Amara's back.

"Please, my girl. Leave me be. I am sorry. I never chose this for you. I hate this wretched town. Let me leave and never come back," Dietrich sobs, pushing himself back, his hands slipping on the floor. Each thump of his body against the floor sending winding blows through him.

"Cargill," Amara whispers neutrally. A statement, not a question.

"No. No, I am not. I am Dietrich!" he smiles.

"Cargill," Amara confirms.

"You are descended from Cargill. You continue to imprison her," Nadia says. Amara steps towards Dietrich, slow and soft, firelight dances across her pale skin. Her white dress floats at her knees, her hair rippling just above her clavicle.

"I do no such thing. Damn the youth of this damned place. Damn you all!" Dietrich refutes.

"You have lived far too long, Viktor. Humans are not meant to spend so much time on this earth."

"Don't you claim heresy of me, young lady." His eyes flicker to Nadia for a moment, then back to Amara as she draws closer.

"You have lived far too long, and Amara has been kept prisoner for even longer. Humans are not meant to live this long; souls are meant to move on. Don't you see, you've held her back. You, your father, Dietrichs and Cargills have sapped energy from her." Nadia pushes off the wall of the room. Feeling confidence build in her.

"Witch!" Dietrich hurls an insult, staring it at both Nadia and Amara.

Nadia laughs, "That's what they called her. When she merely helped save women from slavery through rape. Men controlling the world with their impulse. Men grown on greed. Men who cast judgment on Amara and tortured her before they killed her. Raping, slicing, tearing and choking her". Nadia's voice lifted, pain seeping in her throat. Amara steps finally to Dietrich, his eyes lift to her, weak and frail. She reaches her hands down to him, gripping his suit jacket and picking him up. Though much smaller than Dietrich at full standing height, she has no issue lifting him. Her hair floats a little higher around her shoulders, and Dietrich floats in mid-air.

"Put me down! I command you!" Dietrich shouts.

"You command no one," Nadia declares.

"Put me down now!"

"She will put you down," Miss Pendleton says, stepping into the room and gripping Nadia's hand. Their hair begins to drift back as if pushed by a continuing gust. "Once you have paid your debt." The old woman's piercing gaze chills Dietrich.

Amara shows no burning fury, no disgust on her face for the man before her, though her eyes flare violently. Dietrich begins to whimper, knowing full well what lies ahead.

"You might want to avert your eyes," Pendleton says to Nadia. "A young girl like yourself doesn't need to see the kind of violence she will evoke."

Nadia continues to watch the floating old man and the spirit stare off. "I've seen more violence and horror this weekend than any human could ever imagine. I'll manage."

Amara raises her hand to Dietrich, pointing at his stomach, the man blubbers confusion as his belly inflates. A bump growing in his abdomen. Within seconds his distended stomach bursts free of his shirt, a pale pregnancy, levels of uncomfort push through his expression. Her hand lowers to his groin, her nails extending, glistening white. With a sharp jolt, her hand turns scarlet. Dietrich cries in pain, his head whipping back. The old man's genitalia rest in Amara's hand, feeble skin and organ. She drops it, a wet splat echoes out of the room and down the corridor. Amara lifts her other hand, hovering them over the man's abdomen, admiring his bump. She tilts her head slowly to the side and back as she runs her long talon nails across him. Looking like a gentle, affectionate touch, the reality shows gashes spilling blood from growing wounds as her nails tear easily through flesh. She continues for many seconds, casually slicing the old man's skin open. He continues to cry, somehow not passing out from the pain or blood loss, the shock being held back in his system.

Amara's eyes focus on the bump, both hands now dripping red, cupping around the man's wicked womb. Her hair rises higher, whirling fiercely. She closes her eyes and dips her head.

"What is she doing?" Nadia leans to Pendleton.

"Releasing the curse, sending it back to the bloodline that started it."

Amara whips her head back, her hair dancing like a flame, exploding from the back of her head. She screams, dark energy releasing itself from inside her. The bump bubbles, skin deforming from inside. Dietrich's body begins to tremble, spasming uncontrollably. Nadia squints at the pregnant belly. *Is that, oh god no. That's fingers.*

The skin stretches, whitening as the pressure pushes blood out of the expanding skin. Fingers and knuckles becoming clearer and clearer until they rip through the belly. Hollow gurgles and splutters burp from Dietrich's open mouth. Air barely able to fill his lungs for him to scream in pain.

Fingers pull the flesh, ripping it further, enough for them to breach. Infants emerging from their eggs, the hands pour out of the erupted belly. Spreading out over the old man's body. Children looking to feed upon their dying parent, they begin to grip, rip and tear at his body. A few emerge into the world and, identifying more valuable means, return inside Dietrich to pull out his innards. Yards of intestine thrown out from inside. Organs and other viscera discarded as if animals burrowed new dens internally.

Amara's hands raise above her head. The breaching hands from Dietrich ascending in line with her. They reach his chest and create a collar around his neck. Three circle around the back of his head and grab his hair, pulling his head back and holding it in place, ensuring his eyelids are held open. The collar of hands throbs their fingers in unison before Amara bursts her fists open, the collar wraps around Dietrich's throat and squeezes.

They're doing to him what they did to her. Nadia watches, second-guessing if she should have taken Pendleton's advice. The gathering pool of blood and human insides tainting the air with a coppery sweetness.

The hands tighten around Dietrich's neck, spurts of blood choke and cough out of his mouth as his airway is closed. The nails on the hands begin to dig into the flesh, and with little resistance, they cut the old man's head free. The three hands pulling on the hair rip the last flesh fibres off and drop the head into the pile on the floor.

Amara's hair floats back down to rest on her skin, her banshee scream silences, and she turns to face the two women in the room with her. Nadia looks into her eyes and sees the pale grey of emptiness. Pendleton sighs.

"She is free."

"What happens to her now?" Nadia asks.

The old lady sniffs, a small tear gathering in her eye. "She is free to move on to wherever she wants to. To make her own choices. To be happy."

"And...and the hands?" asks Nadia, seeing the body of Dietrich still floating, headless and gutted.

Amara lowers her head as if releasing tension from within. The hands swarming over Dietrich's body quickly begin to return from their origin, bundling inside the bodily remains, disappearing into the red black hole they'd created. The last few slow their pace as they make their final journey. A sorrow at leaving their maternal spirit. They look weaker as the last one enters Dietrich's abdomen, almost dying.

With the last hand gone and only a floating corpse remaining, it drops to the ground. Crumpling on top of organs, flesh and blood. Amara inhales a deep breath, her lips curling ever so slightly at the edges.

"I guess that answers that, then," Nadia nods. Amara looks into the back corner at the gramophone and points. Pendleton frowns and shuffles over to the corner, carefully avoiding the blood as it expands outwards. She reaches down and picks up the cracked record.

"What is this?" She asks Amara. The spirit doesn't answer, doesn't scowl, doesn't smile. Her business completed, she begins to walk out of the room, working her way down the corridor at a slow pace. Nadia and Pendleton follow after her, rushing in a dazed confusion.

"Where is she going?" Nadia asks.

"I know as much as you at this stage, dear." They hold silence as they follow. Pendleton tucking the record under her arm as they descend the staircase and walk through the building. The corridors and rooms feeling even emptier than before. A euphoric trance-like feeling tickles the woman's brains as they follow Amara. Hearing voices from each room, giggling, chatting, laughing together, thanking them for the freedom they've been granted.

Thank you. Oh heavens above, thank you.
So much suffering, no more.
Her pain. Our Pain. Lifted.
Prisoners of hatred, no more.
Dear lord above, thank you for our release.

Amara walks to the bassment staircase, her feet echoing fleshy pats as she descends. As they reach the bottom step, Amara glances at the ceiling. Pendleton and Nadia halt behind her, peering into the darkness to see shapes. The lights above fizz and crack, a dim light growing inside them. Amara continues down the corridor, the lights illuminating and darkening above her. Pendleton and Nadia shrug at each other and follow after.

"There was a room at the end of this corridor," Nadia says, recalling the horrors she'd witnessed.

"Storage area," Pendleton confirmed.

"No, all these rooms were storage areas," Nadia disagrees.

"These rooms held storage for supplies. The room at the end was a storage area for the more comatose patients. Those that were experimented on. Believe me girl, the history of this building and it's occupants challenges even the atrocities of the holocaust."

"They stored patients?" Nadia asks, checking to see if Amara also reviled such thoughts.

Pendleton nods. "Indeed. They would reduce patients diets to test their boundaries, dose them with stimulants and relaxants, keep them awake for weeks on end. Once they'd reach a comatose state, they'd leave them down here to rot. Claiming the experiments were continuing and they needed to see the results."

Nadia sneered, imagining the stretchers and make-shift beds in the room with decaying bodies. Limbs losing fat and muscle, skeletons draped in flesh, too weak to plead for help. Worse still, too weak to plead for a merciful death.

"Do you think they died of neglect, or do you think Amara killed them?" Nadia whispered to Pendleton.

"I'd rather not hazard a guess," Pendleton replies. Amara gives a slight look back over her shoulder, a glisten of a tear under her eye.

They reach the open room, the pillars look different to Nadia now. Placed randomly throughout the room, she could almost imagine them separating different classifications of decomposing former patients. No doubt summarised in some disrespecting way. Extreme fatigue, forced starvation, and psychotic shutdown. Nadia could imagine the staff referring to them in even more insulting terms. The mouldy ones, the rotters, the puss sacks. None of these patients will have been admitted for these conditions. People who had turned to science for help and aid, and instead had been thrown into the bowels of hell for humanity to make claims against poorly founded hypotheses. Neither the patients nor the staff knew of the tortured soul lingering in the land looking for vengeance.

Amara continued in a straight path, she knew exactly where she was going. Crossing the room towards a door at the back. Nadia's heart skipped a beat, *that's the door that shouldn't be there. That's where we found...her home.* Gripping Pendleton's hand she pulled the old woman close. Hugging her arm for security.

"It's alright, dear, we'll suffer no more pain. I swear," Pendleton said as they continued to follow the spirit.

Before Amara reached the door, the handle turned of it's own volition. Wheezing a long creak as it leaned open, the door clunked against stone wall. The corridor Nadia had been expecting was on the other side. However, it was clearly not as long as before. Nor did the corridor close in to a claustrophobic hole. At the end of the corridor, Amara spotted the red door. Scratches breaking the red paint. *Are those from Amara's hands, or are those from her victims trying to escape?* Nadia wondered. Fearful of enquiring to the spirit in front of her.

As the last door had done before, the handle turned by itself and the door swung open. There, before the two women, was the other world. The same red-stained leaves cover the ground. The same forest huddling around the wooden cabin. The same sky that stretched the imagination of just how big this world might be.

"Oh my," Pendleton said as they stepped through the doorway, soft crunching of leaves under their feet. She looked around, admiring the beauty before looking at Nadia. "Look at all this, isn't it stunning?"

"I've seen it already," Nadia replied.

Pendleton stopped herself before she enquired, lifting her eyes to the back of Amara and sighing.

"Oh, my dear girl. You've been through so much." Pendleton's expression relaxed. Nadia wondered how she'd never seen the old woman look like this. So considerate, so human.

"It's fine," Nadia said and stepped after Amara. The spirit stepped inside her hidden realm home.

Inside, a fire calmly welcomed them in. A table stretched out in front it with plates of food. None of the food looked like anything Nadia recognised or would consider appetising, though she would not judge. *This must be food from her time.*

In the far corner, Nadia watched as Amara settled into a bed, again far from looking like something Nadia could appreciate. The spirit lay back and pulled a large cloth cover over herself. Nadia looked around the room and then to Pendleton. Unsure of what their next move should be.

"Thank you," a voice spoke from the corner. Nadia was so struck by how normal it sounded, she barely realised that it had come from Amara. "Thank you, young girl. You have been my saviour. I have spent too many years in this place, terrorised by the will of a bloodline not my own. Please, do not let your past control you like mine has. Do not let the terrors cast upon you mould your future." Amara closed her eyes.

"Thank you, Amara. It has been a pleasure to meet and assist my ancestor," Pendleton said, seeking some sort of appraisal, Nadia thought.

"Go now," Amara replied. She breathed deeply, a woman in blissful meditation. Her breaths lifting and falling, slowing.

Slowing.

Slowing.

One final breath seemed to exhale for so long there could never have been enough air in her lungs. *Why would she need to breath air?* Nadia thought to herself. Seeing Amara's chest remain, she realised it had been the final breath they would see of the spirit. *Perhaps that was her spirit leaving?*

"Come on," Pendleton said, taking Nadia's hand in hers and pulling her out of the house. The old woman wiped tears from her cheeks with her free hand.

"Are you alright?" Nadia asked as the two of them stepped back into the corridor. The red door gently creaked closed again.

"I'll be fine," Pendleton answered. They continued through the corridor and back into the open room. The door closing behind them, Nadia felt a weight leave her, unnoticed tension lifting.

They walked across the open room, around a few of the pillars. Stopping in the corridor, back to the basement stairs. Nadia turned back.
    The door had gone again.
    She hoped she would never see that door ever again in her life.

33

Belfry would never be the same. Not to Pendleton or Nadia, that was certain. They'd returned back to the main street, discussing what they could possibly do now that the place had been reduced to a population of two.

To Nadia's relief, a few of the locals had decided that going to the pub that night was not for them. They had managed to avoid being eviscerated by Amara and, better yet, had managed to avoid noticing anything strange going on whatsoever.

Nadia's parents had both survived, neither of them being fans of drinking. Nadia hadn't noticed, but amidst the slaughter, there had been the parents of some of her friends. Johnny's father, Gary's parents, Tom's father, Abby's father, the rest of her friend's parents had been the lucky few who had rested up.

Unsurprisingly, those people who had unknowingly survived the massacre were quite disturbed to find the aftermath. Police were called in, real police, of course, not more young men abusing their power.

Pendleton regularly checked up on Nadia during the investigation. Nadia believed that was more for the old woman's benefit than it was for hers.

The police still have not made a concrete decision on what happened that night. The remaining living of Belfry had been questioned, and seemingly none of them had been there. What was more confusing to the police during their investigation was that fingerprints were found all over the building. More fingerprints than could be believed. Madness had ensued when word got out that the fingerprints came from people who had died long ago. Some were patients of Lockwood. Yet further horror and mystery was raised when the investigation searched Lockwood, finding yet more fingerprints all over the place. The owner, Viktor Dietrich, was nowhere to be found. His assistant hadn't heard from him in days; her last record was that he was heading to Belfry on business. With the police intelligence and skillset being thrown into question, it was smothered over with bureaucracy and confusion. There were not enough voices left in Belfry to chase for justice. With the level of massacre that had unfolded, the town wanted to move on more than anything. Nadia and Pendleton quietly thanked that they needn't have to face what happened on that weekend any further.

Five months after everything had happened, the town had calmed down. Press and police no longer hounding the streets. 'For sale' signs starting to pop up on buildings all over. The last of the funeral parades through town finally over. Distant family members who'd never been to Belfry, holding their breaths as they wandered the streets dressed in black and following coffins to be buried.

Nadia swung by the library to check in on Pendleton. She hadn't been as regular at making contact in the past few weeks. Walking into the library, Nadia didn't find the old woman at her desk but instead sat at one of the communal tables. Spread out in front of her were books upon books. Some open at pages, some closed and tossed on top of each other at funny angles. A scene of a woman tumbling down a rabbit hole.

"Miss Pendleton, are you alright?" Nadia asked, the old woman took a moment to notice another presence in the room. Releasing a sharp screech, she turned to face Nadia.

"Oh, Miss Hussain. You startled me. Oh, yes, I'm quite alright. Quite alright indeed," she smiled, her cheeks looking cracked and red. Her eyes bloodshot, heavy bags underneath. *How long has this woman been awake?*

"What are you doing?" Nadia asked, stepping up to look over the texts in front of the old woman. Pendleton glanced at her table of mess, nearly throwing herself over it to keep her embarrassment or hide her objective.

"I'm sorry, my dear," she sighed, giving up the defences. Nadia picked up one of the books, it looked to have a record of people's names. Families, their children, their date of birth and age when they died.

"What is this?" Nadia frowned, tossing the book back on the table, wiping the dirty feeling the book gave her on her jeans.

"I haven't been able to let it all go," Pendleton explained. "Ever since that night, I've felt like there was something missing. I'd long known that Dietrich held dominion over my Amara. The problem is I didn't know how," she said.

"I think it's best if we just move on, Miss Pendleton."

"Yes, mmhmm, yes, I think you may be right," the old woman sighed again, another human's presence pulling her back to humanity. Nadia continued nudging paper and books around as she investigated. Nudging one book of the educational record of Belfry for the past fifty years, Nadia noticed beneath all the paper was something black, an almost plastic shine. She nudged the surrounding items out of the way.

"Is this the record we found?" she said, gently lifting the cracked record off the table.

"I've no idea why I decided I needed it. It just seemed like the right thing to do in the moment, I guess. It gives me some sense of proximity to Amara when I hold it. I can almost feel her near me. I know that sounds strange. Maybe I'm just a withered old woman now. I'm turning crazy. Don't bother yourself with that now, give it here," she reached out. Nadia held the record close.

"It makes you feel close to her?"

"Please don't make fun of a poor old woman." Pendleton's dark bags under her eyes pulled her eyes down, a weak plea for warmth.

"Miss Pendleton, after everything that happened. You feeling close to Amara when you hold this sounds like the most normal thing in the world." She handed the record over.

Pendleton rose, carefully running her fingers along the edge of the record.

"I've listened to it time after time. Long into the night on occasion. I'm surprised nobody has made any complaints about the noise"

"Nobody lives close enough to hear it anymore. They're all…dead…remember," Nadia reasoned, swallowing down sorrow. The poor woman before her had kept herself to herself all these years, researching Dietrich, researching Amara's past. Too weak to take the fight into her own hands. Now the only person she'd been looking to help was gone, and she was truly alone in this world.

"Perhaps." Pendleton crossed the library and pulled a rolling tray from behind a shelf. A gramophone sat on top of the tray. Pendleton carefully set the record down onto it, gently resting the needle down, clicking the device on. "It's got so many cracks in it that the melody is not perfect, but…well…" The old woman closed her lips. The fuzzy buzz of the gramophone rising before a woman's voice hummed out.

Pendleton was right, the cracks in the record stabbed little jumps into the audio of the record, but the melody could still be made out enough. Nadia felt herself shift a little, a dizziness spinning in her head.

"Nadia, are you alright?" Pendleton rushed over to stop the young girl falling over.

"Yes. I-I-I'm fine, I think."

"Oh dear girl. Don't tell me you've been drinking again."

"No, no. I haven't had a drink since that night," said Nadia. She'd been too scared to touch anything that might affect her control.

"Have you eaten today?"

"Yes. I-I just…"

"What is it, girl. I'll take care of you, don't worry."

"I think I know what that song is," Nadia said. Pendleton's eyes quivered, her lip dropping. Nadia could see she'd stolen a breath from the old woman.

"What do you mean?"

"I mean, I've heard it before," said Nadia. Pendleton looked down, searching for a clear reason in her head. She released Nadia and sat back down at the table in front of her research. Nadia sat down in the chair next to her and rested a hand on the old woman's.

"I heard that song from Amara," Nadia began. Explaining the strange vision she'd had when Amara had attacked her and subsequently left her alive. How she'd seen the life Amara had lived centuries ago. Living from the land, embracing nature, feeding wildlife, gathering plants and herbs. How she'd found a lover, a man who sought not to live in a society with many others, who sought a quiet life. A man who could hunt and provide for Amara. How the two of them had found happiness in living on the outskirts of society. How they'd only make contact with the people of Belfry when they'd sought Amara for her skills in medicine. How Amara had only ever wanted to help those who sought her out. Never asking questions, never doubting that people were good.

Pendleton's bloodshot eyes glazed over as tears formed while Nadia told her she'd seen how

Amara was taken from her home. Judged by people who barely knew her at all. Sentenced by a man who'd assumed witchcraft and the Devil was inside her. She didn't tell the old woman that she had been forced to experience all the torture Amara had in her last moments.

"That song, that's the song she used to sing to her lover," Nadia finished. Pendleton lowered her head, wiping the tears away.

"What was her lover's name?"

"I never found out," Nadia exhaled.

Pendleton smiled through her tears and looked back into Nadia's eyes. "It's alright, dear. It's not important. What's important is you've helped me yet again. That song must be how Dietrich controlled Amara. In moments of extreme torture and violence, spirits can get trapped; they cling to their most loved memories. My Amara had a lover, and that song was her connection, in my estimation," she breathed, whistling out a pain as she held her best smile again.

"But this was centuries ago. Must have been hundreds of years before they even made records or had gramophones. How did they get the song onto a record?" Nadia asked herself.

"My dear, you said it already. Perhaps it is best if we move on from this. Some things are better left in the past, and some are better left

unanswered." Pendleton reached out and held Nadia's hand. Nadia smiled back at her and nodded.
Yeah, maybe you're right.

34

The day felt warmer and brighter as Nadia said goodbye to Pendleton and stepped out of the library.

What am I going to do with the rest of my day? Nadia thought. Putting one foot in front of the other, she let herself walk without a destination in mind. Letting her mind calmly saunter through whatever thoughts came.

Waving to the few local Belfry folks she passed, Nadia realised the town felt like a nicer place. For as small a place as it was, it had felt busy. Had that been because there were so many strange businesses and individuals in the town? Maybe. Those "entrepreneurial individuals" with the quirky businesses were unsurprisingly amongst the slaughter. What remained now was the people running more normal shops, hairdressers that only cut hair, corner shops that only sold milk, crisps and booze, not side hussling with low-quality furniture.

Did it feel nicer because Nadia wasn't drinking anymore? Maybe she hadn't touched it since the incident and had no intention to touch it in future. Her skin felt clearer, she was breathing easier, and she'd even managed to get herself out for a few jogs around town. There was less clouding her brain now, less poison to further cloud it as well.

Was it because there were little to no bad influences around town now? Maybe. The rest of the locals appeared to have taken a similar approach to Nadia; they didn't drink anymore. People went out for long walks, often outside of town. There was no longer a young police authority in town to brush trouble under the carpet. There was no need for a policing unit; the locals just walked by each other and gave polite waves. With Tom killed and the heightened police activity after the incident, there were no drugs coming into the area either. Not that anyone would want anything mind-altering. They'd all been well and truly scared straight.

A horn blasted her train of thought as Nadia stepped onto the main street road. Frowning and turning to roll into her old self, ready to shout obscenities at the car, she stopped as her eyes locked with Abby's mother.

"Oh, Nadia, I'm so sorry. I didn't realise it was you. Are you alright? You've got to be careful on the roads, you know." The woman leapt out of the car, rushing over to check on Nadia.

"Huh? Sorry. I, uh, my mind was elsewhere." Nadia's eyes awkwardly danced. It was the first time she'd seen Abby's mother since everything had happened. She hadn't wanted to bother the woman; she'd lost her husband and daughter after all.

"No, no. It's alright. I'm just glad we're both fine. So much has happened recently. You are alright, aren't you?"

Nadia's lips adjusted, but with no words. Abby's mother's shoulders dropped, assuming the worst. Before she could begin mothering her, Nadia managed to breathe out words, "Yes. I'm doing fine. As fine as can be expected, you know?" She let out an empty chuckle.

"Good, good." Abby's mother lingered, nodding at the young girl.

"Where are you going today? Anything exciting?" Nadia asked, quickly changing the subject.

"Not too exciting, I hope. I'm, uh, I'm leaving town."

"What?"

"Yes. Nadia, you might not understand this, but I'm sure with time you will. There are reasons to stay in places and reasons to leave. Your heart will inform you on both. For me, I simply cannot be here any longer."

"Oh, but…what about…" Nadia began, not knowing where her words were going. Only feeling like she was losing something else. Like Belfry was losing another person.

"Nadia," Abby's mother interrupted. "It's fine. I'll miss you. Abby always loved you dearly, and I do too. I'm moving to Glasgow. If you are ever there, you are more than welcome to come and see me."

Nadia opened her mouth to ask more before stopping herself. She exhaled, smiling at Abby's mother.

"Of course. I'll come through sometime to see you." Nadia extended her hand to Abby's mother. The two of them shared a quiet politeness.

"Goodbye, Nadia."

"Goodbye, I hope you have a happy life," Nadia said, feeling a small burn of regret as she saw the blossom of emotion form in Abby's mother's eyes. *Oh god, I've made her cry.* Abby's mother turned and got in the car before she broke into hysterics. The car rolled off down the road. Nadia gave a wave, watching it grow smaller and smaller and disappear. Letting out a sigh, Nadia began walking again, a hollow warmth nuzzling in her chest. She would miss Abby's mother, but she hoped the best for her.

Without thinking of it, Nadia arrived at the park. The same place she'd spent the past few years loitering around with her friends. For all the good that she'd been thinking the town now had, she felt a sting of painful guilt.

She no longer had to deal with Amara, she hoped. She wished she no longer had to deal with the rape. Somehow, that felt secondary to what had just happened. At least there were no drugs and alcohol influencing her now. She wouldn't let anything influence her anymore. She also had no friends to speak of now. She had no boyfriend. No best friend.

Walking towards the swings, Nadia nudged one of them, the chains of the swing creaking, small clouds of rust falling from them. She could remember sitting on those swings the first night Gary had made a move. They'd both finished off a bottle of Gin together, having snatched it away from the rest of the gang. Gary sat on one swing, she on the other; they'd talked for an hour or so about how cool it would be to live in Los Angeles. Gary finally mustered up the courage to get off his swing and kiss Nadia, lifting her up in the swing. She'd felt like a fairy lifting off the ground as their lips touched. Something out of a romance novel.

Nadia kicked the swing, it flopped and flung around as she decided not to remember Gary for the heinous act he had committed. After witnessing so much horror and so many murders, the rape wasn't on the surface. *Hopefully that fades away over time, hopefully before I've recovered from Amara.* In a strange way, it wasn't something that bothered her; she was stronger than it. Hell, she'd survived an ancient monster, right? What were a few feelings to deal with?...right?. *Better to hold onto the good memories,* she figured. Knowing full well that in future she'd likely face intimacy with another boy. That time would come, and she'd face it head-on. If a boy liked her, then she was more than strong enough to deal with it. After all, she'd survived being attacked by a hundred-handed ghost thing, right? She rubbed her stomach, smiling at her belly, feeling a light kick. *Whatever boy I meet, he'd better be ready.* She smirked.

    The bushes rustled as Nadia made her way over to the roundabout. She stepped onto it and put her hands in her pockets. She'd spent too many evenings to remember on this roundabout. Lying back and looking at the sky as Johnny or Tom spun it to try and make them dizzy. Tom had moaned when they'd returned the favour one weekend when he lay down on it. Nadia and Abby had spun it as hard as they could; the spinning did nothing to help the concoction of weed and alcohol in him, and he violently threw up, still gripping the roundabout. Sending a ring of spew out. Everyone thought it was hilarious except Tom, of course.

The strongest memories Nadia had of the roundabout were of sitting on the edge of it with Abby. The boys sitting on the other side or off chasing each other around the park, doing stupid boy things. She'd talk with Abby about things, *real* things. Not about the boys or which one was the cutest. Not about the movies they'd seen or the homework they had. They talked about things that made them adults.

Nadia would tell Abby about how she wanted to live when she was grown up, fantasising about living in some beautiful place. Spain or New Zealand, or the Bahamas, something like that. She'd have a house that led down onto the beach, warm sand at her feet and calming lapping waves to watch as the sun crept under the blue cover of the horizon.

She always felt a little silly when Abby would smile and nod at her before talking of her dreams. She was so incredible, didn't want to just escape town, didn't want to find a nice house and a nice husband to settle down with.

"I just want to do something meaningful in this world. I want to achieve something, you know? Travel the world with just the clothes on my back and discover the real meaning of life. Cure a disease, teach kids in a third world country, become a doctor and invent something that changes people's lives for the better," she'd say as she looked off into the distance and took a swig from whatever bottle of booze they'd snagged that week.

Nadia had never told the boys what they spoke about. Abby had kept it secret as well. No doubt if they found out, they'd take the piss out of them. Nadia was just looking to be some taken wife living in the Caribbean, and Abby was being some pompous know-it-all as usual.

Abby's dreams, though, gave Nadia hope. If someone who lived in a place this small, remote and shitty could dream that big, then maybe there was a chance that Nadia could find some level of happiness.

Biting her lips and sniffing back tears, Nadia spun the roundabout. *You did achieve something, Abby. You never realised how much of a difference you made in this world to me. I know you wanted to achieve amazing things someday, but you can't achieve truly brilliant things unless you start by achieving one significant thing. I am that thing, Abby. I loved you and I always will.*

I'll never forget you.

Acknowledgements

This book was written from a love of horror stories and movies I grew up watching. I've always enjoyed a creature feature, and after many ideas of different monsters, I came to settle on my first, the 'hundred hands monster'. This initial idea then morphed into the story of Amara. I've been fortunate to have people around me who have been open to looking over my work, early drafts, discussions, etc., and I'd like to give a few thanks to those involved in my madness.

Alaine Canavan, a very big thank you for providing me with some extremely helpful feedback. While writing this book I may have got excited about making a spooky scary monster but your insight gave me a good reflection to step back, look at the wider picture and consider the importance of what's happened to both Abby and Nadia.

My partner, Rachael, you've always been supportive of me, even if you steer to the other side of the road to avoid horror. My life is better for having you in it, and I'm thankful that you are open and honest with me.

    Lastly, I'd like to thank the book club I attend for giving me a comfortable place to discuss all things book. Though few of you will read books like I do, I appreciate the discussions we have had. You have helped me gain insight into the reader's mind and shown me that not everyone cares for the graphic and brutal stories I tend to read. That said, I'm not stopping reading or writing those stories. And I'm sorry, girls, it's doubtful that I'll tread into the realm of reading romantasy.

Printed in Dunstable, United Kingdom